In Search of Sons

ISBN: 3-9808084-8-3

J. Sorie Conteh

Cover design by Isiata N. Conteh

In Search of Sons

First published 2007
Sierra Leonean Writers Series / Africa Future Publishers
c/o Binty International Ltd.
P.O. Box 30265 KIA
Accra, Ghana

In Memory of:

Colone Conteh - *Mother*
Rahima Konne - *Granddaughter*

With Infinite Love
Rest in Peace

CHAPTER ONE

Kunaafoh's residence stood majestically facing the Atlantic Ocean. One Saturday evening, in April, she sat alone in a contemplative mood, looking at the flawless horizon. Such was the rhythm and dynamism of the oceanfront that it always provided her with unceasing mental stimulation. She watched two ferryboats coming from opposite directions; one took passengers to the airport as the other took travellers to their destination, Freetown. She saw fishermen in dugout canoes rushing ashore while anxious customers awaited their arrival. Seagulls flew overhead as if they were navigating the fishermen to their destination. The calm sea was at its most magnificent as nature prepared to end another brilliant tropical day. For Kunaafoh, the ocean, was one of the abundant testimonies of God's infinity. Each time she sat viewing its vastness, many thoughts circulated through her mind. On that Saturday evening she was thinking about her early life in Talia and about her parents, Hindowaa and Giita, and their quest for sons. It had all happened such a long time ago.

Kunaafoh was the only girl among three children. After her mother's third pregnancy, no other babies were born, much to the displeasure and dismay of their father who wanted many more children, preferably sons, to pass on the family name and inherit the land. To have only two sons was distressing for her father, Hindowaa.

Hindowaa was a tall, slender, delicate looking man. The knowledge that he was the only son of his mother had eroded his self-esteem and made him insecure and sometimes irritable. He had sisters, but was convinced that one was more secure in life with many maternal brothers. This belief was so strong that he would sometimes sink into a state of depression as he reflected on his condition of being his mother's only son. Many people in his home town and beyond, understood his situation and sympathised with him for he was known everywhere as a very friendly and kind man with a great sense of humour. He had an enormous appetite as well. One of his sisters had written him off as a man who would not succeed in life because he loved food far too much and was always telling stories to make people laugh. How can a man be that foolish? was her comment on Hindowaa's behaviour. However, Hindowaa continued to entertain people and people liked him.

1

Kunaafoh's mother, Giita, had been Hindowaa's wife for thirty years and mother of his three children. She was a very beautiful woman who attracted a lot of attention on account of her good looks, polite demeanour and kindness. When she was younger, before she got married, her exceptional physical assets tantalised men. People used to say that on festive occasions when she dressed appropriately and passed by, carrying herself rhythmically and with dignified elegance, men would salivate, their attention focused on every movement of her succulent body. They found her thighs, which were seldom exposed, tantalisingly seductive. Yet, unlike some women in the town of Talia, Giita had never been excessively interested in her own looks.

Like many women of her generation she was, devoted to her family of three children, her husband and relatives. However, Hindowaa's displeasure over what he considered the gender imbalance in the family, coupled with the fact that he himself was the only son of his mother, never ceased to distress Giita since she bore the brunt of Hindowaa's unhappiness. She herself came from a large family of eight sons and three daughters. Her father and mother were happily married, but the family resources were often stretched to the limit when the sons grew up and took wives. The bride price, which they had to pay, left a depressing hole in the family finances. Sometimes her father owed debts to many of his friends after a marriage transaction was over.

When Giita became of age, she had had many suitors. Her mother had secretly mentioned some of the potential candidates to her. Among them was a very famous hunter, whose knowledge of the forest was legendary. *He* did not qualify, however. There was also another well-known medicine man, who had attracted the attention of the town and beyond because he could cure what people considered chronic diseases. He had cured a chief with a festering and chronic sore, which everybody thought was due to the fact that he practised witchcraft.. The Chief had travelled far and wide in search of a cure, but had never succeeded in finding one. The healer who wanted to marry Giita cured the Chief, but he too was rejected by Giita's father. There were many other well known men who were interested in Giita, but she was never interested in any of them. In the end, the decision as to whom she should marry was made without her consent, and Hindowaa emerged as her husband.

After the marriage was consummated, Hindowaa's mother, Kigba, commonly addressed as '*Yeea*(meaning, 'mother') Kigba' started counting days, nights, weeks and months, wondering when Giita would become pregnant and bring forth grandsons. She had not fully expressed her opposition to Hindowaa's marrying Giita, though she had heard from her peers in the town that Giita's grandfather had possessed the most powerful and deadly Mende fetish called *ngelegba*. If a pregnant woman saw it, she would suffer an abortion; and any guilty person taking an oath on it, would be struck by lightning wherever he or she might be. It was the most dreaded Mende fetish.

Yeea Kigba believed that children from such families would have difficulty having children, and she planned to confront her son with this information when the time was right. She even started contemplating the prospect of his marrying another woman. She was convinced that her son's fixation on Giita was due in part to the fact that her beauty had hypnotized him. Women from Giita's town were well known to dominate their men and *Yeea* Kigba was determined this would not happen as long as she was alive.

While these concerns became her preoccupation, the social rhythm and pulse of Talia continued as usual. People went to their farms every day of the week. People went hunting or fishing even on Saturdays and Sundays. Normal life was only interrupted by festive occasions.

Hindowaa knew his mother liked bamboo wine. She cherished the drink because it was more potent than palm wine and as she grew older, had acquired an enormous appetite for it. However, it was more difficult to process than palm wine, so Hindowaa only gave it to her as a special treat. When he came home one day, his mother was resting on a mat spread under the large mango tree at the back of the house.

"Good afternoon, mother," Hindowaa greeted her.

"Good afternoon," she responded. Her voice was subdued, which was not the response Hindowaa was used to and he suspected something was amiss. However, knowing his mother's variable moods, he pretended that things were normal and said,

"Mother, I have an average-sized gourd of bamboo wine for you. It was difficult to get. I hope that you will enjoy it in the evening."

Still lying on the ground, his mother made no comment. That was when Hindowaa knew for sure that indeed the atmosphere was hot.

"Hindowaa, my child," she started in an aggressive tone. "Do you know how long you have been married?"

3

Hindowaa was surprised at the question and saw no reason for his mother to be asking it and in such a manner. He put the bamboo wine gourd on the ground and sat on the only bench nearby.

"Mother, it has not been long since I got married - just about three months, if I remember correctly." Hindowaa replied, still not sure why his mother had asked the question. She now asked him a direct one.

"When is Giita going to be pregnant and give me a grandson?"

Taken aback by this even more unexpected question, Hindowaa did not reply straightaway. Finally he said,

"Mother, I am sorry. I do not have an answer to that question because I do not know the answer."

His unsatisfactory reply made *Yeea* Kigba sit up and Hindowaa noticed that she was sweating.

"When I married your late father, two months later you were conceived. Yes, only two months; but as for you, after three months going on to four, Giita is still not pregnant. Remember, I told you about her background and you ignored me. Now you have started to understand what I told you. Since you like your stomach, she will make sure that you remain silent on important matters and concentrate on eating. She knows how to cook. She knows your weakness," *Yeea* Kigba told her son angrily.

Under the cool mango tree, which provided abundant shade for both mother and son, Hindowaa was sweating too. He said,

"It has not been all that long since we got married. I know friends whose wives became pregnant only after six months or a year. Mother, I want to give Giita a chance. Let us give her a chance."

"Hindowaa, I want to have grandsons while I am still relatively strong," *Yeea* Kigba replied. "I cannot see this happening with Giita for the reasons I gave you a long time ago. I now want to tell you that I have earmarked a girl for you to marry while you wait for your wife to become pregnant after six months or one year."

After listening politely, Hindowaa said,

"Mother it is too early to come to a decision that I should marry another woman."

His attitude so annoyed *Yeea* Kigba that she launched into a tirade.

"Ah, ah, ah. Hindowaa," she exclaimed. "What are you telling me, my son. You are a big man now so you do not accept my word and

4

advice. What has gone into your head? Don't you know that I am your mother who carried you in my belly for nine good months? Your mother, who suffered pain to bring you into this world, suckled and fed you?"

Hindowaa rose from the bench and turned his face towards the east, as if to solicit wisdom. At this, his mother took even greater offence.

"You are turning you back on me. Don't you know that it is an insult to turn your back on someone who is talking to you? Yes, you don't want to look at my face, yet it is I who brought you into this world. I carried you in this belly of mine which is now wrinkled." She grabbed the fold in her belly and flapped it to make her son pay attention to her.

"I know what went wrong. You know women from Giita's town, how they specialize in manipulating their men. That was why I was opposed to you marrying her. She has hypnotized you with some potion which has turned your head around. You cannot think properly anymore as a man. I wish your father were alive to knock some sense into that big and stupid head of yours."

Yeea Kigba continued to lambast her son verbally for the rest of that afternoon, but Hindowaa did not engage her in a verbal contest. He thought the attack was calculated to convince him to marry another woman who would become pregnant and give his mother grandchildren, and felt that time would redress the situation. Eventually, his mother drank the bamboo wine which soothed her emotional turmoil.

Giita had made an appointment to see her mother-in-law on the eve of the graduation of some male students from the circumcision grove. That evening, her mother-in-law wondered what Giita wanted to see her about and why on this particular occasion. She waited in her room, not particularly interested in seeing Giita. She was thinking about the woman she would propose to her son to marry because Giita had not conceived. The issue had weighed heavily on her mind.

There was a tap on her door and she behaved as though she was awoken from a deep sleep, saying drowsily, "Come in, the door is not locked."

Giita entered with caution.

"The night has not advanced and you expect me to lock the door?" her mother-in-law asked her.

5

"*Yeea*, when I was growing up, I was told that every time you want to enter a house or someone's room, you should knock at the door. They said it was bad manners not to knock before entering," Giita replied as she secured a seat. *Yeea* Kigba remained lying on her bed which was very low.

"*Ah, ndupui ,ngi yiinii gbowai a kpindi, kpengbeyawui saa tii miiniiloo nyama,*" she said in Mende, lamenting the fact that she had not slept much the previous night because she had been tormented by bed bugs.

Having expressed her sympathy, Giita said, "*Yeea*, I have been married to your son for three months now. I am very happy to be in this household. As you know it was my father who gave me in marriage to your son. Since we got married, he has on several occasions expressed the desire that I have many sons for him. I come from a big family with five boys and three girls. I have been quite worried about the way he keeps repeating his preference for sons."

Her mother-in-law, who had listened attentively, told her,

"My son and I want sons for good reasons. You know that yourself, don't you? You also know that I have repeatedly told you about my own burning desire to have grandsons. I am getting old and I want grandsons while I have some energy to take care of them. You know that also, don't you?"

"*Yeea*, to have sons, we also need women," Giita argued in a firm, even defiant voice. "I am not saying that we do not need sons, but sons by themselves cannot have sons. This is my only concern."

"If this is what you have come to see me about, or to tell me this evening, you are being very disrespectful. Would you talk to your own mother like that? I will tell my son about the way you have spoken to me," her mother-in-law replied so angrily that Giita now tried to appease her.

"*Yeea*, we are just talking. I am only raising an issue that I think needs to be talked about. I am here to tell you something else. As I said earlier, I have been married for three months in this household. I am here to share a secret with you before anyone else gets to know about it. I did not mean to annoy you and I will never insult you because you are older than me and you and my mother are of the same age. I never disrespect my elders. Please forgive me if you feel offended by my remarks."

Yeea Kigba sat up in bed and adjusted her wrapper. She was a strong woman, despite her age. Her body was firm and she walked upright, and without the aid of a walking stick.

"I am here to tell you two things," Giita continued. "The first is that I am pregnant, and the second, that my first child is going to be a boy. I saw the soothsayer not long ago and she has already confirmed it."

"*Koooh, Ngewoh biseh, Ngewoh biseh lata caca lata* (Thanks be to God many times)," *Yeea* Kigba said, rising from her bed to hug her daughter-in-law who had also got to her feet. "Have you told your husband? Does he know about it?" she asked as they resumed their seats. There was now an atmosphere of friendly excitement in the room.

"My child," she went on, "God is great. Do you know that I have been thinking about you and my son? I have said to myself, when are they going to have children? I prayed to God to bless you with children and God has answered my prayers. Hindowaa is my only son and I have been praying so that he would be blessed with sons. See, God has already answered my prayers. You see, you are a newcomer, a stranger in this our town. *I* know this town very well. People are interested in other people's business. You will find that out later. I am sure there are people here who have been asking secretly, when Hindowaa is going to have children, now that he has married. They have started counting the days, weeks and months. This is how things are in Talia."

"*Yeea*, I think what you are saying is true," Giita remarked. "Each time I go to the river to bathe, I sense that some women are looking at me as if I am a stranger. I have been curious about it, but now I know why. They want to see if I am pregnant."

When, Giita finally left the room, both she and her mother-in-law were comforted and slept very soundly. The bed bugs in Yeea Kigba's bed did not bite her that night.

The birth of, the first son of Hindowaa and Giita caused much jubilation in the family. Hindowaa knew that the family name would be continued, which was a primary consideration. There was a lavish celebration. Many goats and chickens were slaughtered and the ancestors were adequately propitiated in appreciation for the birth of a son in the family. He was named Hinga ('men') as a welcome to a family that had had no children.

To ensure Hinga's survival, both Giita and Hindowaa took the baby to Gbandama so that an old medicine man could ward off any evil spirits hovering over the baby.. The medicine man would also enhance Hinga's masculinity. He would be treated against snakebites and other venomous elements. This process would be repeated for subsequent children. It was simply a rite of passage.

Hindowaa's mother loved the baby boy, Hinga, her first grandson, and spent lots of time with him. She almost took possession of the baby as if he were her own, which suited Giita because she could devote her time to addressing the numerous chores she had to deal with in addition to caring for the baby.

"*Nya hinii* (My husband)." That was how Hinga's grandmother fondly addressed him.

She was holding Hinga while sitting on the veranda late one afternoon. The breeze was calm and cool and diluted the sun's heat. Giita was busy in the kitchen, cooking. They had not gone to the farm as she was expecting some relatives. The news had gone forth that she had delivered her first child, a son, and they were coming to see him.

"When you grow up, you should be as tough as your-grandfather," *Yeea* Kigba told the baby as she gazed fondly at him. "He was a tough man. You resemble him. Your father too resembled him. Oh, even the way you smile resembles him. I wish he had lived to see you. You look so much alike. Believe me, you are grandpa come back. Look at your forehead. It is exactly like his."

The baby looked up at his grandmother and smiled as if he understood what she was saying. "Oh, your smile is beautiful," she exclaimed. "So you heard me. But when you grow up, don't fight people like your grandfather used to. Oh! Yes, he fought with just about everybody around him. But he was also a nice and kind man like your father."

Absolutely delighted with her grandson, she continued talking to the child, as if he was listening and could understand what she was saying.

Even while Hinga was still small, his grandmother had started praying to God and asking the ancestors for Giita to have another son. She had already decided that the second son would be named after her own father, Soohgbandi (meaning, 'hot aggressive horse'), a name given to warriors. She waited and prayed. Hindowaa, on the other hand, spent very little time with his son though, as the boy grew up, he supervised his development. He saw him through the circumcision rites and then on to the most famous Kpa-Mende initiation into the Wunde society. People remarked that aged two, Hinga was still being breast-fed and his mother was not pregnant. This situation generated much concern in Talia. However, many people said that it was not unusual for children to continue breast-feeding even when they were two years old. Some people observed that they knew of children who had been breast-fed when they were even three years old.

Hindowaa, his mother and Giita, were becoming increasingly worried. They were worried because the issue of Giita still nursing Hinga had become the talk of the town. People in Talia would talk, they would gossip about anything. That was why the Hindowaa family was getting worried.

"Giita, what is happening to you? Hinga is a big man now. He talks very clearly. He will soon grow a beard. When is the next child coming?" Giita's mother-in-law asked her one evening as they were preparing a meal in the farmhouse. Hinga was outside, playing with other children.

"Ah, *Yeea*, I was going to tell you that I am two months pregnant, and I have even consulted the soothsayer. She told me that this time I would have a baby girl," Giita answered.

"Eeeeh, a baby girl?" *Yeea* Kigba asked. She sounded disappointed.

"Yeea, that is what the woman told me. I also need a girl to be close to. Hinga will grow up being attached to his father, so I need someone that I, too, will be attached to," Giita replied. Her mother-in-law said,

"I will ask Hindowaa and you to allow me to give the girl the name of my older sister who never had children. You know my older sister, don't you? She will appreciate that very much."

Giita's pregnancy soon became the talk of the town when her belly assumed such a size that she could not hide it any longer. She was sensitive about the way people looked at her, knowing that the second child was coming. She took her time over telling Hinga that his sister was on the way. Hinga could not understand what his mother was talking about and kept asking where his sister was. The discussion never lasted long. Hinga would disappear again either to go and play or to go to his grandmother.

Giita's second labour pains came unexpectedly and, as had happened with her first confinement, did not last long. She soon delivered her baby with the traditional birth assistants in attendance. Hindowaa was away that day, having travelled to visit some friends in another town.

The second child and the only daughter in the family, was a welcome relief and joy to both parents, though more particularly to Giita. Giita adored her first daughter who was named Kunaafoh, meaning that she should live forever. It was a term of endearment given to her by *Yeea* Kigba who announced that Kunaafoh looked like her older sister, whom everyone called Kunaa. Hindowaa was less convinced about this but kept his opinion to himself so as to avoid an unnecessary misunderstanding.

Yeea Kigba also adored Kunaafoh. Many a time people believed that *she* was the baby's real mother. She put Kunaafoh on her back and went everywhere with the child. She would sing songs to Kunaafoh when she cried. She would feed her when she was hungry, and she would put her to bed. Even though she would have preferred another grandson, she performed her grandmotherly role with religious commitment. Once again, Giita appreciated her assistance.

Kunaafoh combined the physical features of both parents. She grew up to be taller than her mother but not as tall as her father. People noticed that she was quite different from her brother, Hinga who looked more like his father - tall and slender. Hinga also had good looks, but later became arrogant as a result of his attractiveness to girls. He was aggressive, often bullying them, and insensitive to their feelings, whereas Kunaafoh was sensitive, polite and friendly to her friends and elders alike.

There was no doubt that Kunaafoh was the brightest pupil in her class. The Catholic nun had remarked on her brilliance to her father, and everyone in the town, including the Paramount Chief, liked and respected the nun. With the Catholic fathers and other missionaries, she had become very popular in Talia. People said that they had become just like the locals and there was sense in their observations, for the missionaries all spoke Mende as fluently as if it were their mother tongue. The people also said that Mother Kono was at ease with the local food, especially the famous *saaki-tomboi* (cassava leaves sauce) when cooked with goat meat. People admired her and the other missionaries in Talia and the chiefdom.

As Kunaafoh grew older, she was also perceived to be an ambitious girl. Many people, who had watched her grow up, said she had such an iron will and so much determination that she should not have been a woman. She was so clever that some people even believed she had psychic powers, but in spite of this, many in the town loved her

Hindowaa's mother started praying that Giita's next child would be a son. She knew that daughters in the family would bring wealth when they got married, but she still preferred to have more grandsons. She kept asking Giita when the next son would come, which made Giita uncomfortable. *She* also kept praying for a son. She appealed to her maternal ancestors, who she felt would be more sympathetic towards her. She was convinced they would grant her wish for more sons, though there were times when she would cry for fear that she would not have any more. She lost count of the number of times she prayed each day.

Giita went to visit the old soothsayer to find out if she would become pregnant again and have a son. On her way to the woman, she continued to pray.

"I hope you don't get angry with me," she told the soothsayer. "I am here again to find out whether I will be pregnant and have another son. I have been having sleepless nights over this matter."

They were alone in the hut which smelt of smoke. The smoke in the hut did not disturb Giita, however. She was too busy thinking about what the old woman would tell her.

"You know, Giita," the old woman said, "I sympathise with you each time you come to see me. I know how you feel about this. I know many women here in Talia who have had to go through your experience. I myself wanted more sons, and God answered my prayers. I was lucky and my marriage survived because I never wanted co-wives to have sons for my husband when I did not. When he married other women, it was not because of sons, but because he wanted more women, so I did not feel inadequate. To feel inadequate is not good. That is why I am happy, and that is why I understand your situation and sympathise with you."

Giita listened impatiently to the old woman's history because she wanted her to make a pronouncement about her own concern.

"Your daughter Kunaafoh has grown up nicely. She is a lovely child and I am sure when the time comes for her to be initiated into the Sande Society, she will attract many men when she graduates," the old woman continued as she consulted some pebbles on the floor. "Oh, you are lucky," she said suddenly. "The son is coming. He is on the way. Soon, you will be pregnant and you will have a baby boy. I see the way the pebbles are assembled."

"Thank you, *Yeea*. Thank you very much."

Giita was delighted as she left the hut.

Kafo (meaning 'a son born at midday') was Giita's third child. Unlike Hinga he looked like his mother. His parents welcomed his birth. Hindowaa was relieved for he had been secretly afraid that he would have only one son. The birth of Hinga and Kafo dispelled his fear and restored his self-esteem. His confidence in his ancestors was solidly reinforced as he had prayed to them many times so that he would be rewarded with sons.

Hindowaa's mother was the happiest person when Giita had Kafo. She had danced and sung songs of praise for the ancestors. She thanked them for having answered her prayers for Giita to have another son, and more pregnancies with more sons. Everyone in the household, noticed how much attention *Yeea* Kigba paid to Kafo. Her devotion was remarkable.

Giita would have loved to have as many sons as Hindowaa wanted, but after Kafo, conceptions mysteriously ceased. Hindowaa was visibly worried over this development, and failed to accept that fate had intervened. He knew some people who had similar experiences but had overcome them and had gone on to have more sons. This matter preoccupied his mind for he could not understand why a healthy man and woman like himself and Giita should stop conceiving children. In Talia, anything was possible, but he was not prepared to be the victim of malevolent forces at work. He would fight them if the need arose. He was determined that such evil forces would not seal his fate. He thought, I shall go and tell the Paramount Chief that I want to hire the *ngelegba* medicine man to come to Talia so that I can put a curse on all those who are bewitching my family. He knew that once the *ngelegba* fetish was mentioned in the town, all the witches would repent of their deeds or disappear. The *ngelegba* was the fearsome and potent fetish used to bring order to the community when things went out of control. It was

12

efficacious - lethal and swift, and sent fear and panic into those who flouted the moral order of the community. Hindowaa was not sure the Chief would grant his request, because he knew that there were stringent conditions for the use of the fetish. He wondered whether he would fulfil those conditions, but would not resign himself to accepting what he thought was Giita's fate. Something would have to be done.

These family developments were of great concern to Kunaafoh. Many a time, she would sit in lonely silence trying to figure out her own place in the family sphere. She wondered why her mother's wishes for more sons had not been fulfilled. Above all, she wondered why her father would not be content with three normal, healthy children, two sons and a daughter. She and her mother were united in their distress over these matters, but Hinga and Kafo were far too busy trying to navigate their youthful orbit to be bothered by such matters.

CHAPTER TWO

Behind the house where Kunaafoh grew up, there was a very wide river, the main river in Talia. It was the biggest river that Kunaafoh ever saw during her childhood. The river had been there since time immemorial and people talked about it with awe and reverence. It was the lifeblood and hope of the community for it provided them with water to drink, and to bathe, as well as spiritual sustenance. People believed that the spirits of the underworld dwelled there and in time, the river acquired supernatural attributes for the community. Many people claimed that when they went to sleep and woke up in the heat of the night they would hear voices coming from the river that would pierce the darkness and rave through the forest. The voices were those of the spirits of the river. Those like Kunaafoh, who were gifted in the art of the supernatural, could understand what the voices were saying and interpret the messages of the river spirits. It was because people were afraid of the river at night that children and women were told not to venture there unless accompanied by adult males.

Kunaafoh had been told lots of stories about the river, many of them by her mother and grandmother. Some of the stories were horror stories and others just folktales. She never believed many of the stories that she heard and developed such a critical approach to them that her sceptical attitude earned the disapproval of some of her elders. However, some stories left their imprint on her memory.

She remembered in detail the fascinating story of the mermaid who could make people rich as well as poor. She would give people a golden comb, but to obtain it, one had to be lucky. One needed to surprise the mermaid, as she sat on the banks of the river, naked and combing her long, black and silky hair. She would get startled, drop the golden comb and dive into the river. The lucky person would then be able to take possession of the golden comb which would then become the source of riches. People believed in the mermaid story and prayed to see her at least once in their lifetime.

Kunaafoh was also told stories when she behaved in a defiant manner, and she would reflect on them when she was alone. One was the story of the beautiful girl who would not accept all the suitors that her parents had proposed to her. Maagainda was the prettiest girl in the

14

town of Makonde. The news of her beauty had gone beyond Makonde. Potential suitors travelled from afar to come and see the beautiful girl and offered to marry her. Her parents pleaded with her, but to no avail. One evening, a man was passing by the town. It was late in the evening and he asked for accommodation because it was dark and he could not proceed to his destination that night. The man said that he was lucky that nightfall had caught up with him in Makonde where the most beautiful girl lived. He asked for an audience with Magainda, even though it was late and his request was granted though many people thought he was a nonentity. The following morning, Magainda informed her parents that she had at last met the man she wanted to marry. They gave their consent and organised the marriage.

As the story is told to this day, the couple's wedding night was a memorable one. It was past midnight when the town heard Magainda's voice, pleading to be rescued. Her husband had turned into a boa constrictor and had started swallowing her. Fortunately she was rescued and never defied her elders again.

One hot and humid afternoon, Kunaafoh went to the river where her mother had gone without her knowledge. Consumed by her anxiety over Hindowaa's concern that no more sons were forthcoming, Gitta would sometimes disappear without telling anybody where she was going. She needed moments of solitude to commune with the ancestors, the spirits of the river and the forest. Many people in distress did the same. On this particular day, Giita had gone to the river under the pretext of washing some of her clothes.

There was a huge granite rock near the river. People said that it had mystical powers and had turned it into a shrine where they went to pray about their problems, and ask for forgiveness from the spirits and ancestors. They would cook rice and leave it by the rock for their departed loved ones.

The human traffic to the rock was usually heavy so when she arrived at the spot, Giita was delighted to find that the crowd had diminished. She walked slowly and placed a red cloth, known as *tafti* with eleven red cola nuts and rice flour on the rock then kneeled beside it and asked her departed ancestors to grant her requests. She was not supposed to look back once she had perfumed the ritual, so she collected her belongings and went into the water to do her laundry.

As Kunaafoh recalled it, the afternoon was steaming hot and the town was silent. Occasionally, she would hear a goat or sheep bleating by the roadside and dogs barking at passers-by. The noises of these creatures of the town would resonate at the far end of the forest in splendid symphony with the women pounding their clothes on the granite rocks by the river. As Kunaafoh walked towards the river that afternoon, she could feel her mother's pain - the anguish of not having enough sons to please her husband, Hindowaa.

As she walked on the footpath and through the dense green vegetation, Kunaafoh broke a twig from a shrub and started fidgeting with it. From the distance, she could hear the pounding of clothes on granite rocks by the river. She walked at a snail's pace so as not to scare her mother whom she had spotted. Half of her mother's body was submerged in the river. And, as she hit the clothes on the rock, her bare breasts swayed in rhythmic vibration to the tune of her singing.

Giita was singing a sad song about her distressing situation. She was asking her ancestors why they had abandoned her - why her repeated prayers for more sons had not been answered. She wanted to know what she had done wrong - if she had transgressed any of the sacred codes and principles on which the moral pillars of the community were founded and sustained. She was prepared to make amends. Her singing echoed and re-echoed in the stillness of the forest. Kunaafoh stood still for a moment listening to her mother's song of sorrow then, filled with emotion, burst out crying. Tears, warm and tender flooded her eyes and drenched her cheeks. Her mother also began to weep loudly. She stepped out of the river and warmly embraced Kunaafoh.

"Don't cry my child," Giita told her daughter. Their tears of pain and anguish fell freely even as they soothed their shared suffering. When they unlocked their embrace, they looked at each other in silence. Giita's big eyes were red and most of her body was wet.

"Have you been here for a long time, listening to me?" she asked.

"No mother, but I have been here long enough to absorb your songs of grief," Kunaafoh replied. "Let me help you with the laundry so that we can finish quickly and go home."

"Mother, remember, you promised to tell me the outcome of your meeting with Daddy," Kunaafoh said when they had worked in silence for a while. "I have been itching to hear from you. Please tell me now. This is the best moment and place to tell me about it. Please."

There was another interval of silence between mother and child. Giita felt mental pain as she looked into her daughter's expectant eyes.

"My child, I don't have good news to tell you. I wish I had." Kunaafoh stood up instantly, her heart pounding.

"What is it, Mother? What is it? Father is going to take another wife? Tell me. Tell me."

For a moment, Giita hesitated, thinking it was perhaps the wrong time for her to tell her daughter the news. On reflection, she decided that it made no difference if she told her there and then or later. Since Kunaafoh had asked, she would tell her now that they were together.

"Yes, he told me few days ago that he would marry a new wife and I have been wondering how to tell you. Your grandma has been instrumental in persuading your father to have a second wife, but she thinks that I do not know what she has been up to. She is a wonderful mother-in-law. I will not even bother to tell your brothers. They are men and have never shown any concern about my situation. In fact they are not even aware of my situation. One day, they will learn. I wish them well," Giita said as Kunaafoh listened in silence and dismay.

"Do you know that your father has also decided that you should marry the Chief while your brothers go to Freetown to continue school there? He has a half brother in Freetown, who is working for the Railway."

Having unburdened herself, Giita felt a great sense of relief. These matters had troubled her mind as she wondered how to tell her daughter and what Kunaafoh's reaction would be.

"Mother, do you believe that Daddy would really marry another wife just to have more sons?" Kunaafoh asked.

"Yes, Kunaafoh. He means it. Men can give any flimsy excuse when they want to take another wife. You are too young to understand. If a man does not like your food, he will use that as a pretext for taking another wife. My child, they may even take another wife if they don't like your hairdo. There are so many reasons why a man would want to take another wife. The odds are always against us women. You will experience it yourself when you get married."

"Mother, in that case why marry? Why?" Kunaafoh responded hotly.

17

"Don't ask such questions, my daughter. And talk quietly. The river and forest have ears. There are people around who might hear our conversation and report back in town about what we talked about when we were doing our laundry. How can you ask such a question?"

"Mother, if Daddy marries a woman of my age, why don't you pack up and go to your parents? You will get another man. You are still beautiful and attractive. You will get another husband."

"Ah, it is so good to be a child," Giita remarked with a sad smile. "I am grateful for your observations. But let me tell you this; my parents would not take kindly to me leaving Hindowaa because he decides to take another wife. No. They will not accept my logic, especially my father. He will pack me up like a bundle and send me back to your father. My dear, remember, my father received a fat bride price from your father. How could I defy tradition and culture and go back home? My mother would also plead with me to return and bear the burden of a bitter marriage. Ah, Kunaafoh, I wish you were old enough to understand my situation. I shall stay on and keep praying to God and my ancestors to have more sons for your father."

"But mother, is this going to be your permanent state in life?" Kunaafoh asked.

"My child, I have prayed enough and shall continue to pray to God and my ancestors to change it by giving me more sons. I am optimistic that they will respond favourably. When this whole thing started - I mean marrying your father - your grandmother thought I would never have children, but I did."

"Mother, why?" Kunaafoh asked, dismayed to think that her grandmother was not the good person she had believed her to be.

"My daughter, it is a long story and I do not want to bore you with it. To begin with, your grandmother never wanted her son, to marry me. She had her own hidden candidate for him. So since I came into this marriage, she developed subtle but effective hostility towards me. She told people in this town and beyond that I come from a family with a history of barrenness and therefore I would never have children. She did not tell her son, though. When I had my first child, she was ashamed and embarrassed and came to me in secret and asked me to forgive her. That is your grandmother, your father's mother. This has been my situation in this house."

"Mother, why have you never told me these things before," Kunaafoh asked, "Why?"

"My child, these things are meant for adults. Moreover, I did not want to distress and poison your young and innocent mind."

"Mother, as for me, I shall not marry the Chief. Let me tell you in advance," Kunaafoh warned.

"My daughter, don't say that. Don't say it loudly for other people at this river to hear you. What else would you do? What else? If you defy your father, he will say I am responsible for your defiance. My child, I will be in trouble. My parents will say the same thing. It is always the mother who is blamed under such circumstances. But when things go well; the credit goes to the man. If you refuse to marry the Chief I will live a more miserable life than I am now experiencing."

There was a short silence, as if they were both digesting what Giita had said, then Kunaafoh repeated her warning that she would never marry the Chief..

"Mother, there is no compromise on this matter," she said. "I will not marry any man who has another wife or wives. I will not, because I am educated. If this means I will never marry, then that is fine with me. It will not be the end of the world."

On hearing her daughter's words, Giita stood upright in alarm.

"My child, what is happening to you today? Tell me, what is happening to you? How can you say these things as a woman? How can you stay unmarried? How would you have children? Please don't say these things, I beg of you – not now, not ever." She sounded distraught but Kunaafoh remained unyielding in spite of her mother's concern.

"Mother, I don't have to be married to have children. I don't. That is the truth. I cannot see myself as wife number one, two or three. That much I can tell you today and in secret. It is a secret between mother and daughter."

Realising that her daughter meant what she said, Gitta replied, "You see, Kunaafoh, you are only a child. You are my child and only daughter. You should listen to me and stop entertaining those views of yours. It will affect me here in Talia and in the chiefdom if people know that you think that way. They will say I am responsible for your ideas and I will be in trouble, not only with your father and grandma but with the entire community."

She had stopped washing the clothes she held in her hands and looked seriously worried. She tried to make eye contact with her daughter, but Kunaafoh continued doing the laundry. She seemed to have made up her mind on the matter even though she knew that her mother was disturbed by her views. Eventually she said,

"Mother, I wanted to tell you about my dreams for a long time, but I did not want you to be worried about them. I already knew what you were going through; that was why I decided to keep my dreams to myself. I have dreamed about the mermaid three times and I know that if I want to see her I can see her and ask her to grant your wish. If she asks me what I want for myself,, I shall ask her to help me to go to the white man's country and become a doctor."

"My child, do not talk like that," Giita pleaded after listening to her daughter with even greater anxiety. "You know that people already believe that you are psychic and attribute lots of things to people they think are gifted in that way. You are a child. You know nothing much about the mermaid. She may not like you and this may lead to problems. And if she likes you, she may decide to take you into the water with her. It has happened a lot in this area. I beg you, have nothing to do with the mermaid. You are my child and I appreciate your concern, but please avoid the mermaid."

"Mother, I understand that if you ask the mermaid to do good things for you, she will not refuse," Kunaafoh persisted. "I intend to ask her to do the good things I want for you and me."

"Then from this moment, I shall make sure you never come to the river by your self," Giita told her. "I shall tell your father, grandmother and everybody in the house to watch your movements. I shall also tell your teachers about it. This is a big risk you want to take. What if the mermaid loves you and takes you away? That will be an additional problem for me, Kunaafoh. Do not try it, my child. It is dangerous and you are too young for that. Do not be stubborn, I am warning you. And tell me more about going to the white man's country, Kunaafoh. How do you intend to go there without money? How do you expect to travel there. How long will you remain there, my child?"

"Mother, the mermaid will address the question of money," Kunaafoh told her mother. "If you only allow me to meet her, she will solve the problem."

"But Kunaafoh, even if you had the money, how will you actually go to the white man's country? And will you return and find me alive? I also want to remind you that even if going there becomes possible, there are important issues that I cannot ignore. You know that you have not yet been initiated into the Sande Society. You will have to be initiated before you go. I hope you will not attempt to go to the mermaid for help. Avoid her intervention in anything that you desire until you are an adult. Please, my daughter. Do not ignore my advice. I am your mother."

There was a moment of silence as Kunaafoh contemplated her answer.

"Mother, first and foremost do I have to be initiated into the Sande Society?" she asked.

Giita felt as if a razor had pierced her heart. Her heartbeats redoubled.

"My child, are you all right or out of your mind? How can you ask such a question? What is wrong with you? Have you ever heard of a woman who has not been initiated into Sande? How can you be a woman, marry and bear children without being initiated into Sande. When did you ever hear that?"

Giita was now beginning to feel angry with her daughter.

"Mother," Kunaafoh told her patiently, "I know that the Catholic nun has not been initiated. I know that all the white women here at the Mission School have not been initiated; and some of them are married and have had children."

"Kunaafoh, don't push me too far. Do you hear me?" Giita warned. "I don't like what you are saying to me about white people. I am talking about you. In fact, let us drop the subject before people hear about it in Talia. This is why people say it is not good for women to go to school. This is the problem. How can you be saying such things today? Let me tell you this. You are not a woman until you are initiated into Sande. You will remain a child in an adult's body. Do you know that? If your father hears this, he will disown you and drive you from his house. And he will put the blame on me. The whole of Talia will know about it and our household will be the talk of the town and the region. I pray to my ancestors that such a day never comes when we shall have a grown-up daughter in our house that has not been initiated in the Sande Society. The ancestors will be angry with me and they will punish you severely."

21

Hoping to appease her, Kunaafoh said, "Mother, don't get upset with me. I shall do it in the white man's country when I get there. I am sorry that I have annoyed you."

"Kunaafoh, my child, I am not against your going to the white man's country, but not through the mermaid," Giita replied, somewhat relieved. "I have stated this clearly and I don't want us to repeat it anymore. My concern as I said before is simply that you should come back and find me alive. There are lots of stories about people going to the white man's country to study and never returning. We know people here who have gone there and have never come back. Some were there when their parents passed away and they did not even come for the funeral. Can you imagine that? Not to bury your parents because you are in the white man's country? My child, there are stories like that in this chiefdom."

"I shall come back when I finish studying to be a doctor." Kunaafoh assured her mother, but Giita had not finished.

"People said that some of those who had gone to study in the white man's country came back and were mad because they had too much of the white man's knowledge. This one is true. Even people who get too much of the Arab man's knowledge sometimes go insane. I shall pray when you go to the white man's country so that you come and find me alive and well and that you also return with your senses intact. Do not take in too much of the white man's knowledge."

Kunaafoh listened to her mother, but not seriously and even felt amused. For some moments after that neither mother nor daughter spoke; then Kunaafoh resumed the conversation.

"Mother let me tell you something. You were saying that people had gone to study and stayed on and did not come back. You are right. There is reason for this. When they went and did not succeed in whatever they had said they were going to do, they were ashamed to come back. And if they came without accomplishing what they had gone for, the family at home would be ashamed as well. Those who succeed come back home and make the family proud."

Unconvinced by Kunaafoh's explanation, Giita asked, "Where is this place you have in mind to go and study more? Is it far from Saaloon?"

"Mother, many of us at school, if given the opportunity, would like to go and study where Sister O'Connor and the others come from, in Ireland which is very far from Sierra Leone." Whenever, Sister O'Connor's name came up, Kunaafoh would chuckle because her mother and many others in Talia always found it difficult to pronounce the Catholic nun's name and called her Sister or Mother Kono. She was chuckling again as she spoke.

"How long will the trip take if you go by lorry?" Giita asked.

Kunaafoh now burst out laughing - so loudly that people downstream heard her.

"Mother, you don't go to Ireland or England in a lorry. You go to Ireland and England by aeroplane," she told her mother, still laughing. Giita was not amused.

"You mean you will fly up in the air in that white man's boat," she exclaimed. "Are you not afraid? My child, I have heard many stories about that flying boat. Now my heart is beginning to ache for you."

"Mother, the nun came from Ireland in the flying boat and nothing happened to her. That is the only way people can go abroad. The other way is by ship, but that takes a long time."

"My child, it is better to go by the ship. It is not good to fly and hang in the air without any support. How long will it take you to reach the white man's country by the flying boat?"

"They said it would take a whole day to get there." Kunaafoh told her mother.

"My child, only God will take care of you when you are in the flying boat," Giita remarked, shaking her head. "And do you eat in the flying boat," she went on. "My child, what if you want to go to the toilet?"

"Mother in the flying boat, they give you food, and you can walk around and go to the toilet if the need arises."

"Who will hold you when you want to walk, my child?"

"Nobody, mother, I shall do it myself."

"No, my child, please, if you have to walk in the flying boat ask someone to assist you. It is too much to walk in something that is hanging in the air." Giita pleaded as Kunaafoh continued to laugh.

"I still want to appeal to you not to involve the mermaid in all you intend to do," Giita said. "I have told you the reasons. I shall not repeat them, and I hope that you will heed my advice as your mother and never come to this river by yourself."

The rest of their conversation focused on Hindowaa's plans to marry a second wife who would give him more sons, marry Kunaafoh off to the Chief and send her brothers to school in Freetown. While deep in their discussion of these matters, they heard the chattering of two monkeys in the trees overhead. They were engaged in acrobatic exercises. Giita and Kunaafoh looked up and watched them with as much interest as if that was the first time they had seen monkeys playing in the treetops overlooking the long meandering river.

When they had finished the laundry, they trudged back to town. They were both tired. Their hands were sore, their stomachs empty and their hearts bruised. They were united in anguish as they continued to contemplate Giita's future and Kunaafoh's determination not be one of the Chief's wives.

CHAPTER THREE

It was during the early hours of the evening when the stars were defiantly brilliant and the moon illuminated the entire town that Hindowaa ventured from his house to visit his old friend and confidant, Nyake (meaning, 'my father'). He lived 'down town' as they used to call that part of Talia. As he walked along, Hindowaa heard the deafening and continuous noise made by the girls in the Sande grove. He recalled the meeting he had with his mother. The issue they had discussed weighed heavily on his mind.

"When is Giita going to be pregnant and give me another grandson?" his mother had asked yet again.

The question kept coming up in his mind. His mother had repeatedly brought the topic to his attention. He was tormented by it. It gave him sleepless nights and even his once healthy appetite was affected by these concerns.

Hindowaa had never told his mother that he was aware that she had been behind the rumours that Giita would not have children because she came from a family that possessed the *ngelegba* fetish. This rumour had circulated in Talia. He had felt offended by it, but kept his anger and frustration to himself. At the time, when Giita was being considered for marriage, she was magnetically attractive and he would have done anything humanly possible to marry her. He knew that many men had wanted to marry the pretty girl. When he became the lucky victor among so many important contestants, he felt infinitely grateful to Giita's father.

What he and his mother had in common was their desire that Giita should have more sons. On that issue, they were solidly united. He wondered what advice his friend and confidant, Nyake, would give him if he brought up the subject of marrying another woman to improve his prospects of having more sons. He could never predict Nyake when it came to giving advice.

As he approached his friend's house, a sense of despondency gripped him. How could Giita fail to give him more sons? He was aware that he had become the talk of the town, the man who had only two sons. He was restless and agitated as he continued to walk towards his friend's house. He knew Nyake to be very frank person with people who sought his advice.

Hindowaa had at one time entertained the idea of visiting another friend outside Talia to seek advice, but he had swiftly abandoned it because of the cost of the lorry fare. The other friend was more accommodating, more sympathetic to people who sought his wise counsel regarding their problems. That was not the case with Nyake, Hindowaa kept thinking as he walked slowly toward his friend's house that night.

Nyake, was lying comfortably in his hammock on the veranda when Hindowaa arrived at the house.

"*Ndakei, biwah biseh* (My friend, good evening)," Hindowaa greeted him.

Nyake and Hindowaa always referred to each other as 'Ndakei'. This is common usage only among peer groups.

It would have been an insult and inappropriate, for a younger man to refer to his elder as 'Ndakei'; and elders do not refer to younger people as 'Ndakei', either.

"*Biwah, biseh, kahuin yehnah,*" Nyake returned the greeting as Hindowaa secured a raffia chair and sat directly opposite him.

"Ndakei Hindowaa, this is what you found me doing. Let us drink. The palm wine is fresh, the night has just started and tomorrow, I shall not be going to the farm early. I may, however, be going to Moyamba to sell some of my ginger. I need the money, not to marry another wife, but to pay school fees for the children." Hindowaa listened and cleared his throat, as he smelled the inviting freshness of the palm wine.

"Komeh!" Nyake called one of his children to bring a cup for Hindowaa.

Nyake was one of the wisest men in the town. People respected him and would consult him whenever they were faced with problems on a number of issues that ranged from politics, family, legal, and land matters, and many more. Hindowaa was one of those who consulted him regularly. Nyake was always ready to offer his advice and he did so without fear or favour. Many people loved him for his brutal honesty and objectivity, but there were others who disliked his frankness and preferred not to consult him when they had problems. This did not bother Nyake, however. He continued to render his services to those brave enough to seek his opinion.

One of the solid bonds uniting Nyake and Hindowaa was that they had taken the same title of 'Ngumbuwa' in the Wunde Society. This was a very prestigious title and conferred great respect on its recipients in the community. The Kpa-Mende people considered the Wunde Society the repository of all the mystical, military and traditional values and mores that identified them. In Talia, both Hindowaa and Nyake were highly respected members. They would often spend time together talking about the good old days of the Wunde Society. With a sense of nostalgia, they lamented the fact that things had changed and the society was losing its traditional role in the community.

The friends heard singing coming from the Sande grove. It was soothing and rekindled old memories as they both reflected on the good old days.

"Ndakei Nyake, as far as I can remember, I have never witnessed any Sande initiation that generated such interest in our town and beyond like the current one," Hindowaa remarked.

Nyake did not respond immediately and appeared to be considering what his friend had said. His silence gave Hindowaa an opportunity to take another gulp of his palm wine. A cool wind had diluted the heat, and moonshine had effectively enveloped the entire town. There was a festive mood in the town as people listened to the songs coming from the grove of the young Sande students.

"Ndakei Hindowaa, this Sande is the talk of the town," Nyake said. "But last year I was told the same thing. Every year our Sande initiation gets best commendation. Let me tell you why. It is because your mother is head of the Society here. She has been in the business for a long time and is very knowledgeable."

Hindowaa made no comment and poured himself another generous portion of palm wine.

"What I know is that people have short memories," Nyake continued. "The Sande initiation has improved. I know this as a matter of fact. People have forgotten that some time back the people of Khortuhun were well known for initiating the best Sande girls. People used to rush there to look for wives. You know that I married two of my wives from there. They are still pretty. It took a long time before they lost their coveted position. It is so sad."

Hindowaa was hardly listening to Nyake as he wondered how to broach the subject of his mission to his friend. He took another drink, this time, to summon up his courage. He suddenly interrupted his friend.

"Ndakei Nyake, I am thinking of taking a wife at the end of this Sande session. I have been thinking about it. You know my problem. Giita has stopped having children and I only have two sons. I don't know what I have done to the ancestors."

Nyake poured himself more palm wine as he listened.

"Do you have good tobacco? I feel like smoking." Hindowaa enquired.

Nyake offered him some tobacco and Hindowaa started wrapping it. He was, anxious to hear what his friend had to say, but went on, "I am also thinking of sending my two sons to Freetown to continue school there. They will be in the care of my younger brother who works at Loco (the Sierra Leone Railway). As for Kunaafoh, she should get married to the Chief. You know my family has never given a wife to the Chief. I feel bad about it and my mother feels the same. Our chief is a good man. I feel bad that no one in my family is married to him. I wish one of my sisters was married to him, but I don't trust the one I had earmarked for him. She is too worldly and I don't want her to bring scandal to my house."

Nyake listened attentively as his friend spoke. He took his pipe, which was on the floor, stuffed it as best he could, pressing his right thumb down to see if it was full enough.

"Ndakei Hindowaa your mother is the *Sowie* (head of the Sande Society) in this town. She has had a wonderful career and she is well respected," he said as he began to puff smoke into the cool air circulating in the veranda. The singing from the Sande grove continued to entertain the two friends as well as sounds coming from the people in the town who had not yet gone to sleep.

"Ndakei, Hindowaa, I have heard you very clearly regarding your desire to take a wife in addition to Giita. If you are here to seek my counsel, I would like to be frank with you. We have been friends for a long time. We are both '*Ngumbuwa*'. The one difference between us is that I have three wives and you have only one beautiful woman. I have known Giita since she joined us here after you persuaded her father to let you take her away from her town and people. You are a lucky man to have married such a beautiful woman."

28

Hindowaa who was listening attentively this time, felt that, as usual, Nyake was deliberately beating about the bush instead of getting to the point. He became more insistent.

"Ndakei Nyake, I have told you why I have come to see you this evening. It is a very serious matter that has caused me serious headaches and even some sleepless nights. I could have been sleeping by now, but decided to come and see you. I am itching to hear what you have to say."

Nyake cleared his throat and took another gulp of his wine, leaving just a tiny bit in the cup.

"The reason you have given for wanting to take a second wife is not convincing to me," he said. "If I were in your position, I would consult our ancestors. The way I look at it is this; you do not have any guarantee that if you marry another woman she will give you sons. I know many people who are in the same position as you. Also, my brother, the white man has told us that women, I mean girls, can do anything these days that we men can do. So, if you ask my advice, I would say let Kunaafoh continue her education. I mean it. Tomorrow she could be a doctor, a lawyer or an engineer. Who knows? Look at the number of white women who are doctors these days."

Hindowaa listened but said nothing in response, anticipating that Nyake would continue.

"Also, don't you believe that it is God that gives us children and it is He who decides whether you should have boys or girls? Are you not content with God's decision? The ancestors will be angry with you one day. I am warning you so that you reflect on this before you decide on marrying a second wife for the wrong reasons. I know as well as you do that a long time ago a very stubborn chief insisted on marrying for the wrong reasons, after much harassment of two of his beloved wives. The new wives actually gave birth to spirits, but we have not learned from his experience."

Hindowaa looked uncomfortable but said, "Ndakei Nyake, you are not in my position. For the past two years Giita has not been pregnant, and my mother has been on my back about it. I know if my father were alive, he too would have expressed concern over this matter of the need for me to have more sons. Now as for Kunaafoh, look how her breasts are full. It is not good for girls not to be married. I am also the only member of a well known family that has not given a wife to the Chief. I am worried about these things. I know about women who are doctors. I have been to Freetown and gone to the hospital. I have seen some of them at the hospitals at Moyamba and Bo. The only thing that concerns me is that I think there are some illnesses that women should not treat. Imagine if you have hernia of the scrotum which is so common in our society, is a woman going to treat you?"

At this, both Nyake and Hindowaa burst out laughing. They laughed so much that Hindowaa felt as if he was choking. Nyake was remembering his late father who had developed the swelling, and how embarrassed their household had been because it impeded his walking.

"Ndakei Nyake, I came here hoping you would sympathise with my situation and encourage me to take another wife and give Kunaafoh in marriage to the Chief, but you have not helped," Hindowaa said once their laughter ended. " No. You have not helped at all. You know that I have a very big piece of land in this town. I need sons to take care of it when I die. *You* do not have this problem because you have many sons. As I said, my mother is also very worried about my situation and she has repeatedly asked me to do something about it. She and my wife are poles apart on this matter. Sometimes she even accuses Giita of having a male spirit that is jealous of her and has decided to arrest her chances of having more sons."

Though Nyake listened as his friend continued to make his case for taking another wife, he was not impressed. Their positions on the matter remained entrenched and polarised.

Hindowaa gave serious thought to appealing to his ancestors even as he refused to give up the idea of taking a second wife and marrying Kunaafoh off to the Chief. He would find it impossible to tell his mother that he had given up the idea of marrying a second wife, when it was a very common and acceptable practice in his culture. In the case of Kunaafoh's marriage, what could he possibly say against this, when so many girls of her age had been married as soon as their breasts began to show? No. It was not defensible. For this, he did not have to consult the ancestors. He knew the answer. Kunaafoh should get married to the Chief. The decision was his alone and he would allow no one to influence him on the matter.

Hindowaa knew how stubborn his friend was when he believed his ideas were the right ones. He also remembered a proverb that said, "Don't rub powder on the back of a crocodile, it is a waste of effort."

He abandoned all efforts to persuade Nyake to change his position and they continued to drink as the night advanced.

"Ah, Ndakei Hindowaa, how time flies," Nyake remarked eventually. "I remember when you were about to marry Giita. I mean it is not so long ago when you think of it. We saw her almost naked in her town. She was provocatively seductive and pretty. She was a good dancer and singer. You used to say she would be the only woman that you would marry and that you would have her alone for life. What has happened to you? The woman is still beautiful even after three children. Have you forgotten so soon? Remember one day when we went fishing and we almost quarrelled because you spent most of the time talking about Giita and how you looked forward to marrying her? You said that you were already in contact with her father and that he had promised you that for as long as he was alive, it was you who would marry his daughter? You see my friend, we all need daughters and we love beautiful daughters who will attract suitors. The daughters will then give birth to the sons that you and I so desire."

Feeling frustrated that his friend did not seem to appreciate the seriousness of his concerns, Hindowaa did not respond to Nyake's comments. The town was getting sleepy as it was now late. The moon was still generous and continued to illuminate the town.

"Now, Hindowaa, tell me in confidence. Did you ever tell Giita about that competition, when you won the first prize? You know what I mean. If I were you, I would tell her. She will be told one day by someone in this town."

Hindowaa laughed though he felt a bit irritated. He knew his friend was referring to an eating competition organised by the white man. There had been other events but Hindowaa competed in the eating event and had won first prize. He had kept his prize sacred and was proud of it.

"Ah, Ndakei, I know that you just want to provoke me," he said. " I have not told her about it. Now that you have brought it up, I shall tell her at the appropriate time. Thank you for reminding me."

"Tonight, the Sande initiates have been singing beautiful songs, maybe that is the reason you are so adamant about marrying a new wife. The songs have also reminded me about my own efforts to marry the two women from Khortuhun. Those were the best of times, when men were men. I still recall how many men were vying for my first wife after

31

the initiation was over. There were men who were famous and wanted her desperately. Do you know what happened, I had a friend who said that he knew a famous medicine man who would prepare something for me that would attract my future wife's father? He gave me directions where to find the man."

"And were you able to find the man?" Hindowaa asked, interested in hearing Nyake's love story.

"Ndakei Hindowaa how can you ask such a question when the answer is so obvious? That is why I was able to marry my first wife. I traced the man and he gave me all that was necessary for me to charm my future father-in-law. In fact, to this day, my father-in-law and I are the best of friends."

"Well, let me tell you that if I have to charm the father of my next wife, I shall go to the man who helped you. I shall engage the services of any famous medicine man to get married and have more sons. For now, I do not see any need to hire such a man."

"Oh, so you have already been assured by the girl's father and you came to inform me after you had already started the process. When do you intend going to 'put kola' for her (have a formal engagement)?" Nyake asked, surprised that Hindowaa had gone so far in the process of marrying a second wife.

"You know Nyake, if your mother were alive, you would understand my situation. My mother has a lot of influence on me as the only son in her life. People don't seem to appreciate my predicament. My situation is not an easy one. Perhaps, if she had had many sons, my situation would have been different. My mother suffered a lot for me, because I was the only son. Father was rather lukewarm towards her, and her co-wives used to tease her because I was the only son she had. Poor mother, she suffered a lot for my sake. This is the source of my problem. Each time I tell you about needing more sons, you show no sympathy. All you do is lecture me."

Hindowaa thought, he would win Nyake over after he had so passionately told him the source of his problem for the first time. They were still drinking and enjoying the evening. The Sande initiates continued to sing at regular intervals and both friends continued to enjoy their songs.

"I appreciate all that you have said, my friend," Nyake replied. "I only hope that you have not misunderstood me. You can marry another woman, but not for the wrong reason. You can marry two, three, four women because you want to marry and have children. Nobody will scold you for that. However, do not say you are doing so because you want the other woman to have sons. What if the other woman has girls? Would you marry another woman, and then another and another if they gave you daughters? That is my concern. My other concern is that you seem to have forgotten, perhaps for good reason, the famous story of Kinni Kposowa. I know very well that it is a story that should have guided many of us, but it seemed not to have served us all well. Kinni Kposowaa had harassed his two wives for not giving him sons. In the end, his third wife and the youngest gave him four sons. I am sure that you know the rest of the story. If you remember, one of the boys was expelled from school for smoking and drinking alcohol. The second boy became wild and made several girls pregnant, which was a serious case for the parents, because he could not even afford a pair of decent trousers. The third son decided to look for quick money and went to the challenging District of Kono to prospect for diamonds. He never came back. The fourth son simply told his father that he had no plans and roamed the chiefdom aimlessly. He was confused, a confused son." Hindowaa was not amused by the story and waited for Nyake to continue.

"If the four children were girls, they would be married, have children, who in turn would have children and continue to populate the chiefdom. At least they would give the census people work when the time came."

Hindowaa made no comment and continued to drink his palm wine, so Nyake said, "Ndakei, as of tonight, I shall pray for you so that when you marry your second wife she will bear sons. I promise you, I shall pray for you. You can trust me as a good friend."

He felt relaxed, as they continued to drink and listen to the songs of the Sande initiates. The atmosphere was calm, peaceful and the palm wine tasted even better. The spirits of the night were awake as the two friends continued to drink and talk the night away.

They were both startled when someone greeted them. He stood outside in his tattered clothes. Both friends burst out laughing, then Nyake asked loudly. "What do you want? Why are you not sleeping? It is late."

The man laughed, when spoken to by Nyake. He laughed loudly enough for Nyake's neighbours to hear.

"You are also awake, and I also see someone passing over there," the man answered. "He too is awake. He is not sleeping. I want you to give me some tobacco. I want to smoke, but as you know, I do not have money. Many people in this town owe me money. I do not like to call debts from people. That is my fault but many people owe me money. They think that I am mad. They send me on errands and promise me money, which they never give me. How do they expect me to live? They only give me food. How much food can I eat in one day? One day, I shall go to the Chief and summon all those who owe me money."

Mboma was the most famous madman in the town. He was there to beg for tobacco because Nyake was puffing away and he had smelled it as he passed by. He was harmless and would dance for children if they sang his favourite songs and clapped their hands. People would send him to go and fetch water from the river or firewood from the bush. He was always a willing messenger. A few times when sent to fetch water, he would overstay and come with firewood instead. There were other times when, sent to buy snuff across the street, he would go down town for it and when queried, would say that was the best snuff in town even though he never ate snuff. Nevertheless, people liked him and continued to send him on errands.

"Mboma, where is your friend?" Hindowaa asked him.

"I have many friends, which one are you referring to?" he responded quite coherently.

Nyake and Hindowaa were not surprised at his answer. They were among those who were of the view that Mboma was not really mad, but possessed by spirits which attacked him periodically. However, other people were convinced of Mboma's madness. How can a young and handsome man like Mboma be in tattered clothes all the time, walking from one corner of the town to the other? they asked.

"I am talking about the only friend of yours that I know, Kasilo (a spider). I don't see both of you together." Hindowaa told him. Mboma smiled and moved a step further toward Hindowaa.

"Ndiyaamu, Nyake, tell your friend that I am not like Kasilo. Kasilo is a madman and he wants me to be his friend. Am I not your friend, Ndiyaamu? So how can he say Kasilo is my friend? Are you Ndiyaamu a mad man?"

Nyake and Hindowaa laughed at Mboma's question.

"I have seen many people come and pass by since I have been standing here and you have not asked them why they are not sleeping. Why don't you ask them? Maybe tonight I shall come and sleep on your veranda. It is a long time since I slept here, not so my friend?"

He was referring to Nyake.

"Some people think I am mad," he went on. "The children say I am mad because when they sing I dance for them. I dance because I know how to dance. I am not like Kasilo who eats dead rats and bats. Have you ever seen me eat dead things in this town? So why do you think I am a mad man?"

Hindowaa and Nyake remained silent.

"I know people who try to provoke me and tell me that I am a mad man. One day, I shall go to the Chief and tell him about it. I know all of them in this town who say I am a mad man. However, they have never seen me sit down like Kasilo and go to toilet while the children watch me. So, I am not like Kasilo."

Nyake gave him some tobacco.

Mboma had earned fame during one Ramadan month. The whole town was eager to spot the new moon, which would usher in the period when Muslims would start the fast. Every evening, people would stay outdoors watching the sky in search of the new moon. The exercise had continued for an uncomfortable period and the moon was nowhere to be seen. There was also the myth that the person who located the moon would go to paradise. One day, the Muslim community decided that an emissary should be despatched to Freetown to find out whether the Muslim community there had indeed spotted the moon.

One day, after many people had given up trying to spot the new moon, there was a loud cry of, "The new moon. The new moon. There it is, the new moon." It was Mboma, the mad man, and many people ignored him, saying that it was only Mboma, the madman. But he insisted as he pointed east and convincingly showed the crowd around that the new moon had appeared. He was correct. Many in the crowd saw the moon and were pleased with Mboma, the mad man. He was showered with compliments. Some people even felt he was about to recover fully from his madness.

As the jubilation over the moon continued, Mboma shouted again and told the still jubilant crowd that he had also spotted a second

35

moon in the west and tried to convince his admirers that indeed there were two moons. People laughed and said Mboma's madness was incurable.

Hindowaa walked home that night, determined that he would proceed with his plan - marry a second wife in search of sons, marry Kunaafoh off to the Chief, and send the two boys to continue school in Freetown. However, he also decided that he would consult his ancestors about these things. As he walked along, he knew that he was not the happiest man in town. He reflected on these matters, wishing the ancestors would come up with a solution.

CHAPTER FOUR

The news of the sudden and mysterious disappearance of Kunaafoh emotionally paralysed Talia. The town was shaken by a sense of fear and incomprehension such as it had never experienced in its long history. The entire town was enveloped in a collective state of nightmarish anguish and anger. Everybody asked the same question. Why should it happen in their town? And why to the Hindowaa family?

The older generation gathered in little groups to reflect on Kunaafoh's disappearance. The younger generation was even more apprehensive, feeling that it was their group that had been targeted and assaulted by the devil. They were filled with a sense of awe and uncertainty. The atmosphere was intensely sombre.

The Hindowaa household was immersed in a funereal atmosphere, understandably so since it was the most directly affected by the sudden disappearance of Kunaafoh. Many sympathisers, old and young, trooped to Hindowah's house during the day as well as at night to pay their respects and offer their condolences.

Death or mysterious disappearances always brew fresh memories in the families of those who have left this world. Hindowaa and his mother recalled the passing away of his father many years before. That was the time when the family became split because of speculation and suspicion that his death was the result of internal foul play. It was said that Hindowaa's father had used his influence to grab some land from a very close family member who then decided to take revenge. The battle for the land had taken a long time to resolve. In the end, it was Hindowaa's father who won the case and he had started boasting. However, when he died, it was never proved who was responsible for his death, though the speculation persisted. The entire family never fully recovered from the rancour and incrimations of the incident.

"I have lived for seventy-five years but cannot recall anything like this happening. No. I cannot recall anything like it." *Kinie* Ndovo ('Mr. Toad') told the elders assembled at Hindowaa's house. Some bowed their heads as he spoke. Others nodded in support of what he had to say about the affair. He went on, "Talia has never been associated with such things. I know that other towns have had similar incidents in the past, but not Talia. We have to investigate the matter and make sure that the sinister witchcraft practised in other places is effectively arrested here. We should make serious efforts to discourage such things."

"*Kinie* Ndovo is right. I agree with what he has said." *Kinie* Fefegula (meaning, 'Wind Garment') remarked after *Kinie* Ndovo had spoken. His father was a renowned medicine man who detected and chased people with evil spirits as well as those involved in witchcraft. People travelled from faraway towns to come and seek his assistance when they had problems. Some people believed that it was because of his presence in Talia that evil spirits and witchcraft had disappeared till now. "I am older than him, but I do not remember such an incident happening here. Our town is a peaceful place. However, look at what is happening to us now. This world is not safe. We are not like Kanibu, where all manner of witchcraft exists. It is at Kanibu that women go to fetch water and do not return. It is at Kanibu that children go in search of firewood and disappear. We will not allow Talia to become like Kanibu."

"As for me, I do not have adequate words to express my feelings," another elder observed as the others continued to listen. There followed a moment of subdued silence on the veranda where they sat that evening, as if each person was pondering what measures to take to avoid such a thing happening to him. Each of them felt personally affected by Kunaafoh's sudden disappearance.

A sharp and piercing outburst of wailing came from inside the house, first from Giita, then from an entire chorus of women's voices. The pitch was low at first, then like a musical graph, took a high tone for a brief moment before levelling off. The women were all seated on the bare floor, their wrappers rolled up, their legs outstretched. Some of them had loosened their hair and removed all jewellery from their bodies.

"*Yeea yoo, yeea yoo* (meaning, 'Oh, my mother')" Giita started crying again, alone this time. She called out to her deceased mother. "Where are you today? My child is gone. She has gone to the unknown. Will you take care of your only granddaughter? Without Kunaafoh my life has no meaning. My sweet daughter has gone forever. Kunaafoh, I warned you repeatedly about the mermaid but you defied me. It is the mermaid that has taken my daughter. I know it and Talia knows it. The mermaid took away my daughter. *Mama Kemah yoo. Mama Kemah yoo,*" she wept, calling out to her deceased grandmother. "*Eekeh Vamboi yoo. Ekeh*

Vamboi yoo," she called out to her deceased father. *"Maadaa Ndomahina yoo. Maadaa Ndomahina yoo,"* she called out to her grandfather.

Appealing to them all to come to her aid, she cried, *"Ah wa wey awah. Gboh ngi piia. Ngi monehnga gbama ndunya."* She told them she had struggled in vain in the world because Kunaafoh had now disappeared.

Others entered the room to sympathise with Giita and, amid silence, went round telling those who continued to wipe tears from their eyes to stop crying. Then all of a sudden they too burst out crying, wailing loudly and continuously as they pulled at their loosened hair. They wept for a long time before another moment of silence ensued.

The sympathisers stayed on until very late at night. The rest of the town was preoccupied with Kunaafoh's disappearance and started speculating about why she had disappeared. Some even suggested that she might have eloped with a boy friend, but that idea was dismissed. There was no missing man. Then some suggested she might have drowned in the river if she had gone there without the knowledge of her parents. Indeed, if the river overflowed its banks, and the community had not appropriately propitiated its spirits, they often took offence and held a member of the community as ransom or hostage. There were those who also believed that because Kunaafoh was a known psychic, she might have decided to join the spirits of the forest because the *Ndogbowusui* had been active recently.. A short dwarfish creature with in a brownish country-cloth garment sewn with cowry shells and amulets, *Ndogbowusui* was a well-known spirit of the forest who would mislead his victims and hold them ransom for a long time while the community went looking for them. He always carried a bag suspected of containing powerful medicines which he used as charms. When he trapped his victims, he would make sure that their vision became blurred and all the roads out of the forest erased. He would take his victims to the river, give them a fishing net and ask them to collect water from the river with it and fill a container. This was an impossible task meant to frustrate his victims. Was this the fate of Kunaafoh? They wondered. What was well known was that the spirit of the forest never killed its victims. They would resurface far away from their own homes or towns to tell the story of what had happened. They were never harmed, but people feared the spirit of the forest and continue to do so to this day. Other people based on what Kunaafoh had told them about their conversation at the river, believed that the mermaid might have been responsible for Kunaafoh's disappearance

When the sympathisers had gone, some to their own homes and others to temporary accommodation, Hindowaa went to visit his mother, *Yeea* Kigba. Since Kunaafoh's disappearance, she had entered a virtual state of solitary confinement for though she was not very fond of Giita, she had an immense love for her granddaughter. Kunaafoh's disappearance had made her grandmother extremely unhappy. She could not eat or sleep properly. Her countenance was morose and sour. She recalled in infinite detail how she had helped to take care of Kunaafoh as a child. She recalled the songs she used to sing to her when she cried, and how she used to cuddle her when it was cold and Giita was away at the farm. She recalled how she used to tell Kunaafoh to start walking soon so that Giita would get pregnant again and produce another son. All these tender and loving thoughts, brought warm grandmotherly tears which dripped freely from *Yeea* Kigba's eyes and soaked her dry cheeks.

"*Yeea*," Hindowaa addressed his mother who was lying on the floor, tired and despondent over her only granddaughter's mysterious disappearance. "*Yeea*, when the mourning is over and we have made all the necessary sacrifices to the ancestors, I shall go to Rogbohun in the north to see the venerable soothsayer, the *Moimu* (Muslim priest). He will tell us what happened to Kunaafoh, my only daughter. We should be able to discover the facts. I am determined to find out what happened. You know that when my father died, I wanted to find out who was responsible but people prevailed on me not to proceed because they said whoever was responsible would be punished by God. I refrained from pursuing the matter and you agreed with me. This time, I am going to investigate what happened to Kunaafoh. God will understand my anger, my grief, and my pain as a parent. I want your support. Your only granddaughter is gone, perhaps dead. Why?"

His mother coughed slightly. She now looked frail and many in Talia thought she might die at any time. Some people even thought that she had tuberculosis though they kept such suspicions to themselves.

"My son, with my seventy-nine years of living, experience has taught me of the infinite possibilities of evil. This world is a place where people make others their prey. There is too much wickedness in this world. Why should anyone hurt Kunaafoh? I think that someone is trying to hurt you, to hurt the family. Think about it also, I always suspected that some people in Giita's family were not clean. You know the family she comes from. I have discussed with you many times the fact that she has not had more than three children. I am suspicious but you always dismiss my suspicions. The town she comes from is full of witches, very powerful witches. It is the only place I know where witches even eat unborn babies. What is more painful is the fact that my granddaughter has not yet been initiated into the Sande Society. She is going about as an uninitiated girl. It is a shame for the entire family. Her breasts are now ripe." *Yeea* Kigba stopped speaking to cough. Hindowaa found it painful to watch her struggle to clear phlegm from her throat.

"Mother, I have heard all you have said. I shall see the soothsayer as I have promised. The only problem is that after all these things, I have no money to go and see him. I shall have to take a loan from friends to pursue this matter. If I have to sell all my goats, I will. If I have to pledge my rice barn, I will. If I have to sell all my ginger, I will. I will do all that is in my power to come to the root of this matter."

"Have you consulted with Giita since the disappearance of Kunaafoh?" *Yeea* Kigba asked.

"Mother I want to wait until the sympathisers stop coming. You know that since we found out that Kunaafoh had disappeared the house has been over-flowing with sympathisers. I shall talk to her to hear her own version of the story. We shall find out the truth as long as our venerable soothsayer is alive. Let me say this, mother. I am sure that our ancestors are with us. I know that from experience. I have never abandoned my obligations to them. It is because of this, that our harvest has always been plentiful. Look how full my rice barn is. Look how many goats I have. My ginger harvest this year; is the talk of the town. That is because I have not abandoned our ancestors. Why should this thing have happened to me all of a sudden?"

"My son, I understand. I myself have been worried over these things. To tell you the truth, I have asked myself many times why, why our ancestors failed to give you more sons. Are they punishing you or me? I only had one son. Why do they want to do this to you again? Every Sunday, I go to the shrine and pour libation to them, I leave cooked rice, and rice flour and palm wine by the shrine. You have also done all that you are supposed to do. I don't believe they listen to us. How can they do this to us at this time? It makes me wonder. My heart bleeds, my child. It aches."

"Mother, don't cry, Kunaafoh will come back I swear to my father and grandfather, Kunaafoh will come back some day. She is not dead, no; I refuse to believe that my only daughter is dead. Whoever bewitched her will not succeed. Mother, I am convinced, she is somewhere. I suspect it is the *Ndogbowusui* that has taken my daughter. She will come back some day, she will come back safe and sound and we shall rejoice."

"How is it that no one can say when last they saw my granddaughter and where?" *Yeea* Kigba complained. "No one, not even her mother has a clue, and the school has not helped us. When I was with her the day before she disappeared, she looked extra happy though I could not discern the reason for such a happy mood. She probably knew she was going to disappear. Children who are psychic know beforehand what is going to happen to them. That was why I told you that we should engage a Muslim priest and our own medicine man to get rid off my granddaughter's psychic powers, but you never listened to me. It's not good for some people to be psychic. Some even end up mad."

"Mother, we shall deal with some of these matters in the future," Hindowaa assured her. Abruptly changing the subject, *Yeea* Kigba said, "Hmmmm. My son, I wanted to broach a subject with you, but I have been hesitating because I do not know how you will react to it. It is a very sensitive matter."

Hindowaa immediately became anxious, knowing how his mother brought up sensitive issues at the wrong time. He sighed, waiting to hear what she had to say.

Yeea Kigba scratched her scalp slowly as her son looked on. She then bowed her head as if she did not want to have any eye contact with him.

"Is the door securely looked?" she asked. "People here like to eavesdrop."

"Mother we have been here for some time and the door has been ajar all this time. It is even better for us to leave it as it is."

"My son, tell me, you are my son." *Yeea* Kigba went on. "Tell me the truth, do you trust your wife, the woman you married from that town? Do you know the history of that town and people who come from there? You are a child, my son. There are many things you don't understand. You think you are grown-up and know many things. No.

You are making a mistake. You are still a child, my son. You will always remain a child to me. Get this into your head because it is a fact."

"Mother, I know that I am your son and that you know many things that I don't know. However, also admit that I am grown up now - a married man with a family."

"Aha, Aha, that is the problem. You think you are a big man now and you know everything. Your late father used to tell me how you were too big for your shoes."

Hindowaa began to feel impatient.

"Mother, tell me what you want to tell me," he said. "It is late and this is a funeral period.

Yeea Kigba finally asked him in a stern voice, "Do you trust Giita, Giita your wife from that town? Tell me the truth, I am your mother. Tell me."

"Mother, I don't understand what you are asking. I have been married to Giita for a long time and this is the first time we have had such a problem. I don't understand what you are suggesting."

"You don't' understand what I am…what? What exactly do you mean by that? Let me tell you, Hindowaa, you are my only son and I will make sure you listen to me; listen to what I tell you. You will never be more experienced than your mother or father even though you have grown tall and fat. You are still my child."

"Mother, I know that I am your child. I have never doubted that."

"Then, let me tell you this. You know that Giita is psychic and Kunaafoh is psychic. Do you know that it is possible for the spirit of the river or forest to fall in love with women who are psychic? The female spirits also fall in love with men sometimes. When that happens, they often strike a deal with the man or woman. I believe that the spirit of the river and Giita struck a deal. He would take Kunaafoh so that Giita would have more sons. I know this because I had a dream and my dreams are always correct. I had a dream, Hindowaa, I had a dream. Keep it a secret. These things have happened many times in our town and beyond. You can sacrifice any of your loved ones if you enter into a bargain with the spirit of the river or the forest. You know that is the case in a number of situations. Don't you know the case of Nyamakoro, the richest woman in town? She has no children because she preferred money to children. Everybody in Talia knows that. How else can you explain it? Kortu's wife also preferred money to having children and struck a bargain with the spirit."

Hindowaa was listening attentively and thought his mother's reasoning was plausible, though his sixth sense cautioned him.

"If you were psychic and the female spirit of the river or forest fell in love with you, she would approach you and ask you what you wanted her to do for you. She would give you all that you asked for, provided you abandoned your wife or wives. Don't you know such things have happened here in Talia and beyond?"

"Mother, are you suggesting that Giita would do such a thing? Remember when I married Giita, there was rumour that she would not have children because she came from a family with a grandfather who had *ngelegba*?"

"Hindowaa, where did you get that information? Who told you that story?"

Agitated, Hindowaa's mother was visibly disturbed by her son's reference to the rumours that Giita would be barren.

"My son, this town is full of rumours," she said quickly. "Look what you are bringing up now. I am trying to help so we can discover what has brought this misfortune to the family, and look what you are saying about Giita. All I said is that these things do happen and have happened here in Talia, and I cited the case of Nyamakoro. Do you have such a short memory, my son? Don't you know the case of *Kinie* Kpelewo? Have you forgotten that also? Did he not sacrifice his daughter so that he would win elections? Yes, he did and the water spirits took the beautiful child away. He confessed after he lost the elections. Do you want me to tell you more of these stories which you already know? Let me tell you this. Giita could do anything to have more sons for us. You now consider yourself are a big man and do not believe what your mother tells you. One day, you will find out for yourself; but by then it will be too late."

"Mother, Nyamakoro and *Kinie* Kpelewo were not psychic," Hindowaa pointed out before saying he would also like to ask her a question.

"Mother, tell me, I am your only son. Would you have sacrificed me if the spirit of the forest or river had asked you to do so with a view to increasing your chances of having more sons?"

"Hindowaa, how can you ask me such question? How dare you?" *Yeea* Kigba responded. She sounded angry and bitter. It was a reaction Hindowaa had anticipated.

"You children of today," she went on peevishly, "that is why you will always be in trouble. You do not listen to your parents. You think you know it all because you have put on trousers. Yes, I know you have put on *BEREWA* (meaning, 'big trousers') and you don't listen to what your parents tell you. I am warning you, Hindowaa, to listen to me. If you don't do that, one of these days, I shall curse you. I shall curse you. I will go to the river and undress and curse you. Then you will see who your mother is. You will know what a mother's curse can do to a child. I carried you for nine months in my belly and suffered labour pains to bring you into this world. I dare you to challenge me."

"Mother, I think you chose the wrong time to bring up this subject. I understand how strongly you feel about it, but let us come back to it after I have visited the famous soothsayer. In the meantime, let us give Giita the benefit of the doubt."

There was a painful silence in the room as Hindowaa went away. They had not achieved much by way of agreeing on what role Giita might have played in Kunaafoh's disappearance. Hindowaa was disturbed that his mother harboured such thoughts about Giita and decided to continue assessing the situation.

When he entered the room, he found Giita still awake. Sleep had effectively escaped her. She was in a state of mourning, her hair undone, her eyes sore from excessive crying for she had had to cry along with all the women who came to sympathise with her as well as the rest of the Hindowaa family.

Hindowaa wanted to confer with Giita over the issue his mother had raised. It was a sensitive subject and he felt uncomfortable bringing it up for discussion with her. His mind was in turmoil. He had to admit that his mother was right in the sense that people had conspired with spirits before to enhance their status in life. However, he was equally sure that Giita would not do such a thing. But such certainty could not be sustained in this mournful atmosphere. There was a slight possibility that his mother could be right. Human frailty can lead to fatal consequences, he thought.

Giita was lying quietly in bed. Hindowaa cleared his throat.

"I have always wanted to know if you have *ngafei* (a spirit) in your family," he began. "Tell me, when did you last see Kunaafoh?"

"Why are asking me such a question at this time of night and under such conditions?" Giita replied, sounding angry and surprised.

"I am just curious."

"Yes, I am psychic, and Kunaafoh is psychic. It is in our family, but our own type of psychic power is good let me tell you. It was rumoured that I would not have children, but I have had three. It was rumoured that Kunaafoh would do anything to prevent me from having another child, but Kafo came. They said that Kunaafoh was jealous because she wanted to have all the fatherly and motherly attention and love as the only daughter. All these fabrications came from people with sinister dispositions. I do not think we should go into that at this time of the night. We can do that after the forty day ceremony. Who knows, perhaps before that time Kunaafoh will be back. I am convinced that my daughter is not dead, missing, yes, dead, no. Before you came into this room, I knew you would be consulting with your mother and now you are here to interrogate me."

"Giita, I am not psychic like you and Kunaafoh. However, I also believe that though Kunaafoh is missing, she is not dead. Both of us agree on that. What I am now asking you is a result of my investigations. I do not mean to say that it is because you are psychic that such a thing has happened to us. Moments like these offer us an opportunity to discuss family matters. So please do not misunderstand me."

While Hindowaa started getting ready for bed. Giita was thinking, Sleep was a distance away from her. Her husband's question disturbed her greatly. She felt that both her mother-in-law and her husband were conspiring to make her life miserable. She knew what Hindowaa's mother thought about her and how she was not in favour of her son marrying her. She had not been interested in marrying Hindowaa. It was her father who made the decision. If Hindowaa's mother was instrumental in the affairs of her son, then she should have prevailed on Hindowaa not to marry her. She had accepted her mother-in-law's hostility towards her because she had been told repeatedly that in many marriages, it was the mothers-in-law who caused most domestic problems. They wanted to control their sons and in the process created domestic conflicts. It was as a result of this that she had been told to be cautious in dealing with her mother-in-law. She was told - she recalled, that fathers-in-law were less difficult to deal with.

When Hindowaa came to bed, she said, "Let me ask you, Hindowaa, why is it that it is not Hinga or Kafo that went missing? Have you thought about that?"

"All I can say now is that the truth shall prevail in the end," Hindowaa replied.

"I am glad to hear that, so let us wait and see."

Complying, Hindowaa changed the subject.

"I am grateful to the people of Talia and beyond for the sympathy they have shown," he said. "Many people of substance have been here, including our future father-in-law, the Chief. May he live long to rule over us."

"You know, after the whole ceremony is over, we are going to be bankrupt," Giita observed. "These days, funerals have become expensive. Look at the amount of food that we have been cooking, and the drinks, and this is going to continue for some time. You also have to go and see the soothsayer. How are we going to recover financially from this? Then what if Kunaafoh returns? How do we get back the money we are spending? These days, there are many professional funeral attendants. They go to every funeral because they can eat, drink and even socialize at the expense of the bereaved family. If you are poor and die, only a few sympathisers will come while the majority will stay away. So the professional funeral attendants pray for rich and well-to-do people to die so that they can feast and drink. This is our world today."

Hindowaa thought for a while as Giita's observations sank deep into his mind. He was not ready to fall asleep. The fact that after the ceremony they would have to cope with the cost of the funeral kept bothering him. He had already incurred a substantial amount of debt. Then, he knew he was confronted with another financial matter, the question of marrying another wife. This was an issue of serious concern for him. He had already earmarked the prospective bride. Now he had to deal with bereavement. Why are all these things happening to me at this time? he thought.

"You see, if we had many girls, then when they married we would get bride price," Giita reminded him. "You see my point. When the boys marry, *we* have to pay the bride price, yet the preference is always for sons. Now after the bereavement comes the reality of our situation. Hindowaa, we might end up dying in debt, because even if we sell all that we have, we shall not be able to pay the outstanding debt. I have been thinking about this even as I cry over Kunaafoh's disappearance. It is a serious matter."

Hindowaa agreed, but refused to admit that daughters were therefore more to be desired. His preference for sons had overwhelmed his reasoning process.

"Giita, Giita, did you hear the cock crowing?" Hindowaa exclaimed. "Here we are, lying awake when we should be sleeping."

Giita did not reply, for she had fallen asleep.

CHAPTER FIVE

Not far from Giita's own home town of Farhma lived one of the most venerable and feared soothsayers in the area. Giita had chosen him, not only to seek help in respect of Kunaafoh's disappearance, but also concerning the prospect of her having more sons. She had not been pregnant for two years and her husband continued to threaten that he would marry another wife who would give him more sons. The soothsayer was known to be expensive even as his services were said to be more efficacious than others in the area. . Giita had to take a loan to finance her mission and would remain in debt long after the mission was over.

Her choice of Gbahama (meaning, 'unconquered') was not because she came from that town, but because it had become famous during the ethnic wars of many years ago. Gbahama fought with its neighbours and in each battle it emerged victorious. Its victory over its neighbours was attributed to the great mystical powers of its soothsayers and medicine men. People said that the war lasted for ninety days and left the countryside almost decimated of its population. Gbahama mobilized its hunters and warriors who wore mystically bulletproof garments. Many of the soothsayers who predicted Gbahama's victory in those wars were still alive and continued to practise their profession, so, people continued to patronize Gbahama's practitioners of sacred divination. Giita was one of them, together with her relatives. They undertook the journey after the funeral ceremonies had ended.

Giita, her brother and uncle left very early in the morning for Gbahama. They left when the first cocks started crowing, even before the Muezzin and the Town Crier had started their tasks. Nature was at peace with herself. People were sleeping peacefully and the dreamers enjoyed their dreams in blissful abandon. Giita, her brother and uncle stole away in the stillness of the early morning with a view to arriving at Gbahama before *Kinie* Komawaa's numerous clients arrived from all over the region. The footpath was wet with dew that morning.

In all fairness to Talia, when a family was in trouble, bereaved or had other problems, the town always showed a sense of solidarity and cooperation. In this regard, while Hindowaa and his wife embarked on their missions to ascertain the circumstances surrounding Kunaafoh's disappearance and possible death, the community was equally engaged in its own efforts to locate the girl.

The elders of Talia had met earlier and agreed to dispatch traditional hunters familiar with the forests and traditional fishermen who could dive deep into the river to search for Kunaafoh. These hunters and fishermen were well armed and fearless. They were the custodians of security in the town and were often summoned to defend the territorial integrity of the town when it was threatened or violated. The townspeople were anxiously awaiting the outcome of the hunters and fishermen's mission that could take days or even weeks.

"My daughter had become the envy of the town. I had known that for a long time," Giita told her relatives as they walked along the dew-soaked footpath to Gbahama. The two relatives listened attentively as she spoke and afterwards her uncle remarked, "I always told you that people of Talia town are not as good as we often think. They have some of the most venomous witches in that town. That was one of the reasons I was opposed to your marrying to anyone in Talia. I believe that they are responsible for your inability to have more sons. I have the entire history of Talia in my hands."

"Uncle, I agree with your observation," said Giita's brother. "I totally agree with you. You see, when it comes to a question of making a decision, we the children have no say in the matter. Father had made up his mind who should marry our sister. There was no opposition. Like you said, Talia has one of the worst records in this chiefdom. People seem to have short memories. They have forgotten the scandal that made this town infamous. They have forgotten it so fast, that family feud that was unprecedented in the history of the chiefdom".

"My son, I agree with you. It had never happened anywhere to my knowledge. It was simply unbelievable. How could someone refuse the burial of his brother because he died without paying his debt? What is more scandalous than that in a town? People in some quarters still talk of the matter today. He was told to inherit his brother's four pretty wives in settlement of the debt. He refused and the corpse remained unburied. This was too much. Such things can only happen in Talia. The man's heart was as hard as a stone. Only someone with a stony heart could do such a thing to his own relative, above all his brother from the same womb."

The incident had been one of the most scandalous the town had ever witnessed, and the elders still consider it the worst defilement of the moral sanctity of Talia in living memory. In the end, it was agreed by the town's council of elders that the hardhearted brother should be banished from Talia. Such an incident never recurred after that.

"As my brother has said, our father is to be blamed," Giita said. "I know how he insisted on my marrying *Kinie* Hindowaa. Mother told me that there were other suitors even though I had shown no interest in them, but *Kinie* Hindowaa just appeared from nowhere and ended up being my husband. He has been good, but as you said the people of Talia are full of envy. Look what has now happened to my daughter and my life. *Ngewo* (God) will punish them if they are the ones responsible for my tribulations."

Giita's brother said, "You know, the people here have two faces, one is real and the other is masked. They have been very sympathetic and supportive during our time of tribulation, but they cannot be trusted. One should always be on one's guard. The place has become a very treacherous environment where you can never be too sure of the intentions of your neighbour. How can we live in such a state of mutual suspicion and fear? This world is becoming more and more dangerous."

"At Farmah, the situation is slightly different," their uncle told them as they continued to walk towards their destination. "In our own town, if people don't like you, they do not pretend. They simply avoid you and your business. This is not the case in Talia. In Talia, those who don't like you smile to you often and you are deceived, until they stab you in the back. Then you wake up with a rude shock and ask the question, you also, my brother and my neighbour?"

Giita was pondering all that she had heard. They still had a long distance to cover. The day had just begun, so time was in their favour and all of them were familiar with the road and the distance they had to cover before arriving at their destination. Giita's brother interrupted her thoughts with an unexpected question.

"My sister, tell me," he said "since you have eyes, did you not foresee this incident coming to your household? I am asking you a serious question. We should have known beforehand that something like this would happen in our town, and then taken appropriate measures to avert it."

Unprepared for the question, Giita did not reply immediately. They walked along for some time before she cleared her throat to answer it.

"No, I was not warned. Sometimes even a jinee can be overtaken by events beyond its powers to control. Remember that in the spirit world there is an hierarchy. We humans tend to forget this fact. If I had prior knowledge, of course, I would have taken appropriate measures to prevent what has happened to my family and me. It is too late now and I don't think anyone will benefit by continuing a discussion on this issue. Let us wait and see what the soothsayer tells us when we meet him."

"I agree with you, my sister. I am sure even Kunaafoh was not aware that such a tragedy would happen to her. Children have more powerful psychic powers than their elders. Many people said, Kunaafoh's psychic prowess saved us many times, but this time, she seems to have been deceived. Who knows? I am just speculating."

"As for me," Giita's uncle commented, "all I can say is that we shall soon get to the root of the matter. Even though *I* am not psychic, my dreams are often accurate and precise, but this time, to tell you the truth, I never dreamed about this incident. I am disturbed by that because I ought to have dreamt about such a major event and sought the counsel of a soothsayer. He would have advised me accordingly. That never happened so I am not surprised that both Giita and Kunaafoh were not aware of this matter beforehand."

They had been walking for over one and a half hours. They heard birds chirruping and frogs croaking as they passed through a stream. Giita thought that if she had brought her fishing net along she could have caught some fish to cook when they arrived at Gbahama.

"*Hohnaa blah, ti ghoto ngo Talia,*" Giita's brother said eventually, again commenting on the fact that there were many witches in Talia. He put emphasis on 'many'. His uncle replied, "When we come from Gbahama, if we are not satisfied with what the soothsayer tells us, we should be prepared to ask the Chief to allow us to bring the *ngelegba* medicine man so that we can swear those involved in Kunaafoh's disappearance. We shall see how people start confessing their guilt in this matter. With the *ngelegba*, there is no joking. It is a matter of life and death. No one wants to be struck by deadly lightning. This is the last resort. We should be able to convince the Chief that our case merits attention. We need to weed out the evil spirits in Talia. But let us wait and see the result of our visit to Gbahama. My only other concern is that people in Talia might make serious efforts to implicate Giita in Kunaafoh's disappearance. They might say she sacrificed her daughter to the spirits so that she would have sons. But if I hear that from anyone, I shall attack that person or persons in Talia."

"Uncle, I agree with you," said Giita's brother. "I have also anticipated this and I am ready to confront them if they come up with such a wicked idea. Just imagine!" he went on. "Her father has threatened to marry her off to the Chief, instead of allowing the child to continue her education. My in-law is a very stubborn man. Long ago, they used to say that girls should not be educated because in the end, they would get married and become glorified housemaids to cook and take care of the home, but we all know that things have changed now and there are women who are doctors, administrators, artists, and lawyers. *Demia* would not listen and now, he is in a dilemma. He faithfully promised the chief that he would give Kunaafoh to him as his wife after her initiation into the Sande Society. I believe that '*demia*' was wrong to have decided that he would give Kunaafoh in marriage to the Chief. That might have contributed to her decision to run away. Who knows? By all accounts, the child was doing well in school. We all know that education is very important today. Why was he rushing to marry her off? I have five girls. If I had money, I will allow all of them to finish their education so that they would become independent. In my old age, they would take care of me. But the boys, once they get married, they are more concerned with their own family."

Giita and her two relatives were confident that they were making progress and would arrive at Gbahama early enough to be attended to by the soothsayer. Their conviction was reinforced by the fact that they had not come across any people from Gbahama going to their farms. It was still very early in the morning. And they continued to hear all sorts of noises as birds, frogs, monkeys and baboons realised that day was about to take over from the calm and peaceful morning.

Giita's uncle said in a very serious tone, "As for me, I am not educated, but I want all my children to go to school. If I had been educated my life would be different. Look how well the people who have gone to school live. When the month ends, they get money. I work on the farm and only when the harvest is done can I sell my produce to get money. And that is just once a year. If I were a clerk, I would get paid every month, which is good. That is why I shall do all that is necessary for my children to become educated."

Giita was walking behind her brother and uncle. As she listened to them talk, she began to cry. It was not loud weeping. Tears just streamed from her big, brown, lovely eyes. They heard voices coming from the opposite direction. As they became more audible, the three relatives listened carefully. They knew that they were not very far away from their destination. The people who were talking were farmers from Ghahama who were going to their farms. Farmers who ventured out early in the morning to tend to their farms did so in order that they would have accomplished a lot by the time the sun took over the day. Some also went early to inspect the animal traps and fish-nets before tending to their farms.

As the two groups crossed each other, the farmers from Ghahama, two men and a woman, greeted the travellers from Talia.

"Good morning people, how are you? And where are you coming from so early in the morning?" People were always curious to know why others were travelling because doing so as early as Giita and her relatives were doing suggested a matter of importance. People who ventured out that early on a journey might be going to a funeral, to see a relative who was reported to be seriously ill or to mediate in a serious family palaver.

"We are coming from Talia and going to Gbahama to see *Kinie* Komawaa." Giita's brother replied, which told the three farmers that something was wrong. Having heard about Kunaafoh's disappearance, one of the people in the party asked, "Ah, you are coming from Talia where the child went missing? Oh, people, please accept our sympathy. We heard about it and we found it difficult to believe that a child could go missing just like that. Please accept our sympathy. It must be painful for the parents."

She seemed genuinely touched by the incident of Kunaafoh's disappearance. "Oh, people, but Kinie Komawaa has been ill for a long time even though he is getting better now. Many people came to see him but had to go back because he was unable to attend to them. The old man almost died in our hands," the woman went on.

Giita was extremely distraught with the news of Komawaa's illness. Her stomach churned. She felt sick and anguished at the information. She felt it was a bad omen for her. Why should this happen to her? she wondered. He tried to console his niece who was struggling bravely to wipe the tears from her eyes as they walked along.

"They say he is getting better. Who knows, maybe in a day or two he will be able to see us. We have come a long way. We cannot return without seeing him. Otherwise, we shall have to go south to see another medicine man and that will be too expensive. Giita you know how much it is costing you just to come this far. Let us exercise patience now that we are here," her uncle said.

Many people from the great to the lowly, all in search of Komawaa's mystical powers, frequented the road to Gbahama. Komawaa himself was from obscure origins. He had acquired his esoteric powers through his great grandfather. He had been born crippled until he was four years old, then, in his sleep, his mystical powers were revealed to him and he was told that the test of the efficacy of such powers would be his ability to walk and resume normal life. His physical rehabilitation was dramatic. From that time on, he was able to predict the future, reveal the past through divination with precision and assist people achieve their ambitions in life. His fame spread like wild fire during the harmattan season. All sorts of people came to see him. The mentally ill sought his art of healing to be restored to sanity. Those who were in debt and bankrupt also came to see him. People came to solicit his help to gain promotion in their jobs. Those who could not have children or had love and marital problems made the journey to Gbahama seeking his help.

When Giita and her relatives finally arrived there, most of the town was empty for the able-bodied men and women had gone to their farms as early as they could. Giita and her relatives were welcomed by the elderly population of Gbahama. The people of Gbahama were used to all sorts of visitors. They were hospitable and offered the three clients accommodation and food. Komawaa's wives were particularly kind. They realised how much their husband's illness had eroded the family's resources. For as long as their husband remained ill, clients came and went away again, so they made every effort to speed up their husband's recovery. Giita and her relatives expressed an interest in visiting Komawaa to offer sympathy and to wish him rapid recovery. Komawaa's first wife granted their request. She had been married to Komawaa for twenty-five years and had eight children for the old man. Her three co-wives were much younger, the last of them being younger than her own first daughter. However, there was a relative degree of amicable co-existence in Komawaa's household of four wives and numerous children.

When Giita and her relatives arrived at Komawaa's hut, he was having his breakfast. After they greeted him, he told them to sit down on the benches in the hut.

"This is where you have found me," he said. "Come and join me. It is good to have something in your stomach in the morning, then you can challenge the rest of the day. I knew you were coming to see me. I dreamed of you not long ago."

Komawaa spoke as if he was well, showing no sign of pain. His wife, who had sat down beside him, looked happy with his condition. As he continued to eat, he said, "People, eh, I am happy the way you found me. I have improved a lot. If you had seen me few days ago, it was bad. Ask Boi Tiama, (he was referring to his wife who came from a town called Tiama) she will tell you. They had almost given up on me two weeks ago. I am much better now and know that in a few days time I shall be back to normal."

Komawaa's wife confirmed what he had told them, saying, "*Njabu ngike* (Njabu's father) is right." (The old man had a daughter called Njabu, born when it was raining, which was why she was named Njabu). "The town of Gbahama was about to give up on him. The entire family was distressed. Most nights we did not sleep, expecting the worst. He is much better now. Many clients came and left and he was not even aware that they had come. That is how ill he was. They wanted to kill him. Why? What has he done to deserve death? All he does is to help people. People come from all over this chiefdom to seek his advice, or to get medicine for their sickness. Those who want to advance in their business are also helped. Is this the reason they want to kill him? They want to kill our husband. He has many children and grandchildren. Why are they fighting him?"

"We are happy to know that you have improved," said Giita's brother. "Our ancestors are with you. You do not look like somebody that has been ill for a long time. We came at the right time. *Kinie* Komawaa, you should also realize that this profession is not an easy one.

There is always professional jealousy and competition. It is the same everywhere. People in the same trade fight each other."

"My dear, you have hit the nail on the head," the old soothsayer responded vigorously. "I know other soothsayers have been trying to get rid of me. All over the chiefdom, those in our trade are involved in a mortal combat in the under-world to eliminate each other. In my case, they will not succeed. I have lived long and know how to fight back. In my profession, I am as strong as a granite rock by the river. People go and wash clothes on it and yet it remains unscratched and immobile until eternity. I challenge them. In the end, I shall emerge the victor. Come and join me for breakfast."

Giita and her relatives did not join the old man for breakfast even though he kept asking them to do so.

"I know that I am getting better by the day," Komawaa went on, "but I do not want to talk too much. I know, however, that there are those in this town who want me dead. *They* will go before me. Some of the people here are wicked. I know them and they know that I know them. We meet in the world of the ancestors and, as cowards, they avoid me there. It is here that they try to hurt me. I shall deal with them when I am well. Some of them have started running away from the town having realized that I am about to recover. Let them run away. I shall chase them one after the other. They will have nowhere to hide from me. Children of devils, let them wait until I recover."

The visitors listened with concern and awe.

"*Kinie* Komawaa, these evil ones are everywhere," said Giita's brother. "We have them in our town, Farhma. There, people just die without getting ill. Children also die. Why? It is due to such wicked people."

By now, the old man had finished eating every bit of food in the dish. The wife collected the empty dish and took it outside. She was pleased that her husband's appetite had improved. She remembered that at one time, Komawaa could not eat or even entertain the sight of food. Those were worrisome times. She was happy that the situation had improved and her husband had already shown signs that his generous appetite was being restored. She thanked God and her ancestors.

It was late in the morning when the visitors trooped out of the hut praying for the old man's rapid recovery. They would have to wait for him to recover fully. He had assured Giita and her relatives that he

57

would be ready to address their concerns in a few days, as he was feeling much better. They left him in a buoyant mood, his spirits high.

The people of Gbahama continued to give them hospitality, and told them stories about the old man's enormous medicinal and mystical powers and about the people he had assisted with various problems.

That night, Giita went to sleep, full of hope, mixed with anxiety and great expectations. It would not be until the old man was fully recovered that she would know what fate had in store for her. As she waited nervously, the days and nights seem to advance at a snail's pace. Would she ever have more sons? The question kept tormenting her mind, but she had no choice but to wait for the soothsayer to answer it. So she and her relatives waited.

CHAPTER SIX

Hindowaa knew about *Kinie* Komawaa, having met him on a number of occasions. He first met him when there was a serious dispute about land between the people of Talia and Sembehun Kortuwabu. Talia won the case as a result of Komawaa's intervention. However, this time, Hindowaa had decided to go north while his wife had gone south though with the same objective. He had heard about the presence in the north of the country of a man whose spiritual and mystical powers surpassed all the known medicine men and soothsayers in the area. He had come from Kankan, a town in Guinea known for men learned in Arabic literature and with mystical powers. These men would travel from Kankan to several places in West Africa. They sold their professional services from country to country to those requiring them. There were many, like, Hindowaa, who sought the assistance of these men to address their problems. When he undertook his journey that day, Hindowaa was convinced that he would soon be back with information about the disappearance of his daughter, Kunaafoh and about the prospects of Giita having more sons. Unlike his wife and her relatives who had gone to Gbahama by foot, he had to go by lorry from Talia to the north, to a town called Rogbohun. It was a half-day's journey under normal circumstances, but experiences varied. The conditions of the roads were woefully unpredictable. More unpredictable was the condition of the vehicle one was travelling in. Sometimes, after the vehicle had gone ten or twenty miles, the driver would stop and say, there was a problem with the engine; the carburettor was too hot; and the vehicle could go no further. Another frequent complaint was that the petrol had finished and the apprentice had to go some miles away to buy fuel. There was also the perennial problem of a tyre puncture and its attendant frustration, especially in situations where the vehicle had no spare. This would entail the tiresome process of having to disembark and wait for the tyre to be repaired. Their mission stalled, travellers like Hindowaa, would either suffer in stoic silence or else their heartbeats assumed moments of irregularity.

Hindowaa travelled with one of his sisters. He had declined his friend, Nyake's offer to accompany him because he said Hindomaa had to meet the cost of transportation to the north. Hindowaa was furious and thought that Nyake was not a true friend. They had been friends for a long time and he found it inappropriate for Nyake to have behaved like that at a time when he was distressed over the mysterious disappearance of his only daughter.

On his way to the north he reflected on Giita's mission to Gbahama. He was longing to know what Komawaa would find out about Kunaafoh's disappearance. Was she alive or dead? Would Giita have more sons? These questions challenged his sense of curiosity as the driver sped along on the short stretch of road, which was in good condition.

Manja (the name Hindowaa's sister was given because their mother became quarrelsome when she was pregnant with her) was also feeling very sad as she accompanied her brother. She was one of Kunaafoh's favourite aunts and they had got along very well. She had looked forward to participating in her niece's initiation into the Sande Society where Kunaafoh would be circumcised and thereby attain adulthood before marrying the Chief. For the time being, her expectations had to be postponed, and she wondered why such a calamity should happen to the Hindowaa family. She had other reasons for concern, being the mother of three girls herself. If this pattern of female disappearance continued, she knew that her own daughters would not be safe. More worrisome was the fact that the disappearance of girls was never part of the social structure of Talia society. Why was it happening now? These questions worried her and kept her mind busy as the vehicle sped towards Rogbohun.

Hindowaa and his sister, Manja, were lucky that day though they arrived at Rogbohun very late at night. There were times when the journey took two days because of the frequent technical problems that the vehicles suffered. They were lucky in another respect, for when they arrived at Rogbohun, they found that their host was in town, well and hearty, though he was asleep. The arrival of the vehicle after midnight disrupted the peace of the sleeping town which was amazingly serene and dark. A gentle and cool breeze gave Rogbohun an atmosphere of virgin innocence and tranquillity as the passengers disembarked from the lorry. Nature was at rest

The *Moimui* (Muslim priest) from Kankan-Guinea spoke neither Mende nor Temne, two of the major languages in Sierra Leone. He spoke, Fullah, Susu and Madingo. However, he had an interpreter though some of the clients would have preferred a one to one audience with him as they felt a third compromised their secret.

It was late in the evening of the next day when Hindowaa and his sister were finally summoned. At this point, Hindowaa felt nervous and was glad that he had come with his sister who displayed much more courage and emotional fortitude as the moment of truth approached. Hindowaa wondered what had become of his bravado as a member (*Ngumbuwaa*) of the Wunde Society where he was initiated when he was a boy of nine years.

The last group of clients had just left when Hindowaa and his sister were ushered into the *Moimui's* hut. When they entered, they found that he had just finished his last prayer for the day and was counting his prayer beads (tasbir). The *Moimui* was a slim man with a long, white beard. His eyes were barely visible, which gave him a mysterious appearance. He also had on a small red hat, which was delicately perched on his well-shaved head.

"Tell them I welcome them here in Rogbohun. It is my second home. I have been coming here now for well over ten years. I have many clients in this country. When they know that I am around, I do not sleep as they come in groups, seven days of the week. But I thank Allah. Bismilah."

The interpreter told Hindowaa and his sister what the *Moimui* had said.

Manja, like her brother, spent time surveying the *Moimui's* hut. He was seated cross-legged on the floor, on a sheepskin rug. Manja was impressed by the ritual paraphernalia that hung on the walls and ceiling of the hut. On the sheepskin, was an old book also wrapped in sheepskin. Its contents were almost falling apart. The book was written in Arabic. It was brownish and in the eyes of Hindowaa and his sister it looked awesome. There was another item beside the book. It was a small calabash filled with smooth stones, pebbles from the sea and an assortment of cowry shells. Some people who knew the *Moimui* well said he had another container with the fangs of vipers, porcupine's spines and the teeth of crocodiles. Because of these items, they said it was forbidden for pregnant women to enter his hut. Manja was uncomfortable when she looked at the items that were assembled on the *Moimui's* sheepskin. They looked awesome.

"What is your name?" the Moimui asked Hindowaa through the interpreter. Hindowaa was startled as he was not expecting that question.

"*Nyalaa Hindowaa*, (My name is Hindowaa)", he replied. "*Nya ndi laa Manja* (My sister's name is Manja."

The siblings were seated next to each other. Manja gazed at the *Moimui* as if that was the first time she had seen such a person. The *Moimui* would occasionally fidget with his long and silky white beard as his clients watched him.

"Where do you come from? I have been to some areas in your country, especially in the east, I mean in Kono. I lived in Sefadu, in the good old days. It was a good time when the diamonds were everywhere in that part of the country. I even learned the Kono language and almost married a Kono woman. I still have very fond memories of those days." The *Moimui* seemed energized as he spoke through his interpreter. "I can see that you and your sister are troubled. I can sense it."

Hindowaa and his sister looked at each other, impressed. A moment of silence ensued. The interpreter also monitored the countenances of Hindowaa and his sister after the *Moimui's* observation. Hindowaa said to the interpreter, "*Ndiamoo*" (Friend), tell the *Moimui* we have been troubled all right and that is why we are here to see him. My family has also been troubled. Talia, my town has been equally troubled. It is a tragic situation. You see, I have been married for a long time. I have three children, two boys and one girl. I need more sons and my wife has stopped having children." Hindowaa paused, waiting for the interpreter to tell the *Moimui* what he had said so far. After listening, the *Moimui* nodded and asked the interpreter to tell Hindowaa to continue.

"You see, I am the only son of my mother, all the other siblings are girls. This one seated by me is one of my many sisters. My wife is lucky; she came from a large family of three girls and five boys. I am a farmer and I have lots of fertile land. I have goats, sheep and a few cows. I do not have enough sons to inherit the land. I am troubled by this state of affairs, which equally troubles my wife. It is my intention to have another wife to give me sons."

The interpreter told the *Moimui* what Hindowaa had said. He seemed sympathetic and nodded accordingly.

"We are also here because something tragic has happened to my family. As I was going though this agonizing period of stress and pressure, my only daughter disappeared from Talia. We have made efforts to trace her, but so far we have failed. We have used some of the most experienced traditional hunters and fishermen to comb the forests and swim and dive in the river to see if Kunaafoh could be found. We have not succeeded in tracing her. It is as a result of these developments that my sister and I decided to come to you to find out what happened and what the prospects are that she will be discovered alive. The second point is I want to know whether Giita will bring forth sons. These are the matters that made my sister and I come to seek your assistance. I have had sleepless nights over these matters. I had decided to give my daughter in marriage to the Chief. Next year she should be initiated into the Sande Society and after that she would be married to the Chief. All that is now very uncertain. This is my situation and I need your help."

While Hindowaa was talking, the priest had been fidgeting with his book and touching some of the cowry shells he had assembled on the sheepskin. Hindowaa and his sister looked on with a great sense of anxiety. The room was silent.

"Tell him and his sister that I have heard the story. It is a sad story. Tell him I sympathise with him," the Moimui told the interpreter before continuing, "*Kinie* Hindowaa, yes, you are the only son of your mother. Your sister, who is seated there, is the eldest of all the sisters. She has three children. Not so? Hindowaa, you have many half brothers and there is one in Salone who has custody of your two sons. His wife has no children. Not so? I foresee some problem in that house of your brother in Salone in the future."

These preliminary observations by the Muslim priest left a very positive impression on both brother and sister. How could the priest be so accurate? They wondered and remained baffled beyond bafflement.

"I thank him very sincerely and his preliminary observations are correct," Hindowaa told the interpreter, as the Moimui busied himself assembling the rest of his ritual accoutrements on the sheepskin rug. After he had laid out the pebble stones and cowry shells in a perpendicular position, he laid his right hand on them and uttered a few words, which only he understood. Hindowaa and his sister focused their eyes on what the *Moimui* was doing. Without saying anything to them, he opened his book again and leafed through several pages. He read a couple of pages in silence for a few minutes, then rubbed his forehead with both hands. Afterwards, he stretched out his hand to Hindowaa and gave him four cowry shells and four pebble stones. He then told

Hindowaa to go outside, turn east, and with the cowry shells and pebbles held out in open hands, make his wishes and come back into the hut. Hindowaa willingly complied and in few minutes came back and gave the items back to the *Moimui*.

"My friend, I see that you have gone through a lot of pain. I see this. It is clear. You have a very beautiful daughter. She is tall. Not so? She is also slim and was very close to her mother," the *Moimui* told Hindowaa.

Hindowaa was impressed as the interpreter told him what the Moimui said. Manja was also pleased, but she wanted the *Moimui* to come to the point. Would they discover Kunaafoh's whereabouts? That was what she wanted to know. As far as she was concerned, at the moment, the priest was beating around the bush.

"I see a white person in this whole saga," he went on. "I mean of the events surrounding your daughter's disappearance. The only thing that is difficult to ascertain now is that I cannot tell whether the white person is a female or male. You know what I mean. What I am certain of is that there is a white person involved."

Hindowaa started sweating. His heartbeat skipped. He stood up and in a few minutes went to pass urine outside the hut.

"Could it be the mermaid?" Manja asked. This was the first time she had spoken. "The mermaid became a potential suspect in this whole drama."

"You may be right, that is a possibility. But let me tell you this, your daughter will come back. It may take a long time, but your wife will have her daughter back. That much is certain from what I have discerned from my findings."

Hindowa and his sister were reassured as well as pleased.

"Now about your wife having sons," the *Moimui* said and paused for a while as he continued looking at the assembled cowry shells and pebbles on the floor.

"I can say this much. She will have more children. She will have a son. The ancestors will come to her assistance but only if you agree to the consequences. If you agree and she also agrees that you do not mind the consequences of having additional children, then it will happen. The point is that the consequences are unforeseen; that is part of the deal. It is within the nature of things. If you agree on that, then the deal is signed, sealed and delivered," the *Moimui* said as they listened attentively.

Hindowaa and his sister, almost jumped from their seats with joy when they heard this. They were delighted that their journey was not in vain.

"I thank you very much on my behalf and my sister's. We are immensely delighted. Our enemies will be ashamed. I have been praying every night since my daughter disappeared. I wish my wife knew the result of our mission. Tomorrow, we shall board the first vehicle leaving here so that we arrive home in time for me to tell the people of Talia what you have told us," Hindowaa told the interpreter.

'The entire process entails some sacrifice," The *Moimui* said as Hindowaa, his sister and the interpreter listened carefully. This was the most delicate part of the whole exercise. Apart from the fee for the *Moimui's* services, the sacrifice in some instances could be more expensive than the cost of his divination. It could be prohibitive in money and human resources, so when the *Moimui* mentioned the matter of the sacrifice, both siblings froze, for they had almost exhausted the money they had. Both prayed silently as they waited to hear what the *Moimui* had to say about the sacrifice. Would it entail human sacrifice? They wondered. To their immense relief, he said,

"Before you leave here for your home town, secure a hen. It has to be spotted, mainly with white and black spots. Get a healthy one. When you wake up in the morning, do not talk to anyone. Take the hen to the river, hold it securely and tell your ancestors all that you want to happen to you to. Then leave the hen by the river. Do not let it get wet. Do not drop it into the river. Just drop it by the river bank and walk away. Once you let it go, do not turn your back again as you walk to the town. If it finds its way back here we shall know that your requests shall come to pass and you shall come back to prepare for the final rites that would lead to the realization of you sacred desires."

Hindowaa could not believe that was all he had to do to achieve his heart's desires. He felt impatient. He wanted to run out of the *Moimui's* hut to go and look for the hen so that early in the morning he would be the first to go to the river and perform the sacrifice. His sister too was impatient. When they went to bed that night, they felt emotionally and physically relaxed and dreamed the night away in blissful slumber. However deep, deep down in their minds, they wondered whether the hen would find its way back to the town, thereby paving the way for Kunaafoh's return and Giita's wish for sons to be fulfilled. Only the ancestors could tell so Giita and her relatives waited with great expectations.

The whole town of Talia knew about Hindowaa's journey to Rogbohun to see the renowned soothsayer. His wife was making a similar trip to Gbahama. Kunaafoh's disappearance had shaken a community that had been at peace with itself. The mood in the town was nervously expectant; for people were eager to know the truth surrounding the mysterious disappearance of Kunaafoh. As they waited, the days and nights seemed to become mysteriously longer, as if the spirits of the river and the forest had something against Talia. Hindowaa's journey seemed to be taking forever. When would he finally return with news? They wondered. Only Hindowaa had the answer. So they waited in a state of feverish anticipation.

CHAPTER SEVEN

When Hindowaa's junior brother, Kortu (meaning, 'stone'), agreed to have custody of Hinga and Kafo in Freetown, he did it as an act of brotherly obligation. He never thought that it would create problems in his household which consisted only of himself and his wife, Fanday (meaning, thread). The couple had never had children but unlike Hindowaa and Giita, had never challenged fate. Fanday's mother had told her repeatedly that in life, what is destined for you is bound to happen. She saw wisdom in what her mother had told her and accepted her fate. They had been married for a long time and were now over fifty years old.

Kortu was an ex-service man who had seen action in Burma during the Second World War. He was tall, slim and had a receding forehead. Less aggressive than Hindowaa, his paternal half-brother, he was a very disappointed man. Apart from the fact that he never had children, the realisation of his most burning ambition in life had escaped him painfully. He had wanted to be educated and above all to become a lawyer, but instead had found himself in the colonial army. Back home after Burma, he secured a job with the Sierra Leone Railway as a fireman, and worked there for a long time.

Fanday had been beautiful as a young woman. When she graduated from the Sande Society she was one of the most beautiful girls and captivated lots of men in Talia and beyond. She had wanted to marry her childhood sweetheart but was married off to Kortu instead. After that, to her sorrow and disappointment her childhood sweetheart drifted at the periphery of society. Unable to influence fate, she dedicated her life to her husband for the rest of her life. Fanday was one of three siblings, two girls and a boy, so she was painfully familiar with Giita's problem of not having enough sons. Her mother's repeated efforts to have more sons never succeeded, so she felt sympathy for her in-law. Fanday was the senior sibling of the three children. Fefe (meaning, 'breeze') the boy, was the second and Jinaa, a girl was the last of the three. Jinaa was a twin but her twin partner had died soon after birth. She was married and lived in Freetown with her husband, Ndoma, who, like many men of his status, barely managed to get by in life. The couple lived on the fringes of society (the so-called 'poda-poda' men and

67

women). They lived in a rented, one-bed room apartment and were often pursued for failing to pay the rent at the end of the month because Ndoma, had a rather unpredictable job. He was always looking for better paying work, but his situation was made worse by his lack of any formal education.

Fefe, the boy, had himself left Talia where he was a farmer and drifted to the diamond mines in Kono to seek a quick fortune. That was the trend in those days. Unable to make progress in the diamond mines, he soon cut off communication with his sisters. After that his existence became a matter for speculation as news spread about the ups and downs of the diamond area where death was the common denominator of everyday life.

Relatives from the provinces frequented Kortu's house. Some of them had nothing in particular to do in Freetown but were captivated by the bright lights of urban life. They came, without notice and they came often. Some of the visiting relatives came to seek financial assistance, some to seek help to pay school fees for their children, buy books and uniforms, others to ask Kortu and his wife to help raise money to settle a court case that had gone against them. Some also came to ask Kortu to help them raise money to marry a new wife. They kept coming without prior notice and would stay for a long time, even after they had secured what they initially came for.

Hinga and his brother, Kafo, shared one bedroom in the house while they stayed with their uncle and attended school. Kortu's responsibility for his brother's children was limited to the provision of free accommodation. Hindowaa paid his children's school fees, bought school uniforms and books. He also provided them with food and paid for their transportation to and from Freetown during the holidays. They had one main meal a day. Apart from the food, Hinga and Kafo organised their own social life in the city. There was nobody to supervise their studies. Hinga developed a passion for football but Kafo had no particular interest. He drifted with the wind and would later become a seaman, whereas his brother became one of the best soccer players in the country and would later become captain of his football club. It was a dream he had cherished and was happy that a boy from Talia could captain a team in Freetown. Talia was also proud of him. However, Hindowaa was disappointed because he had wished his two sons to become a doctor and a lawyer.

There was no love lost between Fanday and Giita. It was as a result of this that Giita was uncomfortable when her husband decided that the children would be going to Freetown to stay with his brother. Giita, like many other women and even some men in Talia and the township of Ginger Hall where the Kortus lived, believed that Fanday practised witchcraft which was why she could not have children. The frequency of these rumours had eroded Fanday's self-esteem and made her so bitter that her once beautiful features had faded. She aged prematurely. Her tall frame withered and at only sixty years old, she already stooped slightly. She however showed a remarkable resilience in enduring life.

Fanday took her domestic responsibilities very seriously. With a degree of religious commitment she cooked food on Sundays, the only day of the week she stayed home with her husband. After church, she would prepare several sauces and soups, which would last the household for a week. It was generally agreed that she must have acquired her culinary skills when she was a student in the Sande Society. Many people speculated that it was because of her culinary expertise that she was able to retain her husband who had a very generous appetite. Fanday loved him for this. Women often took exception to husbands who ate only a little after their wives had expended enormous time and energy in preparing food. Many women would even suspect that such husbands were being fed by girlfriends. Fanday's husband spared her such speculation.

Hinga and Kafo, the nephews of Kortu, were curious about their uncle and aunt's way of life. They had heard a lot of the gossip about Fanday that was circulating both in Ginger Hall and Talia. On their way from school one day, they decided to brainstorm about their domestic situation.

"I look forward to going on holiday. I miss mother a lot," Kafo told his elder brother who was holding his books against his chest and pretended he was not listening.

"You are just a spoiled son," Hinga told Kafo as they walked along with other students behind and ahead of them. "I don't intend going on holiday this time because I want to stay and do some football practice. My team as you know has been doing well. I need to be around during the vacation for lots of practice."

"But you don't have to spend the entire holiday at home. You can go for one week and then come back to Freetown and resume your practice. I will not enjoy the holiday without you and don't you think that our parents will be angry with you for not coming on holiday?"

"I shall give you a letter for Daddy and I shall explain to him why I am not coming on holiday. I hope that you will read it properly to him and to Mother. Do you hear me?"

"Yes, but brother, I still feel that you should go for one week. Our parents would like to see both of us. Other students will be going on vacation. This is the longest vacation of the year and most of the students here in Freetown will be going home. All parents are looking forward to seeing their children during the long vacation."

"Kafo, you are the younger one," Hinga told his brother. I do not need any lecture from you. I have told you that I need to stay and practise with my team. Don't you understand simple English? Please do me a favour. As I said, I shall give you a letter to take to Daddy and our mother. Make sure you read it to them carefully. That is all I am asking of you. I wish to thank you in advance while anticipating your full cooperation and understanding on this matter."

Kafo laughed, but his brother was not amused, so having understood that Hinga was serious about not going home on vacation, he changed the subject.

"Ngo Hinga," he said, "I always wanted to ask you a question but I have not been brave enough to do so until now."

"Ask about what?" Hinga said in a stern but surprised voice.

"Is it true that Auntie Fanday has a *koko* (a witch-bird that appears mostly at night and is believed to suck the blood of children,) and practises witchcraft. I am just asking because the rumours are floating all over Ginger Hall. I sense it sometimes when I am passing through the neighbourhood by myself. One day some children actually told me that my auntie has a *koko*. I was scared and denied it. I told them that if she had *koko* you and I would not be alive."

Hinga abruptly stopped walking and stood without speaking, His brother also stopped walking. They blocked the path, looking at each other in silence. Then Hinga started off again. They walked for a while in total silence.

"Kafo, you should know by now that Ginger Hall is full of rumours," Hinga said at last. "I have also heard such rumours and I have decided to ignore them. So should you, otherwise, you will not have time to attend to more serious business. As for me, I have no time for rumours in Ginger Hall. I need all my time for practising my football. By tomorrow, you will hear another rumour, like how a man attempted to bite a dog, because he said the dog was looking at him with evil eyes. Or like the last time when they said that a man had gone to the hospital to complain that he was pregnant because during a urine test there was a mistake. The doctor had exchanged his test with that of a pregnant woman. It was the wildest rumour Ginger Hall ever heard. A pregnant man! That is Ginger Hall for you."

Kafo laughed until he almost fell to the ground.

"Brother, do you remember that our mother was against our coming to uncle? It was because of such rumours and suspicions in Ginger Hall. They have been there for a long time. Mother was very concerned about our safety."

"Yes, yes, but Kafo, we have been here for a long time and we have not even suffered from headaches. How do you explain that?" Hindo remarked.

"But brother, tell me why their room is full of trunks and lots of bottles with amulets attached to them? And it is always dark. What is inside those trunks and bottles? Also, on Sundays, uncle spends most of the day in the room. *I* am afraid," Kafo told his brother.

"Kafo, you are not thinking like a man," Hinga said as they continued walking along. "Why were you initiated in the Wunde Society? Now that you are a man, you should be strong. The *koko* bird only attacks children, not big boys like you and me. Our mother was just being motherly. Like all mothers she would be worried to know that someone suspected of practising witchcraft would be living in the same house as her children. Let me also tell you this, our uncle was in the army, the colonial army. He fought in the Second World War. Have you learned about it in history yet? He is an ex-service man. When these people came from the army, from overseas, they came with lots of things like the trunks you are talking about. Those trunks contain clothes, uniforms, boots and many other things that uncle brought from overseas."

"Have you seen them or you are just making an intelligent guess?" Kafo asked. Hinga ignored him.

That evening, Kafo's worries were reinforced when, just about the time when people were ready to go to bed in the neighbourhood, a worried mother of four little children announced loudly that she hoped the person with a *koko* would not dare come to her house as she had hired a medicine man to destroy anybody practising witchcraft. After she made the announcement, she also said that the neighbours knew who the culprit was and that people were determined to purge the community of such a malevolent person.

"Ngo, did you hear that? Are you listening?" Kafo asked his brother. "It is just today that I told you about Auntie Fanday and what the people are saying."

"Did they call her name? Did they say she had ever killed someone's child?" Hinga replied in a firm voice but Kafo remained apprehensive.

"I now understand why our mother was worried about our coming here. I am getting more and more worried about our safety. I intend writing to her to report what is happening here. I told you about the trunks in their room and about Uncle Kortu spending all of Sunday in the room."

"What do you expect uncle to be doing for you after six days of his back-breaking job at the railway?" Hinga asked scornfully.

After the night that the woman with four children made the announcement, the atmosphere at the Kortu's household became tense. Rumours about Fanday's association with witchcraft became more focused. She had to take short cuts to her house whenever she decided to go out because people started throwing hints at her as she passed by. Her life was becoming miserable, but her husband supported her and was convinced of her innocence. They were united as they endured life in their neighbourhood.

"Fanday, I am looking forward to my retirement so that I can go to Talia and live the rest of my life in peace," Kortu told his wife as they lay in bed one night. Fanday was visibly disturbed by the sordid innuendoes about her connections with witchcraft.

"How can we live a peaceful retirement in Talia," she retorted. "I know that your brother's wife is one of those slandering me even though I sympathise with her condition. She does not appreciate my sympathy. She has poisoned the innocent minds of her children. I know because Kafo looks scared of me. However, I am comforted by the fact that his elder brother is comfortable with me. I thank God for that. Have I ever eaten somebody's child? Have I ever killed anybody in Ginger Hall? Just because I go about my business without consulting anyone, I have become the centre of attention and suspicion. Just because I do not go to people to beg, take debts, or borrow clothes and just because I do not sleep with other men, I have been targeted for scandal. I don't foresee a peaceful retirement in Talia, my dear. I am being honest with you. I cannot tolerate Giita, your brother's wife. She is working against me though I don't know what I have done to her. Let me tell you this, I shall fight Giita. I shall show her that I am also a woman. I shall tie my wrapper very tightly from now on and confront her in one way or the other. I swear by my Sande Society. That is all I have to say for now."

"Don't hurt her or any member of her family and bring ill repute to our home," her husband said after listening to her angry words. "I am warning you. The ancestors will fight for you."

"The ancestors, oh, the ancestors. Why don't the ancestors tell all those who are slandering me to stop. Why encourage them? What evidence have they produced to show that I am a witch? Just because I have no children they assume I am a witch and have a *koko*. Have I eaten anybody's child?" Fanday asked again. Kortu tried to calm her down by saying, "Everything will be all right when the time comes, Fanday, I assure you. Take my word for it."

"I have heard all this before from you," his wife replied, unappeased. "How long am I to suffer these indignities, these sordid innuendos? The mere thought of going outside the doors of my own house makes me shiver with fear. It is a nightmare. Sometimes, I am afraid of my own shadow, can you beat that? Your sister-in-law, Giita also contributes to these malicious rumours. What have I done to Giita? Tell me what have I done to her?"

"I cannot answer your questions if you are looking for an answer from me." Kortu told her.

"So who do you think I am talking to? Can't you understand my situation? Don't you see and sense the misery I am going through in Ginger Hall? Ah, my dear, don't think I am a fool. I am not. I also have enough ammunition to make your sister-in-law's life miserable. Yes I do," Fanday told her husband, rising from the bed. Kortu sensed how deeply she was affected by the issue."

"What are you talking about tonight, Fanday? And please, let us not talk too loudly; you know that we have visitors here. They would like to sleep even though they are at the other end of the house. Please, don't talk so loudly," Kortu said but Fanday ignored him.

"Your sister-in-law too is not free from scandal, from malicious gossip. That is why our people say that if someone is carrying you on their back don't say that their head smells. I have enough ammunition to destroy Giita. Tell her not to push me too far. Tell her, and do so as soon as possible before it is too late."

Kortu continued to listen with great concern and anxiety, now realising how angry Fanday had become about his sister-in-law's role in tormenting her and her iron determination to revenge herself.

"Fanday, you are throwing dangerous hints at my sister-in-law. Please stop. I don't like it. It is not good. Remember that we are Christians and the Bible preaches against malice," Kortu told her, not knowing that his reference to the Bible and to Christians would further inflame Fanday's sensibilities on the matter.

"Is it only now that you remember that we are Christians?" she sneered. "What about your sister-in-law and her husband, your brother? Are they not also Christians? What are they? I know that we are all Christians. I knew that a long time ago. So why should Christians torment Christians? Why don't you tell your sister-in-law to stop tormenting me? Why don't you?"

"Fanday, it is late at night and I am still in the darkest of darkness regarding this thing about Giita. Please come out plainly. I like plain talk. I am a military man. I am also a Wunde man and in my society men talk plain talk," Kortu told his wife, deliberately keeping his voice low. There was silence, a long silence before Fanday spoke again.

"Kortu, Giita, sacrificed her daughter to the water spirit so that she would have sons. Don't tell me that you are not aware of this? Take an oath on your Wunde Society as a *Ngumbuwaa*. I challenge you. This is now well known in Talia and beyond, and the rumours have started circulating here in Ginger Hall, yet you, Kortu, want to tell me that you are not aware of this. I want you to swear your innocence by your Wunde Society."

Kortu was shaken by these words and began to sweat. His wife had touched a sensitive nerve. She had asked him many questions to which he had no answers. He too rose from the bed and began to pace to and fro in the congested room.

"Fanday, what is wrong with you tonight? What is the matter? Where did you get these rumours from and do you know that these are serious allegations? Do you know what my brother and his wife; and the entire family have had to endure as a result of the mysterious disappearance of Kunaafoh? Fanday, do you also know that it has now been established by a very famous soothsayer that Kunaafoh will return? Are you telling me that you do not believe the soothsayer? Fanday, do you want to ignite a family feud for which no one will ever forgive you? Please, I beg you, think twice. Don't let malice cloud your reason. I do not want to hear this from you again, not even as a rumour. You want to set the family on fire? No. I will not allow it." Kortu spoke softly but very firmly.

"But Kortu, the family is already on fire." Fanday replied. "Oh God! You don't know that yet? I am just going to fan the fire so that it will glow more brightly, as our people say, and everything will now be clear. Giita believes I have a *koko*. She believes that religiously, and has helped to spread the rumour. Look what has happened to her now. Do you know what it means to sacrifice a human being, your own blood for any cause? Well, my dear, many people including myself believe that Giita sacrificed Kunaafoh to the water spirit so that she will bear more sons for your brother who is not happy with his present condition in Talia. He wants more sons. I understand the situation because my own mother had a similar experience. That was why I was sympathetic towards Giita even as she continued to slander me. But God fought my case, and not long after that she sacrificed her own beautiful daughter for sons."

"Tell me Fanday, what if one day as the famous soothsayer has said, Kunaafoh comes back? What will you do then? Tell me, what will you and all those spreading this dirty gossip do? You are a Christian. Just last week, you were in the Church and by coincidence the reverend preached about malice and gossip. You were there, I mean last week in the Church. Just a week ago and now you are doing exactly the opposite. Do you think that God will forgive you? It is not that you are innocent about this malice. God forgives the innocent ones. But you are aware of what the gospel says about it and you are practising it. I warn you,

Fanday, refrain from this and repent." Fanday had listened attentively, but remained unimpressed.

"Hey, hey, Kortu, you talk well," she said rudely. "We call it goo..ood talk. Let me tell you this evening, tonight and today, you went into the wrong profession. You should have gone to study and become a reverend. You talk and preach so well. I tell you something, if you preached like this in a Church to defend your sister-in-law, you would get many converts; but you would get converts only because the congregation does not know you. They will not know that you would defend your sister-in-law who is equally guilty yet vilify your wife. So, Mr. Reverend I am not convinced despite the sermon you have so eloquently delivered to me tonight."

Kortu replied, "Fanday, my sixth sense tells me that you will live to regret what you have said about my sister-in-law and you will repent and wish you had not been party to this malicious gossip about Giita. The day will come when all those who harbour such malicious views about her shall confess and ask for her forgiveness. I can assure you that the day will come and Fanday, you Fanday, shall be in the queue weeping with shame to go and ask her for forgiveness."

"I look forward to that day. I tell you, I look forward to that day." said Fanday. "I also look forward to the day Giita and others will come to me and confess and ask for forgiveness. Until such a time comes, I remain convinced that Giita sacrificed her daughter and she is dead here on earth but alive with the spirit of the river."

"Fanday, you sound like a stranger to me," Kortu said, shaking his head sadly. "You sound to me like someone I have not known for all the years we have been married. You sound like a total stranger. I do understand your feelings and concerns about this issue, but I think you have gone too far. Let me tell you once again that I believe passionately that Kunaafoh will return and all of you will drown in shame."

"And, until such time, I mean when Kunaafoh comes back, I shall continue to believe that her mother is involved in her mysterious disappearance and I shall support those who hold similar views here and in Talia. I promise you that as of tonight." Fanday told her husband. Equally angry now, Kortu moved closer to his wife who was now sitting at the opposite end of the room.

"Fanday, if it were not so late at night and people were not sleeping, believe me, I would have beaten you mercilessly for the first time since we got married. You have provoked me enough and I swear by my Wunde Society I cannot take it any longer."

"Oh, Oh, Oh. I will never believe this. Kortu, I will never believe this. My dead parents will never believe this. You are threatening to beat me because of your sister-in-law, and for your useless nephews. Look at the time, look at it and go and check their room to see whether they there. Your nephews," she told Kortu in a challenging tone. "You are right, since we got married you have never beaten me. But believe me, you will beat me tonight as you have threatened. You will beat me tonight and the whole of Ginger Hall will know why you have beaten me."

As she spoke, Fanday rose aggressively and moved close to her husband, hands akimbo. She tightened her wrapper and tied her head tie around her middle like a belt. Kortu stood still, contemplating his next move. Fanday stood firm, waiting for him. Kortu said, "Fanday, I have told you that I will not touch you because it is too late at night and we have visitors. You are very lucky. You have provoked me enough."

"Ok. We shall continue in the morning," she replied, eyeing him with scorn. "I will not allow you to leave this room in the morning until you beat me because of your sister-in-law and those useless and good-for-nothing boys. Do you know where they get money to buy cigarettes, drink and chase women? And they call themselves schoolboys - school boys my foot! Where do they get the money from, especially that Hinga? But you are not concerned about such things, are you? Tomorrow will come and I want you, Kortu, to beat me. Then I will know that you are a real Wunde man."

By this time Kortu had given up the idea of beating Fanday because he realised what his wife's strategy was and would not allow her to obtain her objective. She wanted to wake the whole of Ginger Hall and bring the Kortu's house into disrepute. He would not give her that pleasure.

"One thing I know, as I go to bed," he said calmly, "is that I remain convinced that Kunaafoh shall return."

"I shall pray for that day to come. Believe me, I shall be the first person to jump at the opportunity to meet Giita and ask for forgiveness because we have bad-mouthed her, as our people will say. I shall also ask her to confess to me, because I have never eaten anyone's child even though I have no children. So I shall wait for that day too. However, for this moment on and until Kunaafoh resurfaces, well and sound, in mind and body, I remain convinced Giita has a foul hand in her daughter's disappearance," Fanday said. Kortu did not respond to her comments and observations, but he was concerned that she was sinking deeper into a quagmire of hatred. He had seen Satan, Commander-in-chief of the devils entering his wife's aging body and mind. Eventually both husband and wife slept through what remained of that dark night painfully exhausted.

CHAPTER EIGHT

Giita and her relatives lived in a state of nightmarish anguish during the eight days and nights they waited for the recovery of the soothsayer they had gone to consult in Gbahama. Giita felt it was the most challenging time in her life. The soothsayer would tell her all she wanted to know about her husband, her prospects for having more sons, whether Kunaafoh would come back and the future of her sons in Freetown. The days and nights got painfully longer as she engaged her mind on an endless journey of imagination. Fortunately, Gbahama had offered her the hospitality she needed to postpone some of those tormenting moments when her mind wandered into infinity.

It was a brilliant Saturday morning and their last Saturday in Gbahama. Giita, her brother and uncle sat at the back of the house, which had a big veranda which was used for cooking during the rains. In the dry season,, the women cooked out doors under luxuriant mango and kola nut trees. As they sat and talked about events, their conversation was interrupted by the sight of baboons and monkeys climbing pawpaw and mango trees, harvesting nature's bounty. These were familiar scenes. They had witnessed the same in Talia. The animals were not afraid of the presence of people. They would come very close to the house, especially the baboons. Sometimes the dogs would bark at them but the baboons would not go away and the dogs would not chase them or go close. When the baboons came too close, the dogs retreated. One baboon watched with visible longing a pawpaw tree with ripe fruits on it. The baboon, a huge creature, stood on its hind legs and went round the tree. It paid no attention to the repeated barking of the dogs. Giita and her relatives focused their attention on the animal wondering what its next move would be. The animal pounced on the pawpaw tree and began to climb it. The fragile tree could not sustain the baboons weight and both fell on the ground. Giita and her companions laughed out loud. However, the animal had achieved its objective which was to get at the fruits. Others came and joined in harvesting the paw paws that had fallen on the ground. Some of the animals grabbed as much as they could. Giita and her relatives were greatly amused. They saw some of the monkeys swinging from one mango tree to the other. It was the season when mangoes were abundant and every day, monkeys would visit the area and help themselves to the ripe fruits which filled the air with a sweet aroma. The animals would retreat towards the end of the morning after they had feasted, dropping the seeds, which would later germinate and add to the already large number of mango trees in the compound.

"I hope one day you will visit Talia, so that I can be your hostess," Giita said, turning her attention to the soothsayer's wife who had joined them. She had been busy preparing food for the visitors. It was about lunchtime and the sun was still bright.

"My dear sister, we do this all the time," the soothsayer's wife told them. "I am used to it now. We are always having visitors here. Like you, some of them find it difficult to go back and come when this place is crowded with customers. So I entertain them as they await their turn."

'Hmm, my dear, in some places it is not always like this. I have travelled a lot and I can tell you that in some places you do not get the type of hospitality you have given us since we arrived. We are very grateful to you and your husband," Giita's brother remarked. The uncle listened and nodded in support of what his nephew said.

"Yes, yes, my brother is right, my dear," Giita said. "I have been to some places and found hospitality lacking. It is true. In some places you are fed but the portions are always small. In other places, you get very little meat or fish and you are left with one impression - pack up and go. You have overstayed your welcome. If you don't get the message, well the rations become smaller and smaller till you start getting starvation rations."

Everyone on the veranda laughed at Giita's observations. The day was advancing and Giita's pulse was beating in anticipation of meeting *Kinie* Komawaa, the venerable soothsayer. There was silence in the town. The animals had disappeared. The dogs, the cats, and even the chickens were resting under the shade of the pawpaw and mango trees.

"My dear, the nature of my husband's work is such that I have to be accommodating. People come here from all over the place, and some, like you, have to stay around and wait their turn. What do you do? Throw them away? Let me be honest with you, I consider myself lucky because during the time I have been married to my husband, I have learned a lot about human beings. I am always around in the room when the clients are consulting him. This is one of the advantages I enjoy as the first wife. The things people come to see my husband for are many and interesting," Komawaa's wife told her guests.

"Like our own problem, I suppose," Giita's brother remarked.

"Yes, but of course, problems vary. Yours are not unique. I tell you, people come here seeking solutions to problems that baffle my mind."

They continued to listen to their hostess with a sense of curiosity. Giita was particularly interested in what she told them.

"This thing called power," she went on, "I mean this their politics. It will kill us in this country. It is going to kill all of us. People stop at nothing when they want this power. One man came here with his wife. I don't even know from which town. He came with lots of money and asked my husband to help him win the election at any cost, even when my husband said that the man's opponent would win because he was a very formidable candidate and was the people's preference."

"What did he want your husband to do after that?" Giita asked.

"My sister, my mouth is too small to say what he thought my husband could do so that he would win the election. My husband told him that in his own profession, he does not subscribe to taking human life, or in spilling blood for the sake of power."

Giita and her relatives were dumbfounded. They had heard rumours of such things before, but that was the first time they had learned first-hand about someone making such efforts to achieve power.

"I tell you people, this man had money," Komawaa's wife added. "He had lots of it because he showed my husband how much he had brought and was prepared to pay for his services. I had never seen so much money at one time in my entire life. To be honest with you, my mouth started watering. The truth is that I had never seen so much money."

"If you have so much money, why do you need power? Money is power in this country. Why do you want to take someone's life in the pursuit of power? People are not satisfied," Giita's brother said, showing his disgust.

"My dear, how can you ask such a question? It is greed and greed is a sickness. The more you have the more you want. Some people will stop at nothing until they get what they aspire to. They become blind," Giita's uncle observed.

"After he failed to convince my husband, the man left. You won't believe this. When he was leaving, he never said good-bye to my husband or to me - after I had cooked for him here for two days. But do I stop entertaining because of him? No."

"My sister, I feel sorry for you. You have a difficult task," Giita told Komawaa's wife. Her brother added. "You know we used to hear these stories. For me, they were in the form of rumours and fairy tales until today. Now I believe what people have been saying about those who stop at nothing in their efforts to get power and money. Sometimes, I don't believe that it is the same God that created all of us when I hear such stories."

"Our old people say that the world is always in a state of balance, harmony. That is why those who do these wicked things pay for it one way or the other. When they pay for their wicked deeds, then harmony is restored. There is a form of compensation and the spirits are there to bring this about. My husband knows this and that is the reason he never assists those who come to him asking for help to take someone's life or blood. The victim's spirits will haunt you. If they don't get you, then they will chase your loved ones. Don't you see how some people end up? Don't you see how all those who acquired their power and wealth through foul means end up, or how some of their loved ones end up? Tell me, all of you here, tell me how many people you know who went to the diamond areas and acquired wealth through foul means and are around today with that wealth. In our own town, they have all disappeared. The things they did to acquire their wealth in the diamond areas was unbelievable. But tell me the truth; are such people happy in life when they succeed in achieving their objectives through malevolent means? Do they go to bed and sleep soundly? Do they enjoy their meals? I wonder."

The soothsayer's wife looked into distant space as she spoke, her voice solemn.

"Madam, you are asking pertinent questions, but unfortunately, we are not in position to give you answers," said Giita's uncle.

"My people, I am serious about these questions. How can you possibly go to bed and sleep properly when you have innocent blood in your hands? Don't you know the victims' spirits will haunt you? Don't you know that the spirits of the victims' parents, relatives and friends will haunt you? Yes, they will haunt you."

She continued to express her concern and there was silence as her audience started absorbing the seriousness of what she had said.

82

"Uncle, despite what madam has said, and she is right, these things are still going on. When elections are approaching, these incidents happen. When people are contesting for chieftaincy, these incidents are reported and they shall continue. What do we do?" Giita asked. Her uncle replied with bitterness in his voice.

"What do we do? My child, we do nothing, but the ancestors and the victims' spirits fight back. Don't you see it happening in real life, how some of them end up? Don't you see? The end of man. The spirits fight back and the rich and powerful men end their lives on earth humiliated. That is why some people believe that hell starts here and some people experience it before they exit this world. They are wicked people and the spirits hit them very hard before they depart. That is the only consolation. This is how harmony is re-established. The spirits take vengeance and re-establish harmony. Vengeance, you see in the realm of the spirits is harmony, it is therapeutic, it deters the recurrence of such events."

"Yes, my dear, you have made a point, and I agree with you. The question of balance and harmony in life. I experience it here in Gbahama. There are good people who compensate for the bad ones. I think that God tried to create a balance and I have always believed that the good people far outnumber the bad ones. I already told you the story of people who come here, stay here overnight or spend a day or two, some even more than that. I entertain them. When some of them depart, they express gratitude for our hospitality, but there are also those who just disappear as if they did not drink water in this house. Do we stop being hospitable to people because of the ungrateful ones?"

Giita's uncle concurred as their hostess continued.

"For me, what is interesting is that I learn a lot from these experiences. All types of visitors keep coming with very interesting stories. Some of them are fascinating. Not long ago, we had lots of visitors here. This town was crowded and my husband was busy. One man and his wife came to seek help because three of their sons had migrated to the diamond areas and they had not heard from them for a long time, and news kept coming every day that the situation in the diamond areas was rough. News of death and accidents were reported every day. They were worried and came crawling on their knees asking for our husband's help."

"So what happened?" Giita's brother asked.

"Well, after my husband's investigations, he told the couple that their children were well and alive but were not likely to come back."

"They will not come back to their town? That is awful," Giita remarked. Amid subdued laughter, Komawaa's wife told them, "Well, according to the story, they all got married to women in that area, in the diamond area. Those women, the story goes, are well known for capturing men and holding them captive indefinitely. They say that the women have medicines, which they give to the men clandestinely to make them completely subservient. To cut a long story short, they say that the women use fetish to tie the men's feet so they cannot leave the area. That is why whenever men are going to the diamond areas, their parents beg them not to take wives from there, otherwise their feet will be tied and they shall never again be seen in their home towns. So the man and his wife came here to ask my husband to help in untying their son's feet so that he could come back home."

"My dear sister, I envy your situation," Giita's uncle told the woman, "you have learned a lot. This is how educated people write about things. If you had gone to school these are things you could tell people about. They are very interesting."

Flattered by the observation, Komawaa's wife continued to entertain them with stories about other clients.

"Talking about people travelling to places and not coming back," she said, "A woman came here some time ago with a similar problem. She was a rich woman. Her son and daughter, according to her, had gone to the white man's country and only the son had returned very recently and after many, many years. They had almost given up on him, as he was now old…."

"Which country of the white man?" they asked.

"My people, she only told us 'Roporto,' (meaning 'the white man's country'). I don't know which one. But she came pleading with our husband to help her. She also asked our husband to help get rid of the bad habits which the son had brought with him and which were becoming a scandal in their town."

Giita and her relatives listened with great interest as she went on.

"The son had returned, the mother said, with a speech problem. He kept talking like someone whose nostrils were blocked (talking English, the white man's language), instead of Temne. That was not the worst of the bad habits he came with: it was the fact that, to the total embarrassment of the parents, he ate with the white man's hands (a fork and knife). This was a scandal, which rapidly spread through the town."

"Tell me, did he eat foofoo and tola with the white man's hand, the hand that has teeth (a fork)?" Giita's brother asked their hostess. Everybody, including their hostess, laughed heartily.

"What did your husband do for the woman?" Giita asked.

"He assured her that the daughter would eventually come back but he was sorry to say that by the time she returned both parents would not be around to welcome her, because, sadly, they would be dead."

"My dear, to be honest with you, your husband has a tough job. I don't envy you both. It is indeed a tough job," Giita's uncle remarked. The soothsayer's wife went on to tell them that despite this gloomy prediction, when the woman was leaving she gave her money and thanked her warmly for her hospitality during the two days she had spent with them.

"There are some nice people," she told her guests, "so I keep being nice to everybody." Turning to Giita she added, "My dear, I am happy you will be seeing our husband soon, so that he can determine your situation. I know how you have been feeling. It must be terrible to be in your position - the sleepless nights, the dreams in between, the weight of uncertainty that this whole thing has created for you is too much of a burden to carry alone. As I told you and your relatives previously, and as the incidents I have narrated to you show, your case is not too different from that of many other women who keep coming here every day, every week and every month to see our husband. They all have one thing in common, and that is, to find a solution to their problems. They come to seek remedies not because they are not fertile, but because they either have only one child who happens to be a girl, too few sons, or no child at all - the worst of the lot. They are all faced with the same threats of divorce, separation or their husbands' marriage to other wives to improve the balance between boys and girls in the family."

Not long after these observations, Giita's relatives got up and walked away to join the other men on the veranda in front of the house, leaving Giita and Komawaa's wife to continue their conversation.

"Giita, I can assure you that our husband has been able to solve many of the problems women come to consult him about. By the grace of God and the help of our ancestors, he will solve your problem too and put your mind at rest."

Her assurances gave Giita a feeling of relief and relaxation. She felt confident that Komawaa would be able to help her as he had helped other women in the past.

"You see how men are?" the soothsayer's wife observed after Giita's relatives disappeared, "They are all the same. Why did your brother and uncle leave us? They just walked away."

"You are right, my dear," Giita replied. "They are all the same. As for my brother he had started grumbling to me about one of his wives who had had three girls. Poor child. She is the most beautiful of my brother's three wives, but she is now under fire for having three girls. My uncle has similar concerns. Two of his wives have seven children between them. Four of the children are girls and he continues to make a lot of noise because of the gender imbalance."

"My sister, it is a familiar story. As for me, my sister has been running around trying to get more sons. My husband told her in no uncertain terms that according to his findings, the more effort she made to have more sons, the more girls she would have. So he warned her to accept the reality that she would not have any more sons. Do you know that my sister refused to accept my husband's findings?"

"You don't mean it!" Giita exclaimed.

"Oh yes I mean it. And listen to this. My sister now has seven girls because when my husband told her that, she became angry and decided to consult another soothsayer. He deceived her and assured her that by performing prescribed rituals and sacrifices, she would have sons. She spent lots of money roaming from town to town and from village to village, and look what has happened to her. Her husband married two other women."

"I hope that what we women are going through will not happen to our daughters when they become adults and get married." Giita commented. "I don't want to imagine Kunaafoh going through this."

"But my sister, what can we do about it?" Komawaa's wife said. "Our mothers and grandmothers had to endure the same thing."

"I know, my dear but that does not mean our children should be victims of such things. I shall pray for Kunaafoh."

It was now late in the afternoon.

"Ah, look at them. They have started coming again in the same numbers as the morning," Komawaa's wife suddenly observed. She was referring to the baboons and monkeys which had started to assemble. They are coming for their evening meal. They come in the morning, get fed and spend the day resting under the trees, for the baboons and on top of the trees, for the monkeys. In the evening they return and after that we do not see them again until the following morning. They are very clever animals."

"Let us leave the animals alone," Giita laughed. "I am more interested in hearing about the women who come to see your husband in search of sons. Are you aware of cases of women coming to search for daughters?"

There was silence on the veranda, punctuated only by the chattering of monkeys in the vicinity.

"Ah, my sister, you have asked a very sensitive question. You are right. I know of neither men nor women coming here for the purpose of securing girls in the family. Don't they know that to have sons you need women?"

The two women looked at each other in bafflement at the folly of men.

"The whole issue never made sense to me, my sister. Look how men rush to marry now that the Sande Society is in session. You said that your husband has already earmarked one of the girls currently in the Sande grove. Even our own husband has been talking about marrying another girl after the next Sande session. He is old and sickly, but still thinks about marrying," said Giita's hostess. She was clearly not in favour of their husband marrying again.

As the evening approached Giita's countenance changed dramatically. The time of judgment was approaching for her brother and uncle came to say the soothsayer was ready to see them. Her heartbeat redoubled and her legs felt heavy. On their way to the medicine man's house, she felt perspiration dripping around her neck. The soothsayer's elder wife who had been with Giita, joined them. She always attended sessions when her husband had clients. She felt happy for Giita because it was believed that divinations conducted at night had greater efficacy. At this time, the medicine men and women could tame the spirits of darkness.

As Komawaa assembled his ritual paraphernalia, Giita and her relatives looked around his one-room hut. Without any warning, a toad leaped across the room. Giita was afraid that this might be a bad omen. The toad continued leaping and finally disappeared. It was rumoured that the soothsayer himself had a boa constrictor in his hut which he fed with rats and toads. It was just a rumour. No one ever dared to challenge the medicine man in the town of Gbahama.

Giita's eyes were fixed on the manner in which the soothsayer was arranging his ritual wares. Her body was almost wet with perspiration even though it was not a hot night.

"*Nyaha pui* (woman), you come from a big family. Not so?" *Kinie* Komawaa asked Giita as her relatives listened.

"Your mother had only three girls and the rest of the children are sons. Am I correct?"

There was profound silence in the hut. Komawaa's wife stared at Giita who replied, "You are right." She was mesmerized by the accuracy and knowledge the soothsayer was displaying. Equally impressed, her relatives looked at each other.

"Your husband has a relative in Salone. I see a problem in that house. It is not immediate but it will come. These are just my preliminary findings," Komawaa told Giita and her relatives.

On the floor, Komawaa had displayed several of his ritual accoutrements, from cowry shells, peanut peels, smooth pebbles and the fangs of some of the deadliest snakes in the forest around Gbahama.

"You told me about your problems when you came. I still recollect very vividly what you told me even though I was not very well. Do you want me to repeat them?"

"I believe you, *Kinie* Komawaa," Giita replied in a polite and frightened tone.

"You have been married for a long time to your husband?"

"Yes, many, many years back. He married me just when I graduated from the Sande Society. My breasts were full and I had no knowledge of men."

"He must be a lucky man to have married such a beautiful woman," the soothsayer remarked with a smile.

At Komawaa's observation Giita forced a smile in return. It was now charcoal dark. With an outstretched right hand, Komawaa gave her two cowry shells, two peanut shells and two pebbles with instructions to go outside and voice all that she wanted to verify, the content of her mission as she had told him eight days ago.

"*Nyabonda, ndeblaa, ah wooloo nyama a kpindi ngee,*" she said, asking her parents and ancestors to listen to her. She then conveyed to them all the concerns she had related to the medicine man about eight days before. She then went back into the hut, gave Komawaa the two cowry shells, two peanut peels and the two pebbles and resumed her seat.

While Komawaa was busy inspecting the cowry shells, pebbles and peanut peels that Giita returned to him, her brother whispered in her ear, "Did you say everything to our dead parents, our ancestors?"

Giita simply nodded.

Komawaa poured some liquid into a small calabash and asked her to gargle with it and spit it out. This was meant to ward off the malicious evil spirits of the night whose ears only hear evil.

Hindowaa would marry another wife, Komawaa now told her. This was certain. She would give Hindowaa two children, both girls. Giita would also have another son and a daughter who would resemble Kunaafoh. They look like twins.

"I see her as I look at the formation of these articles on the floor," the old soothsayer continued, "but the spirits say these children will come only if you insist, because they have already given you two sons and a daughter. They say your quota has been exhausted, so the choice is yours and the ancestors are right now waiting to hear what you will say. If you accept, then your daughter will return and you will also have twins - a son and a daughter. Your two sons are doing fine but I foresee a serious problem in that household. It will come like a big storm and will leave a trail of destruction. This is also certain. However, in the end, the problem will be resolved in your sons' favour. These things are bound to happen."

The soothsayer's wife was pleased with all that had transpired. Giita thanked him and asked God to let him live for a very long time.

"*Kinie Komawaa, biseh, biseh caca. Ngewo ee bi mahun gbeh. Ngewo ee pieh bi lembie caca caca.*" She added,"*Nya longo ngi hindo lui lee gboma,*" saying that she would like to have another son and was therefore prepared for any eventuality. Regarding the coming storm at Ginger Hall, which he had mentioned, she wanted to know whether there was some sacrifice that could avert it.

"There is no sacrifice," the soothsayer told her. "Certain events are destined by forces beyond human control or manipulation. I am telling you this because people think that we in this profession can alter events that have been destined. It is not true. Any good soothsayer will tell you the same thing. Often, people have the wrong impression that we can perform miracles. However, there is some sacrifice to be offered for all the other matters we have enquired about."

Giita and her relatives became alert. Giita was becoming nervous, as she wondered how much the sacrifice would cost her.

"When a woman delivers a baby, get hold of the placenta. Go and bury it under a kola nut tree that has not yet borne any fruit - a virgin kola nut tree. Sacrifice seven red kola nuts and seven eggs and give all to seven old people, four women and three men in Talia. The people should be about seventy years old. Also, you should sacrifice nine new needles and nine new pennies and throw them into the river. You should offer the sacrifice nine days before you see the new moon and it should be done on the same day. If you do this, all I have said will come to pass. Before you do all these things, be sure that you really want another son, no matter the consequences."

When they trooped out of Komawaa's hut, Giita had already made up her mind that she wanted to have another son, and she received the support of her relatives who had been with her for eight days. Komawaa received his consultation fees and early the following morning, Giita and her relatives left for home. Talia was feverishly awaiting their arrival. The Sande Secret Society's graduation ceremonies were to start on the very day they arrived in Talia. The festive occasion attending the graduation had already affected the atmosphere of the entire chiefdom.

It was during the innocent hours of the morning, when the stars were already in hibernation and it was still charcoal dark, that Giita and her relatives left Gbahama for Talia. Many people were still sleeping. The monkeys and baboons too were fast asleep. Nature was beginning to prepare for another day as Giita and her relatives started walking back home after eight eventful days in Gbahama.

CHAPTER NINE

Hindowaa had decided he would visit his friend and confidant, Nyake, but this time he would not ask him to accompany him to Rogbohun in the north, to ascertain the return of the hen. It was already morning in Talia and people had started trekking to their farms. Some of the farmers would make a detour and visit their palm trees to collect palm wine, while others would visit traps in the bush and fishing equipment left overnight to trap fish. Some of the older women went to the Sande Society grove to visit the students. Soon the town would be empty, providing an ideal atmosphere for Nyake and his visitor. The wind from the river and nearby forest was cool and gentle that morning as Hindowaa strolled to Nyake's house. As he walked towards his friend's house, he saw from a distance the only vehicle in town waiting for passengers. He thought about his first journey to Rogbohun with his sister. The journey had raised great expectations about Kunaafoh coming back home and Giita having an additional son, if the sacrificial hen returned to town.

Along the way, several people going to their farms greeted him. All of them were familiar faces. He had known some of them for as long as he had lived in Talia. Of all the people he knew, it was Nyake and Nyamakoro that he had known for the longest time. He was not convinced that Nyamakoro, the woman who was known to be the most successful businesswoman in Talia had acquired her wealth through foul play. He had become immune to gossip in Talia and admired and respected the 'pancake' businesswoman. The woman had no children. Hindowaa had children but wanted more sons. So neither he nor Nyamakoro were happy with their condition. So what is happiness? he wondered. It is about when you get what your heart desires. Yes, that is what it means. That was why he and Nyamakoro had something in common. So, Nyake must be a happy man, Hindowaa thought. He has many sons and daughters. That is the reason he cannot see beyond his nose. Nyake, simply does not understand that other people want to achieve their own heart's desires and preaches at them whenever they approach him for advice. He had known Nyake for as long as he had known Nyamakoro, but he had never thought of going to the woman for advice, even though she had prospered in her business.

Hindowaa's mind was engaged as he walked towards his friend's house. His thoughts were floating as the time approached for him to find out about the outcome of the sacrificial hen. The whole issue had tormented him. What if the hen did not come back to the town of Roghohun? To deflect his mind from the issue of the hen, he always tried to direct his attention to other less challenging matters, so he continued to walk towards Nyake's house and also continued to greet people he came across on his way.

Nyake spotted his old friend coming towards his house. He had known through intuition that Hindowaa would be visiting that morning. Why? It was just his sixth sense that had told him to expect his friend. Hindowaa, Nyake thought, has never changed in any significant manner. He is a good man, but he has refused to change and has remained stuck to the old ways of our fathers and grandfathers. *Chai*. Look at the amount of time, energy and money he is spending on this issue of sons. Just imagine the loans he has had to take to pay for all his consultations. And look at the pressure he has put on his poor wife. Does he ever find time to sit and reflect on the effect his behaviour is having on her and the rest of the family? I wonder. Yet, when I tell him what I feel about his situation, he says I am not sympathetic. Well, do I have to show sympathy by betraying my conscience? No. I am not prepared to do that and I am ready to tell him the truth each time he comes up with the matter. I have no intention of compromising my principles on these matters for him or for anyone else who comes here to seek my advice. I know that he is going around telling people how callous I am regarding his problems. Let him tell them. Let him tell them now and after I have died, but I shall continue to say what I think about the matters that he brings to me. His mother has not helped either. Kigba also has not surprised me. What is surprising is that she as a woman refuses to understand and appreciate the reality of another woman's situation. I wish Hindowaa's father were alive. He would have knocked some sense into Hindowaa's head and I know that Kigba would have behaved herself. Her husband's death has changed all that now. Look at what the whole household has to go through. These are trying times. I feel so sorry for Giita. Poor woman, Nyake said to himself as he continued to watch Hindowaa coming towards his house, greeting people as he walked along.

Seeing the lorry going to Rogbohun via other towns along the route, Hindowaa thought, they will never leave on time. No wonder people get to their destinations late. He had had what he called a bitter experience before with the lorry which was the only one in the town of Talia. However, the driver and the motor apprentices knew and respected him. The driver, who was called Laundeh, always offered him the front seat when he travelled. He cherished the honour.

Nyake was lying in his hammock, smoking his pipe. The palm wine tapper had already delivered his quota to him that morning. He was lying in his hammock with his head resting on his left arm. The foam from the palm wine filled the veranda with a beautiful aroma which a gentle breeze helped to waft outside. As Hindowaa came within sight of the veranda, he started salivating, knowing he would soon be drinking with his friend.

"*Ndake Biwah, biseh, biseh ah ngendeh jii?*" he greeted Nyake heartily, asking him how he was feeling that morning.

"*Biwah, biseh, kai ee Ngewo maa, nya gahun gbuwa'ngo,*" Nyake returned the greeting, saying he thanked God for his state of well-being.

Hindowaa sat opposite Nyake, eyeing the large palm wine gourd that stood beside his friend.

"Ndakei, when I was coming, I was thinking about the lorry," he said. "It never leaves on time. We have spoken to Laundeh many times for him to leave on time but the boy is stubborn. He does not listen to his elders in this town. When one is travelling it is not good to arrive at one's destination late. The last time my sister and I travelled, we reached Rogbohun very late."

"Ndakei, we are not the only passengers that the driver caters for. He has to wait for the other passengers that come from the surrounding towns. For him to make money and stay in business, he needs a lorry full of passengers. He needs to buy petrol and maintain the lorry. I think that is why he stays around until he has collected enough passengers for the trip," Nyake pointed out.

"So that means people will always be late getting to their destination," observed Hindowaa who was now swinging calmly in his own hammock as people continued to pass by and greet them.

"Ndakei, driving a commercial vehicle like that one is a business and people do it to make money. That is the whole essence of the exercise. It is so simple. I don't know what your problem is. Could you have done it differently and been able to stay in business profitably?" Nyake asked.

"I should have known how you would reply. Always the same. No sympathy."

Nyake ignored Hindowaa's observation and continued puffing at his pipe.

"Ndakei, I am happy you came," he told his friend. Hindowaa sat upright, his mind alert. He thought Nyake would say something about the hen. Rumours, he had heard, maybe.

"I decided to come at the last minute. I had contemplated going to see Madam Nyamakoro but changed my mind and decided to come here instead. Do you have good news for me?" Hindowaa asked. His friend sensed his anxiety.

"How often do you dream?" Nyake asked.

"Dream? Dream? I don't know. I do dream but I cannot remember how often. Why?" Hindowaa replied.

"I had a dream last night," Nyake told him. "It was not a nice dream, by my own estimation. Let us have a drink before I tell you what it was about."

Nyake indicated that Hindowaa should hand him his cup for some palm wine and filled it. Anxious to hear what his friend had to say, Hindowa took a big gulp of palm wine, which left his cup only half full. He held on to it as Nyake began to narrate his dream.

"There was a funeral in this town. It was attended by many people. The town was crowded and the women were crying, wailing and tearing their hair out…," Hindowaa put his cup down on the floor and stared at his friend.

"You dreamed about a funeral?" he interrupted in dismay. "That sounds terrible. Who died, a man or woman, and from which household? Was it from down town or up town?"

"Ndakei, that was the problem," Nyake told him. "I was not able to determine who died and whether it was from up town or down town. However, the funeral took place here - up town. Most of the dignitaries were present."

"Did you spot me at the funeral?" Hindowaa asked.

"Ndakei, are you deaf, I told you that most of the dignitaries of this town were there. You as *Ngumbuwaa* were conspicuously present and very sombre, like all of us who were present."

"Do your dreams usually come true?" Hindowaa asked again.

"Ndakei, we have been friends for ages. Don't you know by now the nature of my dreams? I have told you many of my dreams, and here you are asking me again this morning whether my dreams come true. I mean, in most cases they do. That was why I said I was happy you came to see me this morning. I am seriously concerned about the dream."

"Why don't you go and see a Muslim priest, he may tell you something about it," Hindowaa suggested.

"My brother, even though the majority of my dreams come true, the truth is that I do not like them to be interpreted because I am afraid of being told bad things," Nyake replied.

"Are you not a Wunde man, a *Ngumbuwa* for that matter? What are you afraid of?" Hindowaa teased.

"Ah. Ah. Today is your day, not so? You sound like a bold man. To tell you the truth, I am not afraid of death. However, I do not like to hear unpleasant news. I don't think anybody does, especially where death is concerned. It could be your loved one. Who knows?"

"Nyake, I agree with you. Your dream frightens me. But tell me, is there anybody up town here, or down town that is seriously ill?" Hindowaa asked in a subdued voice, as he remained worried about Nyake's dream.

"Well, unless we enquire from the Chief, I am not aware of anyone who is ill or seriously ill in this town." Nyake's reply gave Hindowaa a sense of relief.

"*I*, also, had a dream a couple of days ago," he said. "It was not really a serious one, but when I told my mother, she told me to go and see a Muslim priest, and I did."

"What was it about?" Nyake asked.

"As I said it was not really a serious dream in my view, but my mother always takes dreams seriously. I dreamed that Fanday, my brother's wife in Freetown, came here, and she looked distraught and remorseful, but I have no details beyond what I have said," Hindowaa told him.

"That does not sound like a good dream to me," Nyake said.

"Did you see the Muslim priest?"

"Yes, my mother and myself saw Karmo Alie. He told me to sacrifice two cups full of clean water and offer them to children to drink, especially when they were going to school in the morning." Hindowaa

"So you feel all right after the sacrifice," Nyake remarked.

"My brother, you will never believe this until you die. That sacrifice became a problem. I never knew that a simple thing like drinking cold water in the morning could turn out to be a big problem. The children refused to drink the water. These are children of these days. They just refused, both boys and girls," Hindowaa said.

"So what happened in the end?" Nyake asked.

"We actually had to beg two children to drink the water and explained to them what it was all about. We were all very embarrassed and ashamed that you could not get children to drink water offered to them, free," Hindowaa said.

"You see, my friend, look at it this way. When we offer people water to drink, in our society it comes along with something else. It comes after people have eaten. It comes when people are thirsty and they ask you for a drink. Think about it, it is rather unusual to ask someone, not a member of your household, someone who just happens to be passing by, to drink water. And in our community water is not such a precious thing that you think by offering it to someone he or she should be grateful. If you had offered the children sweets or soft drinks, they would have grabbed them swiftly and thanked you. Don't feel that the children who refused were being difficult or ungrateful," Nyake's explanation, however, left Hindowaa unimpressed, and he changed the subject as they continued to drink their palm wine.

"Tell me Nyake, do you think *Kinie* Ngolo (meaning, 'baboon' or 'strong man') would make a good Paramount Chief, I mean our next Paramount Chief? His father was a wonderful man, but died, sadly. I hope the next Chief would be like him."

"There is no way you can predict whether anyone will be a better than their predecessor. It is a difficult and dangerous thing to do. Don't you know the story of Chief Bendu, who died many years ago? He was a very nice and wise Chief who was loved by his people," Nyake replied.

"Yes, I know the story. It was a sad one."

"So we just have to wait and see when the time comes. If we get a Chief who is not kind and sympathetic, we shall find a way of getting rid of him or her. We have done it before."

"But what worries me, my friend, is that this town is not changing much," Hindowaa observed. "The people are still the same."

He was now on his third cup of palm wine and feeling more relaxed.

"Ah, Hindowaa, I am glad you are bringing that issue up. You happen to be one of those I think has not changed much in this town since we were children many many years ago," Nyake said to Hindowaa's great amusement.

"You are crazy and funny person." Hindowaa told him, laughing.

'Tell me, Hindowaa, who else has not changed here in Talia apart from you?" Nyake asked.

"Look at that woman, Nyamakoro." Hindowaa said. "For as long as we have known her, she has not changed much. Her business is still the same. She has not aged much either. For a woman, that is remarkable. No wonder people are suspicious about her."

"*I* think she made her money from her business," Nyake replied. "The woman loves money. She never allows anyone who took her cakes on credit to get away without paying. She fears no one. She harasses her debtors to the limit. That is how she got rich. I don't blame her. If she let her debtors go free, how else could she have paid school fees for the relatives' children she adopted?"

The Sande students had stopped singing and there was silence in the grove. As the two friends continued talking and drinking, the morning progressed into the afternoon and the town was silent.

"Ndake, you recall I had gone to Rogbohun to see the *Moimui* about my problem. I came and briefed you about it. I now have to go and find out if the hen returned to the town and I am nervous. I am the only one travelling this time because I cannot afford the transportation for two people. I am having sleepless nights thinking about the possibility of the hen not returning. However, my sister remains optimistic that it will return."

Nyake listened attentively as Hindowaa spoke his mind.

"Yes, *ndake* Hindowaa, I have heard you," he replied. "You have informed me adequately about these matters. My views then and now have not changed. You know my views, don't you? Why don't you believe in God and the ancestors? They gave you three children, two boys and a girl. If Giita has had no more sons, that is what God and the ancestors wish for you. Every Sunday, you go to Church, then you also pour libation to the ancestors at the shrine and pray. They have all answered your prayers, yet you are not content and you roam the country trying to change what God and the ancestors have decided."

"Ndake, Nyake," Hindowaa told his friend, "I think that you are not sympathetic. Yes, you are not. You have three wives and many sons, so every year your harvest is good. It is better than mine, because you have more sons to work your farm. I can see why you are saying that."

"Hindowaa, look how much debt you and Giita have accumulated trying to undo what God and the ancestors have decided. With such a problem, now you are now threatening to marry again in search of sons. You really mean business."

Hindowaa was offended by Nyake's remarks and showed his indignation.

"I may be in debt," he said, "but I have not come to ask you for a loan, have I? In any case, how did you know that we are in debt? There is too much gossip in this town. Yes, we are in debt, but who is not in debt here? Maybe, *Nyahapui* Nyamakoro, the pancake businesswoman. I only came to inform you about developments and look what you are telling me now."

"Have another cup of wine," Nyake offered and generously poured Hindowaa another cupful of palm wine.

"Ndake Hindowaa, I have told you and many others in this town repeatedly that what we all don't like is the truth. When you tell people the raw truth, nothing but the raw truth, they take offence. Our ancestors say that the truth will never hurt you and therefore it will not kill you. But lies do. As for me, I am used to telling people the truth. We all want sons. How do we get the sons if we don't want daughters? By magic or miracle? Tell me. Have you ever heard the saying, that everybody wants to go to heaven, but nobody wants to die? How do you reconcile that? You want to have sons, but you don't want girls." Nyake's tone was serious and sober and he offered no apologies to his friend who looked uncomfortable.

"Tell me, my friend," he went on, "what if when you go to Rogbohun you are told that the hen did not return? What will you do?"

For a moment, silence reigned between the two friends for when Nyake asked that question, Hindowaa felt as if someone had pierced his heart with a razor blade. His saliva tasted bitter in his mouth.

"I shall then go further than Rogbohun, and if need be go to the source of mystical powers. I shall go to Mamu and Kankan in Guinea. I am prepared. I shall increase my present debt, but let me assure you that I will not come to you for financial assistance. If I do, the whole of Talia and beyond will know about it. This much I have to tell you." Hindowaa had already finished his third cup of palm wine. He was not drunk, or even tipsy. He sounded mentally alert. "When many of us come to consult you and have your views, it does not mean that we are stupid," he continued angrily. "We come to you because we believe that you are neutral on many issues in this town. However, now you are treating us as if we are stupid. You treat us as if we don't know what we are doing. You treat us like children."

Nyake listened as his friend vented his feelings, but unruffled and determined to stick to his opinions, he took another gulp of the palm wine.

"When do you plan to travel to Rogbohun?"

"I need to secure the money for the lorry fare, after that I shall set the date," Hindowaa informed him coldly.

"What about the marriage to Boi-Kimbo, the girl at the Sande Society?"

"That issue will be decided after I come from Rogbhun and have found out the status of the hen," Hindowaa responded.

"I shall pray for you so that all your cherished dreams are fulfilled and Giita's also. And I wish you a very safe journey and I await your return so that we can celebrate the good news that you will bring from Rogbohun," Nyake said.

Hindowaa detected his friends' sarcasm and did not respond to Nyake's good wishes.

The weather was now warm and both friends were beginning to sweat. Hindowaa and Nyake spotted the mad man of the village who had seen the two moons. He seemed to be heading towards them. Hindowaa quickly took leave of his friend and promised he would report back after his visit to Rogbohun. The mad man greeted him as they crossed each other's path.

CHAPTER TEN

It was a well-known fact that Kortu and his wife spent several hours in their bedroom. Many a time when neighbours passed by to greet them they would be locked up in their bedroom especially on Sundays, after Church. People said that Kortu had brought lots of money from Burma, where he had fought during the Second World War. The fact that the couple had no children and were gainfully employed also fuelled speculation about how much money they had accumulated. Kortu's nephews, Hinga and Kafo, were also curious about their uncle and aunt's addiction to the bedroom.

On one particular Sunday, the Kortus never stepped out of their room, and on Monday, they did not come out either. It was very unusual for Kortu to miss going to work. His wife also hardly missed going to sell her wares in the market at Ginger Hall where she was well known by the other traders, both men and women. The absences were immediately noticed at their places of work. Meanwhile, in their partially lit room, both Kortu and his wife looked grim and sombre as if a member of the family had suddenly died. They were emotionally numb and devastated. Throughout their long marriage, they had never gone through such an experience. It was simply unbelievable that the most precious of their trunks had been emptied of its contents; and their money was nowhere to be seen. How could this be possible? they asked themselves. All they had in terms of money had vanished from their room. From time to time they would focus their eyes on the empty container, which was still standing in its usual place. They were like two dumb people, for long spells of silence reigned in the room. Many people might be forgiven when petty thieving takes place in a household, but there is one item which when stolen, every effort will be made to apprehend the culprit. That item is money.

"When I talk to you about your nephews, you think I just want to be difficult," Fanday said. "They are not doing well at school; one plays football instead of studying; the other is always with motor boys. What do you expect from them? I even suspect that Hinga has started woman business and even made a girl pregnant. If that is the case, how could he support the girl and concentrate on his studies?"

"Are you suggesting that Hinga is responsible for the theft?"

Kortu asked.

"Who else would you suspect? Tell me. Where would he be getting money from to support his life style? He may also be drinking and smoking, together with his brother," Fanday told her husband in a bitter voice as tears stained her fleshy cheeks.

"I would be careful about accusing anybody right now, if you were to ask my advice," Kortu said in a calm though troubled voice. "It is too soon. The trunk is intact, not broken. We have to determine that no one had access to the keys of the room and the box itself. This looks like a professional job."

"Even if I have to sell all my belongings, I shall do so to find out who decided to inflict such merciless pain on us. I shall never sleep or rest until the criminals are apprehended. I know them. I know who they are. I also know that you know them too, but would rather remain silent," Fanday told her husband.

"How can you say that, Fanday?" Kortu said. The atmosphere in the room was becoming heated. "Now you are accusing me. Fanday are you out of your mind, are you crazy?" Kortu got up and paced around the room, visibly angry and beginning to sweat.

"You know that I am not crazy. Yes, you know that for certain," Fanday responded in a bitter, angry tone. "We have been married for too long for you not to know that I am not a mad woman. A mad woman does not go to the market every day to trade. A mad woman does not take care of a house the way I have done for as long as we have been married. You know that I am not mad. You never said Giita was mad when she accused me of witchcraft. She accused me of having a *koko* and being responsible for the deaths of children. But no, she is not a mad woman."

They were speaking quietly so the neighbours would not hear them and come around. Fanday went to one corner of the room and retrieved some items. She had been spying on the boys, Hinga and Kafo, and had visited their room while they were at school. Kortu looked at the items his wife now displayed on the floor. His eyes were noticeably red.

"Tell me how Hinga could afford these items." Fanday said, brimming with confidence. "Tell me. Even you who are employed cannot afford these items. Where did he get the money? That is my question, since you are defending their case."

The items on display were a sort of unique fountain pen and a new pair of shoes, which Hinga had obviously obtained by mail order from England. They used to be called Langham shoes and were very much in demand at the time. She also displayed an expensive new Terylene shirt - a beautiful shirt. Kortu felt like a mouse caught in a trap.

"I know that you have been waiting for an opportunity to get even with my brother's wife," he said, "but I want to assure you that the law does not accept accusations as proof. You need hard evidence, so I am warning you to be very careful not to accuse my nephews without proof. I have no idea where these items came from. I shall make time to talk to my nephews. However, I am surprised that you would visit their room in their absence and search it. They are big boys and need their privacy. I think you are going too far, Fanday. You are going too far."

"My dear, I was forced to do it," Fanday replied. "You know that it is not my nature to do such things, but your brother's children have become a liability in this house. I was also looking for other items to substantiate my other suspicions. I wanted to see if I could find some women's items, and some love letters, just to prove to you that they are not innocent. Hinga may have impregnated a schoolgirl, and is supporting her. Who knows? These days, boys are up to no good."

Her husband fell silent for a moment as he paced to and fro in the room. "I shall talk to my nephews before I make any definitive comments on your findings," he said. "I shall feel embarrassed though, because you have violated their privacy. I consider this rather unfortunate under the circumstances. I do know that my brother provides pocket money for his children, though how much, I can't say."

"You never told me this before," Fanday said accusingly. "Why are you telling me now? How much is the pocket money? How much of that money would they need to buy these things. Have you ever seen a pen like this? And look at this shirt, have you ever worn a shirt like that in your entire life? And the shoes. Wow! I have never seen shoes like this. These boys are supposed to be students, yet look at what they have in their possession?" She looked Kortu straight in the face as she made her observations.

"I shall not indulge in accusing the boys until I find out the truth of the matter, Fanday," Kortu told his wife. "I do not know for sure that these items belong to the boys. Friends may have given them to them for safe keeping.

Who knows? You see, law is a very interesting subject. You have to have the raw facts to establish innocence or guilt. From all you have said, we cannot make any judgement based on these exhibits. Your evidence is purely circumstantial, so let us wait and see."

Fanday felt offended by her husband's attitude to her accusations.

"Oh, now you are on their side, Kortu. You mean to tell me that you are defending your relatives against me? Your useless nephews are now more important in your life than me. I don't want to believe this. *Ngewo, Ngewo Gbo nyama,*" she said, asking God to help her. So great was her anger and frustration that she put both hands on top of her head, saying, "*Kooh, kooh, kooh, nya bondaa, ahgbo-nyama, ahgo-nyamaa,*" pleading with her people to help her. "I shall get a *Gbator* man," she went on, referring to someone who traces thieves or searches for lost and precious items using mystical means. "He will come and search for the money. I shall pledge all my precious possessions if need be to get the best *Gbator* man."

Kortu felt apprehensive after Fanday threatened to get a *Gbator* man to come and investigate the theft of the money as he was not one hundred per cent sure of his nephews' innocence in the matter. There was a slight possibility that one or both of them could be responsible for the missing money. He was worried about the exhibits his wife had presented, though still convinced that the boys would not be involved in such a massive theft. He knew from experience that an insider would not have taken all the money at once. It would have been stolen piecemeal; so it had to be the work of an outsider. However, he reasoned to himself with a heavy heart, one could not rule out the possibility that it could be the work of an outsider in collaboration with an insider.

The news of the missing money at the Kortus' house was received in Ginger Hall with telegraphic speed. The whole community went into a frenzy of gossip about the Kortus when the amount involved was finally revealed. Some people did not believe the story of the missing money which contradicted the views held by many in Ginger Hall about the Kortus. They were supposed to be in possession of a boa constrictor that protected them. Fanday was supposed to be in possession of the *koko* bird. If these stories were true, who would dare enter their room and steal so much money?

One Saturday evening Kortu disappeared and went to see a little known soothsayer in Ginger Hall. It was a woman who lived on the periphery of the town. She lived alone in her house, having lost her husband a long time ago. She was well known for eating kola nuts regularly and eating snuff. All her teeth were red as a result of her snuff and kola nut eating habits. On his way to see the woman, Kortu felt that the neighbours were watching his movements. He looked uncomfortable and nervous. His short khaki trousers seemed bigger on him than usual as if he had lost weight. He felt awkward in them as he walked along thinking about the items his wife had assembled before him in her efforts to implicate his nephews in the theft. The pen was indeed unique. He had never seen anything like it before. Yes his wife was right. He had also never seen the type of shoes on display or that kind of shirt. All the items were new and well wrapped. The writing on the pen was not legible because it was not in English or any other language he knew or had seen. He started thinking deeply and for the first time, felt that he had not paid sufficient attention to his brother's children who were supposed to be in his care. He wondered briefly why his brother had not entrusted his nephews' pocket money to him. That thought, however, soon evaporated from his troubled mind as he went along.

Kortu's encounter with the old soothsayer was brief and to the point. As he sat opposite the woman, with his heart occasionally skipping a beat, she told him she knew why he had come to see her. The woman said that the person who stole the money was a close family member, but she did not elaborate and Kortu did not insist. He paid the consultation fee and left, feeling in more of a quagmire than before. He started suspecting that his wife's allegations that his nephews were involved in the theft might be true. The soothsayer's reference to a close member of the family started sounding menacingly real. What would his brother, Hindowaa say? How would Giita react? These questions plagued him. He looked forward to an encounter with his nephews on the matter. He would strangle them if they brought shame, feud and rancour to the family.

Fanday had also undertaken a similar exercise though she did not tell Kortu. She had gone to see a male soothsayer. However, Kortu knew that Fanday would make efforts to see a soothsayer.

Fanday travelled to the west of Ginger Hall, and she could sense the way people were looking at her as she walked towards the soothsayer's house. The place was busy that evening as many people had come to seek the man's assistance on various matters of concern to them.

"All our lives we have laboured for nothing," Fanday thought as she walked to the soothsayer's house that evening. "What will they do with all that money? Do they just want to punish us? If they had just pinched some money and left the rest one would have accommodated the situation. The boys never come home in time. You never see them spend valuable time studying like other school children. What do they do? Where do they go? Ah, Ah. Maybe, they go to Big Wharf or King Jimmy to gamble, who knows? They may even be going there to smoke *jamba* (cannabis). The children of today cannot be trusted. Yet look how their uncle is busy defending them so shamelessly. I don't blame him. I blame my parents, especially my father, who married me off to him."

"I knew you were coming to see me. I have known since yesterday," the soothsayer told Fanday when she was seated on a bench near him. As he listened and assembled his tools, she said. "All our lives we have worked hard to save our money. We do not have children. That is what God decided, but we worked hard so that in our old age we would not depend on anyone. Now we have been robbed and there is no future for us. We are not young anymore. Where do we start? That is why I have come to see if you could tell me who stole our money. All our money is gone."

"I understand your pain," the soothsayer replied as he moved his tools around. "Yes, I can see it all. It is very clear, look at the way the peanut shells are assembled. It is very clear. A close member of the family is responsible. That is all I can say. It is an inside job. You and your husband know the person; it is a member of the family, a blood relative. It is not from outside. Look at the things on the floor. Very clear."

Fanday looked on the floor, distressed and further convinced of the guilt of one or both of the boys, especially Hinga. She paid the consultation fee to the soothsayer and left for her home. Her conviction that Kortu's nephews had hands in the theft of the money had been further strengthened by her visit to the soothsayer.

When he returned home, Kortu had an emergency meeting with his nephews in their bedroom. The young men knew about the stolen money but were unaware of developments in the matter.

"Hinga and Kafo, I know that you are aware of the money that is missing in our house. Have you ever seen anyone come into this house while we were away? Kortu asked them.

The boys looked at each other. They appeared innocent.

"No, uncle," Hinga replied.

"I am your uncle, your younger father. If you know anything about this matter, we shall settle it the family way. Don't be ashamed. I don't want your parents to know anything about this. I beg you. If you know anything, we can talk about it as a family. We have spent most of our lives saving money for our old age. All of it has been stolen."

"Uncle, I can assure you that we are not involved in this," Hinga told his uncle with Kafo's concurrence. "We never saw anyone from outside come into this house during your absence. Uncle, I am telling you the truth and nothing but the truth. We know that our parents would be very angry with us if we did something like this. Our father would scold our mother for giving birth to sons who are thieves. Our mother has gone through hard times and we have no intention of adding to her bundle of woes. We do not go hungry in this house. We do not pay rent. Our father pays our fees and gives us pocket money. We have never stolen in our life. I can assure that we are innocent."

Kortu was almost convinced of the innocence of his nephews. However, knowing from experience that some boys were hardened and seasoned liars, there was an element of doubt that he could trust them one hundred per cent. He now raised the sensitive subject and monitored the body movements of his nephews as he spoke, focusing his eyes on the prime suspect, Hinga.

"Ah, there is another thing I want to ask you about. Your aunt was looking for certain things in the house and happened to have gone into your room. She came across certain items, which surprised her, and brought them to my notice. She saw some unusual items in your room. I am referring to a brand new fountain pen, new shirt and shoes. Who owns them?"

Kafo looked at his elder brother, turned his eyes away and focused on his uncle who was still looking at Hinga.

"Eeeeh. Uncle, the items are mine. They belong to me. There is also a pocket watch, a new watch. They are all mine," Hinga replied as his uncle continued to monitor his body movements. He looked perfectly composed and confident. For a moment, no one said anything.

The boys looked at their uncle as if they were anticipating the next question.

"Hinga, tell me very honestly." Kortu continued. "Tell me, how did you acquire these items? Even *I* cannot afford the things I saw. How can you a student, a schoolboy, afford them? Please tell me."

"Uncle, you can ask Kafo here. He will bear witness for me. I play for my club and the club gives us money, good money. You can go and ask our captain. He will tell you that I am telling the truth. It is out of that money that I bought all those items and I have in fact ordered the same for Kafo. Not so, Kafo?"

Kafo responded positively to what his brother had said. "Uncle, because I am not clever in school, I ordered the magic fountain pen from India. Many students do the same. With that pen, I shall pass my exams with flying colours. It is a magic pen and it comes from Poona, India. I have all the order forms and receipts on all those items. The shoes and the shirts are very popular among young boys. These are the most expensive items I have in my possession, Uncle. I am being honest with you. Not so, Kafo?" Hinga told his uncle.

"Hinga, you have this pen, but how is it that you never pass your school exams?" Kortu asked. "You know that you failed the screening test to go to Form Five and take your 'O' Level exams. So far you have been successful in football, but not in school, the main reason why my brother sent you and your brother here. Now lastly, both of you, I want to ask another question which will be a secret among us. I promise you that I shall never tell anyone, including your father and mother, so be honest with me. I was once your age and usually at certain ages, we do things which we hide from our parents, for obvious reasons. So do not be ashamed to answer my questions." The boy were curious.

"All the questions are for both of you. Now, tell me which of the following things do you do or have you started doing. Do you do woman business, smoke cigarettes or *jamba,* drink beer and gamble?"

There was no immediate response as the boys looked at each other.

"Uncle," Hinga replied, "I am over twenty-five now and I have a girlfriend who is a woman. Sometimes Kafo and I go there to eat. She cooks for us and even gives me money. She taught me how to drink and I also smoke cigarettes, but not *jamba*. And I do not gamble at all."

Kafo was startled when his uncle asked, "What about you, Kafo?" "Uncle, me also," he said. "I am now over twenty-two years old, but only schoolgirls are my girlfriends. I smoke cigarettes and drink beer a bit. I do not smoke *jamba* or gamble. I swear, Uncle, by all the good things you do for us. I also swear by my Wunde Society that I am telling the truth as my brother also said. We are telling the truth." Kafo's lips were trembling a little but he looked resolute.

"Hinga, have you ever made a woman pregnant? Do you have children in the street?" Kortu now asked his senior nephew.

"No, uncle," Hinga responded with a little smile. Kafo also smiled, which made Kortu fire more questions at them. "Are you telling the truth? Why are you both smiling? Can you swear that you have never made a woman pregnant? And you Kafo, what about you? Do you know what it means when you make a woman pregnant and you are a schoolboy? They drive you from school."

"Uncle, I only have schoolgirls as girlfriends," Kafo told his uncle.

"What do you mean, you only have schoolgirls as friends? Don't they also get pregnant? You are past twenty-two. How old are your girlfriends. How old are they?" Kortu insisted.

"One is seventeen and the other is twenty, uncle," Kafo replied.

"And you are telling me you only have schoolgirls as girlfriends. Those ones can have children. I warn you to be careful. If you make girls pregnant, you know what you father will do to you. I am warning both of you today to be very careful not to bring trouble into this house."

"You, Hinga, this woman of yours, is she single or married?"
It took Hinga some time to respond to the question.

"Uncle, I think that she is just slightly older than me. She has a boyfriend who is much older, and is a driver. He drives a lorry and most of the time he is away up-country."

"I pity you my child," Kortu said. "I pity you very much. Those are dangerous people. Drivers who make such trips can trap you. One day when he suspects his woman is up to something, he will trick her, saying he will not be back until a certain date, then all of a sudden he shows up at night. Boy, oh boy. You know what will happen if he catches you! Do you know what will happen? He will first re-circumcise you because of his woman. Then he will do the ultimate - murder. You will be dead, boy, cold dead because of a woman. You are taking a big risk. And I suppose you used to sleep there or you still sleep in her place. Do you?"

"Yes, Uncle," Hinga admitted.

"Kafo, where do you sleep?"

"I always come home to sleep, Uncle," Kafo replied.

"You children of today, you are not afraid. Instead of spending your time reading your books, you are womanising. Your father and mother are there, up-country, thinking that you are doing well at school, and here you are fully involved in womanising, drinking and smoking. You make me sick in the stomach. You are losing a very good opportunity, which your parents have given you. If you don't study, you will find out for yourselves in the future that things will not be easy for you. Don't squander your youthful life on pleasure," Kortu warned them. "Pleasure will never pass exams. Do not forget the saying, 'an opportunity once lost will never be regained'. It is true."

He left his nephews with a troubled mind. He felt that the young men had been fairly open with him, but still harboured doubts about their role in the incident. He continued asking himself, how the two soothsayers could have come to the same conclusion that a close member of the family stole the money. Only himself, his wife and his two nephews, who lived in the house, were close relatives. These thoughts started to worry him more and more and he continued to question his nephews on a regular basis. As often as their uncle approached them on the matter, the nephews continued to deny any involvement. The Ginger Hall Community became preoccupied with the subject. It was the talk of the neighbourhood. They marvelled at the amount of money that was involved and admired the Kortus for accumulating so much wealth.

Fanday had obtained permission from her husband to go to a town called Gbendembu to arrange for a prominent *Gbator* man to come and search for the money and the thief. Kortu was shaken. He now believed that one or both of his nephews might be involved. Such a revelation would severely dent the family honour in Ginger Hall and Talia. He had sleepless nights. He had wanted to convince Fanday to drop the idea of a *Gbator* man, but knew that if he took such an approach, then her allegations about his nephews being the culprits would be sustained.

When Ginger Hall learned that the *Gbator* man hired by Fanday was Josayah Kailondo, they knew then that the money would be found or whoever stole it would be caught. That was certain. Fanday had gone to great lengths to acquire funds to support her quest to retrieve the money. She had vowed she would do anything humanly possible to get to the root of the matter, and she had the support of the community. People wanted justice to be done. Her fellow traders at the market also supported her. They knew she was a hard working woman who had acquired her money through self-discipline. Fanday remained convinced that her husband's nephews were the culprits, despite the fact that Kortu had informed her about his meeting with the boys and their collective denial regarding the missing money.

The *Gbator* man, Kailondo, had acquired fame in the art of *gbator* divination a long time ago. He had caught people who had robbed the white man's bank in Freetown. The police had been deployed in the search for the thieves but their efforts proved futile. They were then told to try the native art of catching thieves and retrieving lost items. They declined at first but later, reluctantly decided to proceed with it. That was how Kailondo was summoned. He came with his team of very able assistants, because to put him in a trance and to disarm him after the exercise needed very strong men. When he arrived at the police headquarters, the place was already crowded with busybodies who had come to have a look at this wonderful catcher of thieves who would put the Criminal Investigation Department and police officers to shame.

Kailondo was stripped to his waist. His trousers were short, brownish and made of country cloth with lots of cowry, conch shells and amulets sewn on the material. He was barefooted. Five men surrounded him as he sat on the ground, and started washing his body with a liquid made from herbs and other ritual potions that had been prepared and left overnight in a bucket to ferment. He was given a rod, which he held firmly with both hands. His assistants repeatedly muttered incantations as the police and white men looked on. Then he started shaking as if a spirit possessed him, moving in rhythmic spasms, almost freezing, then moving again. When he finally got up he freed himself from the five men, and started running like a mad cow. People chased him but many could not run as fast as he could. The police and the white men followed the crowd on the chase. They said that he ran non-stop for well over a mile. Those old enough to tell the story said that they never saw anything like that in living memory. They said he ran into a bush and showed the police where the money was buried. Later, he went into the house of the thieves and beat them mercilessly until they confessed their guilt. That was a long time ago. The white men and the police were happy and believed in the native art of catching thieves.

It was on a bright Sunday afternoon that the *Gbator* man arrived at Ginger Hall with his assistants. They were dressed in their ritual paraphernalia. Ginger Hall was emotionally electrified over the event. Since it was not a work day, many people had stayed home to witness one of the most dramatic occasions in their lives. Children were also ready and waiting to witness the event. The weather cooperated fully. It was not too hot. People had already gathered around the Kortus' house. Kortu, his wife and nephews were to assemble on the veranda of their house at five p.m., but by the time it was five o'clock, Kortu had fallen asleep. Everybody said the *Gbator* man could proceed, since it was agreed that Kortu himself would not have stolen the money. Even Fanday agreed, feeling confident that it was her husband's nephews who had stolen the money.

The *Gbator* man's assistants were putting him in a trance. They had a small calabash full of ritual water, which they sprayed on him so that he would enter a state of trance. He had on a loincloth and beads around his waist, but the rest of his body was bare. He had a bundle of whips in his hands and held them tightly as his assistants muttered incantations. Gradually, the *Gbator* man started shaking, then his body became stiff and with the last incantations he cut loose and ran into the house as he continued to shake violently. He combed the house, came to the veranda and went around the boys who sat away from Fanday. The boys were quite composed. The *Gbator* man went outside the house and continued his search. After he had finished combing both inside and outside the house, he started running towards the east of Ginger Hall. His assistants and many people ran after him as fast as he was running. Fanday also went along. People were surprised, but the *Gbator* man went as the spirits directed him, followed by his assistants.

He found the house where Fanday's sister, Jinaa, and her husband lived. That Sunday, they had stayed home after Church, like most of the people in Ginger Hall. The *Gbator* man searched the inside of the house, then went outside and continued the search. He would

111

whip the ground with the bundle of whips then move on. He led people to a spot and asked them to dig there. Volunteers started digging as others watched.

"Dig faster," people shouted as they surrounded the *Gbator* man who was busy beating the ground with his bundle of whips.

"Eeeh, eeeh, look how they have been blaming Hinga and his brother for nothing," one of the onlookers commented as others continued monitoring the digging. "Since they came to Ginger Hall, those boys have never given any trouble. Hinga is always busy with his football and we all enjoy going to watch a game when his team is playing. Thank God he and his brother are not involved. God is great."

The man who was digging suddenly stopped. The hoe had come unhinged from the main handle, almost causing an accident. An interval passed as they tried to fix it. The people were becoming restless. "Let me help him if he is tired," a man volunteered and the digging went on faster than with the first volunteer. People were happy again as they looked on. Not long afterwards, a securely wrapped bundle was retrieved. It contained the Kortus' lost money.

The *Gbator* man then went into the house and started whipping Fanday's sister and her husband. They were whipped repeatedly as they confessed that they had stolen the money. People held their mouths and were heard shouting, "God is great, God is great, Allahuakubar."

Ginger Hall remained in a state of shock not only because Fanday's close relative had stolen the money, but also because when they went back to the Kortus' house, they found that the man himself had died in his sleep. Kortu's nephews were exonerated even as Ginger Hall went into painful mourning for the untimely death of one of the most humble members of the community.

CHAPTER ELEVEN

It was midday in Talia when Giita and her relatives arrived in the town. Before their arrival, Giita took a bath in the long, meandering river, while her relatives went on ahead. The water was so clear that she could see big as well as small fish swimming. She saw a big fish which was being followed by little ones. They were so many that she knew that the big fish was the mother of the smaller ones trailing behind her. As she focused her attention on the big fish, she saw another big one coming from the opposite direction. She wondered whether both creatures were partners, as they seemed to move around each other, surrounded by the little ones. She was thrilled and marvelled at nature's ingenuity. She also saw crabs of various sizes trying to come ashore. All the creatures of the river seemed to be going their different ways, in harmony with their habitat.

"Welcome back, oh, my sister." It was a sharp voice not far from where she was bathing, and Giita was taken by surprise. Another woman from Talia, was taking her bath downstream. She knew that Giita and her relatives had been away on mission to Gbahama.

"Thank you, my sister. Thank you," Giita responded.

"How was your mission, oh? How was it? We have been thinking of you and your relatives. I hope that everything went well," the other women said as she continued splashing water on her body.

"My sister, I thank God and the ancestors. It went well, only that I have to make a sacrifice before my problem is resolved," Giita told the woman. "What is the latest in town, since I have been away for eight days?"

"As you know, the Sande festivities have taken over Talia and the other towns around us. As I am talking to you now, the town is in a festive mood. You will sense it as soon as you leave here. You will hear music which has been going on since morning. It is wonderful," the woman informed Giita.

After her bath, Giita felt ritually cleansed and happy. Talia itself was enveloped in euphoria. The Sande graduation festivities had already electrified the atmosphere in the town. People danced, sang, drank and ate to their satisfaction. Meanwhile, the young teenaged graduates paraded through the town as part of the ceremony. They were dressed in their finest clothes for the occasion and shielded from the sun with umbrellas.

The initiation of the Sande Society always provided an opportunity for the taking of new wives in the community. Parents with daughters looked forward to it as it brought a bride price to the family which was a net gain. On the other hand, the men who married the girls would have to pay money and goods as a bride price. Some people said that it was nature's way of circulating wealth in society. Potential suitors would have earmarked most of the girls even before they had graduated from the Sande grove and would have arranged to pay the required bride price for their future wives. The happiest graduates were those who would be their husbands' first wives. However, there were those who would be joining other wives. Their status was different. In most cases, the young and last to be married would become the husband's favourite wife until he married another one in the future.

The festivities continued in Talia and people enjoyed themselves throughout that period. One evening, when the stars had disappeared and darkness had engulfed the town, Giita went to the room to sleep. Her husband and other men from Talia were sitting on the veranda talking about the graduation festivities. Hindowaa's friend and confidant, Nyake, was also present.

"Last night I found it difficult to fall asleep," Nyake told his companions. "The festivities went on far into the night. Then as I started sleeping, I heard dogs barking. They went on barking for a long time. I thought it was a rather unusual."

"When dogs bark like that, it means they have seen images that we cannot see," *Kinie* Ndomawova (meaning, 'old shirt') told the gathering. "They must have seen the ghosts which came to join the festivities. There is nothing unusual about that. We should be happy because these are our ancestors who have come to celebrate with us."

Many in the group concurred when *Kinie* Ndomawova made the observation. Another man remarked,

"I was fast asleep and did not hear all the barking you are talking about, Nyake. If you did not sleep well, how is it that you are still awake? *I* would have been sleeping by now."

"Eeemm, my friend here will not go to sleep as long as palm wine is around and it is free," another man teased.

"I will not hesitate to say that the reason this other friend of ours is staying up has nothing to do with palm wine. If I were in his position, I would behave the same way. The man is taking a new wife, one of the graduates. Mind you that will be his fourth wife. Do you think he will sleep early?"

There was subdued laughter on the veranda though the man concerned, refrained from commenting on the observation.

"So we are going to be deprived of initiating Sande for another couple of years, after this session," another man remarked. The next one will be at Foyah. Foyah also used to be famous for its hospitality during Sande initiation. We shall be there to patronize it. It is just one year from now. I married my first wife from Foyah, as you all know."

"As for me, while I look forward to the next initiation at Foyah, I have no intention of getting married again," another man said. "I am now looking for a wife for my elder son who is a grown man. Foyah will be the place to look for a wife for him. I have to do it before the boy brings woman damage. These days, the children are so impatient. I can see it in his eyes and I have warned him repeatedly that if he is involved in woman palaver, he may have to be jailed because I do not have money to settle woman damage."

As everybody laughed again, yet another man spluttered, "*Ndakei, Ngonii* (meaning, 'bird'), don't make me choke on my wine. Don't ignite painful memories for some of us here." Those who knew him well, laughed even louder.

"The first time I was put in *ndambeya* (meaning, 'jail', literally, 'feet trapped') was in connection with woman damage. I was young and like my friend said, my father had warned me many times and asked me to wait. But the temptation was too great. I got involved with someone's wife and I was caught. The woman was forced to confess to our relationship. That was my first encounter with woman damage. All the money I made from my ginger harvest that year went into paying for the damage before I was released from jail."

One of the older men now intervened. "If you were to ask my opinion, I would say that we shouldn't be narrating such experiences here tonight. We are here for something serious. I am not saying that what you people have been saying is not serious, but the occasion is inappropriate,"

At this, there was a greater outburst laughter, for the old man's story had generated much discussion and gossip in Talia at the time it happened. He had lost his youngest wife to a schoolboy from another town, not very far from Talia. The boy and girl had eloped to the diamond areas where, it was later learned, they had prospered in the diamond business. The old man never married another woman, much to the delight of his other wives.

When the company on the veranda finally broke up, Giita had still not fallen asleep. She had lain awake, tossing and turning for hours as she pleaded with God to grant her desires. She asked for her sacrifices to materialise. She wanted children; she wanted sons and also prayed that with more sons, Hindowaa would not take another wife. She was in torment over the possibility that he would marry a wife younger than her daughter, Kunaafoh. She felt morally assaulted and emotionally stifled over this matter. She also thought about the fact that when she was taken into marriage, Hindowaa had told her many times over that he would not take another wife. She had not asked for such a promise. It was Hindowaa himself who had volunteered that information. As time progressed, she had felt emotionally secure, her only anxiety being how soon she would become pregnant and have a child. Indeed, Hindowaa never told her that he had a greater preference for any particular sex. At what point did Hindowaa decide to have preference for sons? Giita asked herself. She was convinced that it was Hindowaa's mother who had planted the idea in his mind. How could some men be so fickle? she again asked herself. Hindowaa was a *Ngumbuwaa*. He was a very highly respected person in the community by virtue of his title in the Wunde Society. Why did he not emulate his friend and confidant, Nyake, who was also a *Ngumbuwah*. At least Nyake never told his first wife that he was not going to have another wife or wives. Nyake's first wife, Konah, had told Giita that she had no problem with Nyake from the time they met and married because he had informed her candidly that he was going to have many wives because he wanted to, and that there was nothing wrong with the practice. Konah had been emotionally prepared for that. In the case of Hindowaa, it was the opposite, Giita thought. He volunteered to misinform me very early in our marriage and later turned full circle.

As she lay thinking over this matter which troubled her greatly, Hindowaa came into the room. The Aladdin lamp was dim because the

116

kerosene was running out. Most of Talia was sleeping. The festivities had almost come to an end and nature itself was silent and peaceful.

"You mean, you have not slept since you came to the room?" Hindowaa asked in surprise. "We finished two gourds of palm wine and talked about many things. I had an opportunity to tell my friends about my trip to Rogbohun. You know how people are in this town. Some of them were not happy to hear the result of my trip and what would happen if I performed all the sacrifices that the *Moimui* told me to offer." Giita listened with immense interest as he added, "I shall be going back to find out if the hen returned to the town after I dropped it by the river bank as instructed by the *Moimui*."

He lay down beside her. The lamp was now giving a weak signal that the flame was about to go out. All the people in the house were asleep.

"Are you sure you followed all the instructions that the *Moimui* gave you when you went to release the hen by the river that day?" Giita asked, because she had come to associate Hindowaa with a tendency to forget details.

"How could I forget?" he told her. "Would I have gone to all that trouble to go to Rogbohun about this matter only to forget important details in the end? No. Everything went according to the *Moimui's* instructions. For instance, he told me that one of the vital points in the whole process was that once I had dropped the hen and started walking to town, I should not look back until I arrived in town. I never looked back."

"What if you had forgotten your purse?" Giita teased and they laughed together. It was a long time since Giita had been light-hearted in a conversation.

"Were the people in Rogbohun hospitable?" she asked.

"My dear, when you find yourself in our situation, all you really want is the fulfilment of your mission, so my mind was focused on accomplishing it; but I did not experience any hostility. Thank God everything went well. The people at Rogbohun are generally pleasant. I was satisfied with my mission."

"My own trip was also successful," Giita told him. "The days we spent were useful. The people at Gbahama were hospitable and cooperated fully with us, especially the wife of the soothsayer. She treated us very well. I benefited a lot from the many conversations we had with her and other people in the town. Her husband is a very knowledgeable person in his profession, but you know that by now. He enquired after you and asked why you did not accompany me. I lied on your behalf and said that you had to attend to other pressing matters, and were confident that I would represent the family well."

"It seems the *Moimui* at Rogbohun was also expecting that both of us would be there. I also told him that we decided that one of us should always be present at home to welcome the people who were still trooping into the house to sympathise with us and so on.

"What initially impressed me about the soothsayer in Gbahama was his knowledge about my life," Giita said. "He told me with precision, my background, how many siblings I have, how many children and so many other personal things. How did he know? My uncle and brother were equally impressed with him. At one point when he was talking, I just left my mouth wide open. I was so amazed."

"Oh, yes, I did not mention this before, "Hindowaa said. "On my first visit to Rogbohun with my sister, I had the same experience with the *Moimui*. He told me very personal things, including the fact that I am the only son of my mother with lots of sisters. He told me about you and the fact that you do not come from Talia. I too was very impressed and after that encounter, my sister said that she would believe anything the *Moimui* said would happen. You said earlier that hospitality was fine in Gbahama, especially with the soothsayer's wife?"

"Yes, those people in Gbahama make you feel as if you are at home. My uncle said that he had never had problems visiting or even just passing through Gbahama. He said that once, he was going to Yoni and arrived there at midday. They kept him with them for several hours. They entertained him, and shared the midday palm wine. In the end he arrived at Yoni late at night." Giita paused for a moment, then changed the subject. 'The only thing the soothsayer said that distressed me, was that you would marry again."

Hindowaa changed his position on the bed; his face was now turned toward the wall.

"You know that almost all of my friends have more than one wife," he grumbled. "You know that. I do not see why my marrying another wife should be such a problem for you. You are not young anymore. You should be glad to have someone young to assist you in your chores".

"But does she have to be a child of Kunaafoh's age?" Giita sounded distressed and Hindowaa did not attempt to answer that question.

"Do you remember when we got married?" Giita continued. "Do you remember how of your own will you told me that I would be your only wife? You have forgotten the details, not so? You see, you are good at forgetting details. I never asked you about your future plans regarding wives. *You* were the one who decided to tell me that. I wonder what you were trying to prove then. I know, I know. It is your mother who is now in control of our household, so now you want another woman, and another child."

Ignoring his wife's complaint, Hindowaa said, "Ah, yes, you told me about the sacrifice. At least, most of the items are affordable. It is only the question of the placenta and the deadline - nine days before the new moon. How do we deal with that? I really don't know. It is like my own case. Will the hen ever come back to town, I wonder."

Hindowaa's position remained the same. The Aladdin lamp had finally gone out and the room was in total darkness as husband and wife continued their conversation.

"Throughout our marriage, you never told me you would get another wife," Giita persisted. The threat of Hindowaa taking another wife, especially at his advanced age caused her great distress. She had had conversations with friends in Talia whose husbands had more than one wife. For almost all of them, it was not a very happy experience. Now that it was her turn, she was deeply apprehensive about it.

"You know, of all that the soothsayer told you to sacrifice, the most difficult will the placenta and the timing - nine days after the new moon," Hindowaa remarked as if she had not spoken. "How many women do you know that are pregnant now and besides, when do we know that they will be giving birth.? You and I know that mothers are reluctant to part with their placentas. They might need it themselves, or want it buried at a family shrine. How do you convince them that you need it more than they do? It is a sacred matter that needs to be dealt with carefully. As for my own trip to Rogbohun, my only worry is whether the chicken will have returned. My next trip is crucial and I have been praying for the return of the hen to Rogbohun."

"Ah, Giita," he went on, "what I have learned from all that has happened to us is that most people will not assist us. Look at the amount of debt we have had to take. Each time I explain my problems to friends and relatives, I get very little assistance. I mean money. Look at Nyake, he could not even volunteer to come along with me to Rogbohun. Is that what you call friendship? But of all our misfortunes so far, I think that the most devastating has been the death of my brother, Kortu, especially since we were unable to attend the funeral. What would the people of Ginger Hall think of us? Kortu died and neither his elder brother nor any other member of the Kortu-Tallia family attended the funeral. I think that this is a shame, a big family shame. We need to atone for this. It has been giving me sleepless nights. Kortu has appeared to me several times in dreams, though he did not appear bitter. My reading of the dreams is that he was happy the family was exonerated over what happened at his house."

"One of the ways we could handle this matter, is to attend the forty day ceremony or commemoration of Kortu's death in grand style," Giita replied. "We have to let Fanday know that we were out of town when all this happened. The occasion will also provide a good opportunity for Fanday and I to reconcile, and let bygones be bygones. If we don't do that, Hindowaa, there will be a feud in the family that will take a long time to heal."

Though it was late, neither Hindowaa nor Giita felt like sleeping. It was long time since they had had time to lie in bed and discuss domestic matters of mutual concern. Hindowaa continued to reflect on his brother's death.

"It has had a profound effect on me, Giita," he said.

Giita herself was distressed that they were unable to attend Kortu's funeral. She was grateful that the Kortus had taken care of Hinga and Kafo until they attained adulthood and became independent. She was equally happy about the outcome of the investigations concerning the money that went missing at the Kortus' house. However, she kept asking herself long after Kortu's death whether he had died naturally. The money involved was too much. Had there been any foul play on Fanday's part? she wondered. She, like many people in Talia and Ginger Hall were asking similar questions about Kortu's sudden death. Would the mystery surrounding it be investigated? she continued to wonder. It was alleged that he had died of a heart attack, because, without waiting for the evidence to be substantiated, he had convinced himself, thanks to his wife, that his brother's sons had stolen the money.

Some people blamed Fanday for the Kortu's death and were convinced that she had killed him, through the work of the *koko* bird and their boa constrictor.

By the time Hindowaa and Giita dozed off, it was almost morning. Like most of the women, Giita always woke up early to go and prepare warm water for her husband's bath before he woke up. She would then prepare breakfast for the household before the main activities of the day began. That day was no different. After she had done her domestic chores, she decided to go and visit Nyake, her husband's friend and confidant. Unlike Hindowaa who always took the main road in the town which lead to Nyake's house, Giita used the back road - the road behind the houses and arrived at Nyake's house from the back. She found his wives preparing breakfast after they had prepared water for Nyake's bath.

"*Mba* (a title used for peers initiated at the same time into the Sande Society), *biwah, biseh*" Giita greeted Nyake's first wife.

"*Mba, biwah, biseh ah ngendeh ngii?*" Nyake's first wife returned the greeting. The other women also greeted Giita even as they continued to do their morning work before departing for the farm or going to the Sande grove, depending on the domestic arrangements.

"*Ah mu hinie?*" Giita asked, saying, "Where is our man (husband), Nyake. She was teasing the wives.

"*Taa fakembu,*" the first wife replied. "He is on the veranda."

Nyake's first wife then led Giita through the house to the veranda where her husband was lying comfortably in his hammock, smoking his pipe.

"*Nya hinnie, biwah, biseh,*" Giita greeted Nyake, saying, "My husband, how are you?"

"*Nya gahun Gbuango,* I am well," Nyake replied with vigour, as if he wanted to prove a point. He had great respect for Giita. She was a woman who could hold her head above water. She had never been associated with any scandal. She had remained faithful to Hindowaa and thus made Hindowaa proud and respected in the community of elders. Other women had confessed to various forms of infidelity. Other women had simply divorced their husbands, but Giita had weathered the storms of marital tribulation for over thirty years.

"Sit down, my wife," Nyake teased her.

"Thank you, my man. Thank you. How have you been?" Giita replied.

"I am fine. I don't have much to complain about, only my usual pain around my waist and neck. You know what old age does to all of us. We should be ready at any time after we have attained such an age. We should also be grateful to God for allowing us to reach this age. He has taken good care of us. Look at me. I have so many children and grandchildren. I am not complaining, my dear."

Giita smiled.

"What is funny?" Nyake asked.

"It is about the pain around the waist that you mentioned."

"Yes, it is a constant pain. It comes, as you get older and you can do nothing about it. You just have to be careful about the things you do."

Giita began to chuckle as he spoke.

"Ah, and despite this, you people still get married to young girls," she remarked. "Don't you think that it makes matters worse?"

There was a short silence before Nyake asked mischievously,

"Is Hindowaa having the same problem?"

"I suggest you ask him. He is your friend," Giita replied.

Nyake simply smiled.

"I am sure that my husband told you the outcome of our trips," Giita went on.

"Yes, he has informed me and I am happy to hear that things are going to work out. I am only worried about the sacrifice concerning the placenta, nine days after the new moon. That is not an easy sacrifice, but the ancestors will take care of it. You see, we should be grateful. These people, our medicine men and women, whenever they tell you that you should offer a particular sacrifice, it is done because of the gravity of the particular situation. My wife, let me tell you this, I know lots of cases where the type of sacrifice prescribed was almost impossible to obtain. You know why they prescribe such prohibitive sacrifices, it is to send a message to you that the task at hand is impossible to accomplish. But people never get the message and as they proceed to carry out the sacrifice, they run into serious problems that may cost them everything they own. Do not worry. In your own case, the item prescribed is in my view, affordable."

"My husband, that is why I always come to you, especially when I feel low. You give me confidence and make me feel alive again. I wish we had more people like you here in Talia."

Nyake enjoyed the flattery and boost to his ego as he lay in his hammock, smoking.

Giita was delighted about what Nyake had said. She walked away feeling confident and buoyant with the potent energy of early morning circulating throughout in her body. She was well preserved for her age and she continued to look dignified. She was still on her way to her house when one of the most astonishing things happened in Talia. Giita, like most of her contemporaries, said afterwards that she had never witnessed such an incident in her lifetime or heard about it anywhere else in the region. People said that it was also the most entertaining incident Talia had ever witnessed. The elders said the same. The young and not so young also said the same thing about it. The children said the same thing. Thus, it was universally agreed, that the incident was the most unforgettable thing to have happened in the history of the town.

From a distance, Giita saw that a small crowd had gathered around the famous mad man in Talia and the not so famous mad man. Becoming curious, she quickened her footsteps. She knew from experience that in Talia, any minor incident would generate attention. The crowd was increasing by the minute and all age groups were present. People were laughing very loudly. The not too famous mad man was in tattered clothes, but the famous mad man was not badly dressed. They had walked from opposite directions and without any notice confronted each other.

"You looked at me with crossed eyes (meaning, evil eyes) every time we crossed each other," the not so famous mad man told the famous mad man. There was a moment's silence.

"My father is stronger than your father," the famous mad man told the not so famous mad man to the greater amusement of the crowd.

"What did you say?" asked the not so famous mad man with indignation. "People did you hear him? Did you hear what he said about my father?"

People laughed louder.

"Yes, your father is a woman," the famous mad man told the not so famous mad man.

This made the not so famous mad man furious and he retorted,

"Your mother is a man,"

Both men were calm, showing no intention of physical confrontation. The not so famous mad man smiled and turned around. There was another moment of silence as people speculated on what he would say next.

"My mother is more beautiful than your mother. Your mother is ugly."

The not so famous man thought for a moment, then smiled. His teeth were perfect.

"Yes, you are right, your mother is pretty. My father knows it too, and as you know, my father is a womaniser in this town. That is why people say that you and I look alike," answered the not so famous man, chuckling.

People in the crowd were still laughing heartily as they dispersed, but though she had followed the comments and retorts between the two mad men, Giita was not amused. She never laughed once. Rather, the antics of the two mad men saddened her.

She walked home in a state of melancholy, asking herself why people would derive pleasure from watching two mad men. As parents we should empathise because we too have sons, she said to herself. These are sick people who should be treated. They are healthy, young and good-looking. Today, we are laughing at their madness, but who knows about tomorrow, about the future?

Giita continued to reflect on the matter. The day had started well with her visit to Nyake, but the clowning between the two mad men and the reaction of the crowd, spoiled the rest of it. However, the rhythm of life in Talia continued even as she continued reflecting on the incident she had witnessed that morning.

CHAPTER TWELVE

Hindowaa had gone to bed early in the evening, when the night was said to be in its infancy and nature itself had not quite fallen asleep. He was to travel to Rogbohun the following morning to find out if the hen had returned to the town. That evening, it rained heavily to the surprise of many people in Talia, because the season for the rains was months away. Some people said that it was a good omen. Hindowaa could not sleep immediately, even though raindrops pounded with rhythmic resonance on the zinc roof of his house, whereas even those who normally suffered from lack of sleep slept blissfully in response to the music of the rain on the roof.

Whenever Hindowaa travelled from Talia, Laundeh, the driver, accorded him the front seat. That morning, his wife went to see him off and they walked together towards the lorry. Hindowaa's mother also went along to see off her son while the driver solicited for passengers and waited for others who had to come from the surrounding towns. A polite and plain-looking young woman with a boyish face was one of the passengers in the front seat, sandwiched between Hindowaa and Laundeh. She was about five or six months pregnant and called Teneh.

The atmosphere was damp and cold following the heavy rain the night before. People walked around the town with warm clothes on. The animals stayed indoors and the chicken coops remained closed. People continued to talk about the unusually heavy rain, but life in Talia was not at a standstill, though its rhythm was slower that morning. The air was fresh and pleasant.

"You have my blessings as always, everything you and I wish for shall be accomplished," Hindowaa's mother told him as they stood by the lorry waiting for more passengers to arrive.

Giita listened attentively but decided not to join in the conversation.

People stood in little groups. Some had come to the lorry just to see who was travelling, and where they were travelling to. It was routine. People who were not going anywhere would come and stand by the lorry every morning.

"We have done everything possible," Hindowaa replied. "Now we leave the rest to God and the ancestors. Look at the amount of debt

Giita and myself have taken! None of my relatives has come to assist me. I shall wait until everything is over, then I shall give them a piece of my mind."

"Relatives are supposed to help each other. Assist each other at all times. Look how our house is always full of people coming to eat. They eat breakfast, and they eat lunch and dinner. Yes, we run an open house, but when we are in dire need they turn their backs on us," Hindowaa's mother agreed. "Even your friend and confidant, Nyake, could not volunteer to go with you. All he does is preach to you people. I am disgusted with him."

Yeea Kigba sounded bitter, frustrated and angry at the way some people treated them when they needed assistance. Gitta only listened. She was irritated by the presence of Hindowaa's mother.

The sun was rising, injecting energy into the people, and the pace of activity began to assume its usual momentum.

When the passengers had assembled and the driver felt he had waited long enough, Hindowaa boarded the lorry. As he was doing so, his mother went up to him and said.

"May God go with you and guide you until you come back. I shall communicate with your father during your absence. I shall visit his grave and inform him fully about developments in the family. So, may God go with you."

Giita also said good-bye to her husband. She and her mother- in-law walked away, going in different directions as the lorry started moving. The crowd that had assembled around the vehicle also started dispersing to different parts of the town.

"Today, we have a soldier in the vehicle. But his uniform does not look tidy," Laundeh told Hindowaa and Teneh as the vehicle moved off slowly,, warming the engine, as they used to say.

"Ndake, let us go," Hindowaa replied crossly. "Don't you know that since we became a free people, things changed in this country? When I was a child, soldiers were soldiers. It was the same for the police. They were neat. But now look at what is happening. Let us go and don't spoil my trip for me."

"So you want to tell me that the soldiers and police men used to have nicer uniforms than these?" Teneh enquired. She had not even been born when the nation attained independence.

"No, the uniforms were the same," the driver told her. "What we are saying is simply that nowadays they don't have to be neat. Nobody cares. People are too busy eking out a living to be bothered about clean or neat uniforms. Things have gone down, down, down the drain in this country."

"Why are you people wasting your breath? Why?" Hindowaa asked, still sounding annoyed. "We just passed the only bridge near our town. It was the white men who built it, strong and safe. Don't you see what we have done to it? We have rid it of its railings. Now it is bare and unsafe for both motorists and pedestrians. People have damaged the bridge in order to use the metal to make pickaxes, hoes, machetes and other local utensils. All these are done in efforts to make a living and people do not care what happens to those who use the bridge. This is how bad things have become. Have there been any arrests or efforts to catch the culprits?"

The lorry was going at a slow speed because the rains had made the road dangerous. Hindowaa was angry because it meant that he would be arriving at Rogbohun later than he had hoped. He had wanted to see the soothsayer early and return to Talia.

"Do you know how long it has been since the government promised to build this road?" Hindowaa remarked. "My child, you were not yet born. You were not yet born. It has never been done and when the rains come, the road is a nightmare for motorists and a misery for pedestrians."

"Where are you travelling to?" Teneh asked him, as if she had now gained enough confidence to introduce the subject.
"I am going to Rogbohun in the north. This is my second trip, my child, and the driver knows it."

"Ah, my father, that place, if I had money I would love to go there," The young woman exclaimed. "I understand that there is a famous medicine man from Guinea who performs miracles. I understand people from the entire region go there to have their problems solved. Now that I am pregnant, I want to have a son. I am so desperate that I would do anything to secure a son and more sons for my husband."

"So I am not alone," Hindowaa said. "I am going there precisely for the reasons you have stated. My wife and I have only two sons and a daughter. We have been married for a long time and we have only two

127

sons and a daughter. My mother is worried about this situation and so are many of my relatives. I have spent lots of money trying to remedy the situation. That is why I am going to Rogbohun."

"You know, *Kinie*," Teneh remarked, "I never imagined I would be travelling with someone with a problem like mine. Both of us are looking for sons."

"Tell me, in your own case, what have you or your husband done to look for sons? But you are still young. Youth is on your side, whereas I am now an old man and my wife is not a young woman like you. This is a serious problem for us."

"*Kinie*, my husband is not doing anything," the young woman answered. "I consulted a soothsayer and I am praying to God and my ancestors. My husband has threatened to marry another woman. What is even more difficult is that his mother is encouraging him. My mother-in-law is encouraging her son to take another wife. She is desperate, more desperate than the son. She says that she wants grandsons. What surprises me about her is that she looked like an angel before I married her son. She was very sweet and my parents, especially my mother, liked her very much. Now, after my marriage to her son and the arrival of the two daughters, she has changed from angel to demon."

Much to Teneh's disappointment, there was no immediate response from Hindowaa who was thinking about his own situation. In the silence Laundeh said, "People think that being a driver is not a good job, but I love it. I enjoy being a driver. Let me tell you one good thing about this job. I learn a lot. Listening to what both of you have said this morning has educated me I experience the same thing every time I travel. People in the front seat always have interesting stories to tell. I hear all sorts of stories from people every day. I shall never get this type of education in school. Thank God I am a driver."

"Are you married?" Teneh asked him.

"Oh, yes. I am married and I have two sons, *Kinie* Hindowaa knows my wife and children," he replied.

"Are you going to have more children?" she asked.

"Yes, as many as God gives me since I am young. But I am not going to ask Him to give me only sons. I want many children like my father, but I am not going to ask God and my ancestors to give me five sons and five daughters. I will accept as many as God decides. He will also decide how many boys and girls I shall have. I leave all that to Him and my ancestors."

"*Kinie*, I think I agree with what the driver has just said, don't you? It makes lots of sense," the young woman remarked. Hindowaa kept quiet.

"Do you people believe in God and our ancestors?" Laundeh asked.

The front seat passengers were taken by surprise by the question and there was silence for a while as he slowed down to accommodate an oncoming vehicle. Both vehicles were moving very slowly from opposite directions, each trying to provide enough space for the other so that they would not collide on the muddy and slippery road.

"I visit our shrine frequently and I am also a Muslim. I pray every Friday," Teneh replied.

Hindowaa was not comfortable with Laundeh's question and said, "I know your wife and your two sons. You are a happy man. I also know your father. He has lots of sons. So you cannot understand my predicament. You children of today are insensitive to situations. I know if you were in my position, like my daughter here, you would not have asked such question."

Teneh added, "As I said before, I have two girls but my husband has been uncomfortable about it and has told me he will marry another wife if my next child is not a boy. I have visited a soothsayer and she has told me that I shall have another girl with this pregnancy. She is a very good soothsayer and I believe her. Ever since she told me this, I have not been sleeping well. Sometimes I stay awake, wondering why this should happen to me. My mother had six of us, three boys, and three girls. All my sisters have sons. I am the odd one out. I don't know what I have done to deserve this. Besides, I never wanted to get married. I finished Standard Five and passed the Common Entrance Examinations to go to secondary school, then my father married me off and I lost my education. My sisters suffered the same fate. Now I am married to somebody who is not educated and prefers sons to daughters."

"My child, fathers know best," Hindowaa remarked with emphasis on the word 'fathers'.

The road they were now travelling on was much better than the previous distance they had covered and the lorry was speeding normally. Laundeh wondered whether to comment further on what Hindowaa and

Teneh had said. He thought he had hurt Hindowaa enough by asking the question about their faith though he had done so innocently. However, in the end he said, "If God and the ancestors want to give you children, it is they who decide whether the child will be a son or daughter. If you believe in God and the ancestors, then you should accept it and be grateful. There are people who do not have even one single child. *They* are not concerned about having sons or daughters; they simply want children. What makes God great and infinite is that it is He alone that makes such decisions."

"When I return from my trip, I shall talk to your father," Hindowaa said coldly. "I have known him very well since before you were born. I also know all his children. He had more problems with you when you were growing up than with any of your siblings, and you have not changed. You were always disobedient, rude and cocky. Here you are talking to me as if I am your equal. This woman is my witness. You children of today, you are not afraid of your elders. You talk to them without respect."

Laundeh kept quiet after that, but was inwardly unrelenting. He felt he had said nothing that warranted Hindowaa's hostile reaction.

Teneh, agreed with the driver's observations and said, "When I graduated from the Sande Society it never dawned on me that my husband would threaten to marry another woman if I did not give him sons. I was innocent and never thought it was a crime for a woman not to have a child of the desired sex for the husband. I never thought my husband would marry more women just to have sons. Am I responsible for determining whether I will have sons or daughters? Now, I am going to be faced with the prospect of a mate, a co-wife. My mother always told us girls that having a mate was not a pleasant thing, however nice she might be."

At the back of the lorry the passengers were talking a lot, and those in the front heard noise and laughter from time to time. They had been travelling for over two hours when they came to the main junction. One road led to the north and the other east. Other vehicles that had stopped there, either for refuelling or so passengers could buy food at the junction, which had some restaurants. The passengers disembarked as some had to change vehicles and directions.

There was a crowd at one end of the junction and people were heading in that direction. The driver, Hindowaa and Teneh were among

130

those heading towards the crowd. When they arrived, they found that it was the soldier who had come along with Hindowaa and others that was engaging the attention of the crowd. He was telling them about his war experiences in Burma – how he had fought alongside the white man against the Japanese, and how he had won a medal for his bravery. He showed the medal to the crowd and they clapped for him. He told them lots of stories, especially about his invincibility due to the amulets on his body, which his grandfather gave him when he was going to Burma. He said that in spite of his exciting exploits in Burma, he had missed his native land. When he was abroad with the army, he had studied and excelled in music. He had even won a coveted prize which was a guitar. He loved his guitar with a passion, he told his audience, and took it with him wherever he went to sing songs and entertain people. He and his friends from Sierra Leone used to sing songs that filled them with infinite longing for home. As the crowd listened, he started to sing:

Home again, home again, when shall I see my home?
When shall I see my native land?
I shall never forget my home.
Home again, home again.
When shall I see my home?
When shall I see my native land
I shall never forget my home.

The crowd joined in the singing and as it changed to:

"Na go mi dae go so,
Dain kalma dain.
Na go mi dae go so,
Dain kalma dain."

They went wild and followed the soldier, singing along with him as he started to walk away. The old soldier's trip ended at the junction because he had to cover the distance from there to his town on foot. After that incident, people were feeling very happy as they rejoined their different vehicles to continue their journeys.

Hindowaa arrived safely in Rogbohun and, he was glad to note, not too late in the evening. People were busy having their evening meals and night was just falling. He was well received like many others who had arrived before him and were waiting in turn to see the venerable soothsayer.

His mission was not like those of the rest of the people who had travelled long distances to see the medicine man. He had come to enquire about the hen; whether it had returned to town. He did not expect the ritual involved in this exercise to be long, but he was mistaken.

"For as long as I have been away, I have not been sleeping very well. The thought of the hen not returning and the consequences of that has kept me awake. People even tell me I am looking thin. Yes, if you don't sleep well, you will be thin," he told the soothsayer's elder wife, hoping to find out from her whether the hen had returned from the riverbank.

"How is your family, your wife in Talia and children in Freetown?" she said. "And please accept our sympathy for the death of your brother? We heard about it and we were saddened by it. But it is still better to die in your sleep than go through prolonged illness, like my father did before he died".

Her expression of sympathy pleased Hindowaa, but he wondered how they had heard about his brother's death in Freetown *"Nyahawa,"* he said, (meaning, 'big woman'), "there is a mystery surrounding my brother's death. We may never know what really happened. The wife, that wife of his, my sister-in-law is a complicated woman. She is well known and feared in Ginger Hall in Freetown. Sometimes, I agree with my wife who believes that Fanday is a witch. But to defend the family honour, I have always intervened and reproached my wife for accusing my sister-in-law of being a witch. Fanday's belly is dry and she has a hard heart and no children. How do you explain that?"

"Hmm, it is not easy to understand. And they say she has a *koko* bird. Why? Why? If you are a mother, how do you engage in *koko*. Mothers would not want their babies to be eaten by anything, let alone a *koko*. But people's hearts are hard. That is why we see all these things happening these days. I know what I am talking about because when I was growing up, one of my sister's children was killed by a *koko*. I don't want to talk about it at all."

Having listened with appreciation, Hindowaa said, "I understand all that you have said and I thank you for the sympathy. But tell me, you

132

were with me when I first came to see your husband and when he told me about the hen. What happened to the hen?"

"Ah, my dear, the only person who can pronounce on the return or non-return of the hen is my husband himself, not even his twin sister will tell you anything."

"When do I see him?"

Hindowaa asked. He was restless.

"I cannot promise, but I shall tell him you are here. There are many people ahead of you but because of the nature of your own situation he may see you sooner."

From that time on, during the night and the day, for as long as he was waiting to know when the medicine man would see him, Hidowaa's mind was in turmoil. He could neither sleep well, nor eat well nor do anything well. He felt disturbed day and night. The thought that the hen might not have returned was too much of a nightmare to contemplate. The days and nights of waiting passed painfully slowly in his troubled imagination, and to kill time, he called on some of the friends he had made in Rogbohun during his first visit.

When he met *Kinie* Fatoma he was convinced the old man would at least give him a hint about the return or non-return of the hen. After all, Rogbohun was not that big and news circulated like harmattan wind.

"Ndiamo (meaning, friend), (How are you this morning?)," he greeted his friend in Mende. Since Rogbohun was a border town, inhabited by people from both the major ethnic groups in the country, both Mende and Temne languages were spoken fluently.

"My friend, I am not feeling very well. I think that it is just old age that is making my life miserable," Fatoma told Hindowaa. "My bones are aching. Even to get out of this hammock, I have to negotiate my movements very carefully. It has not been easy for me since you left here."

"I am really sorry to hear this, my friend, but what makes it worse is that you just married a beautiful girl from the Sande Society. It is a pity," Hindowaa replied.

"Ndakei, Hindowaa, I am talking about my health and you are telling about a young girl that I have married."

Fatoma sounded distressed so Hindowaa tried to make a joke out of his friend's situation.

"Well, they say these young girls are factors in our health as we get old. Despite that, I am also in the process of marrying one soon. The next time you come to Talia, I may be in the same situation as you with painful bones and backache. Should we stop marrying because of that?"

Hindowaa did not spend much time with Fatoma because he wanted to visit a couple of other friends by midday. His last place of visit was where he thought he would get some information about the hen. When he went to see *Kinie* Pujeh, (meaning, 'pepper') he was praying his trip there would not be in vain, and that he would at least get some information about the hen. *Kinie* Pujeh was known all over Rogbohun as a busybody. People were afraid of him and used to say that if he found you squatting, the town would be informed accordingly. That was how notorious he was.

Pujeh had just finished eating when Hindowaa arrived. He knew that Hindowaa would be in town and looked forward to his arrival. When he spotted Hindowaa from a distance he got up from his hammock and went to meet him. They met and embraced warmly, for they were good friends.

"How have you been?" Pujeh asked Hindowaa as they walked towards his house, adding, "I have just finished eating, but I will tell my wives to cook for you while you wait. Or maybe there is some leftover food. We always keep food for the unexpected strangers."

Hindowaa was not interested in food. His interest was focused on the hen and nothing but the hen.

"Ndake, Pujeh I am here to find out about the hen," he said. "You know about it. I am now waiting to see the soothsayer so that he can tell me about the hen. But maybe you already have some information about it. That is why I have come to see you."

"My friend Hindowaa, if you want me to be honest with you I will do so. I know about the hen," said Pujeh.

Hindowaa almost jumped from his seat. His jaw dropped and his heartbeat doubled and redoubled. He felt beads of sweat around his neck.

"Yes Pujeh, I was right in guessing that apart from the soothsayer, only you and nobody else in this town would know about the hen. I knew that not even the soothsayer's wife would know anything."

"I forgot to offer you a cup of palm wine," Pujeh answered. "I was in the process of bringing the mid-afternoon palm wine brew when I saw you coming."

"I stopped drinking some time ago," Hindowaa said nervously. "I have some stomach problems." He was now sweating profusely and becoming impatient with Pujeh. "My main interest now is about the hen. Pujeh, you know how long a distance I have travelled for this matter. My mother is waiting. My wife is waiting. My relatives are waiting."

"Hindowaa my friend, you see, according to the ritual surrounding such things, only the soothsayer can make a pronouncement on it. If another person told you about it before him, it would destroy the efficacy of the process. So you have to wait and hear it from him first-hand. That is how the process works. You will see him soon. So do not worry, my friend."

Hindowaa sank in a sea of despondency. When he left Pujeh's house, his feet were heavy, his mood sour, and he felt as if fate was conspiring against him.

The morning he was to see the soothsayer was memorable. He had not slept very well the night before as he had kept tossing in bed, his thoughts roaming from one subject to another. During breakfast that morning, he looked at the food but could not eat for his usually generous appetite had left him. The soothsayer's wife understood Hindowaa's situation and did not force him to eat, much to the delight of the children in the house who looked forward to feasting to their hearts' satisfaction.

"It seems like a long time since you left Rogbohun."
Hindowaa was now sitting in a familiar room and the soothsayer was making unwanted conversation. Feeling as if he was sinking in a sea of uncertainty and despair, Hindowaa kept thinking, what if? What if? What if? The period of divination was over. The period of sacrifice was over, and the moment of truth had come. Naked reality would soon be revealed to him. The ancestors had made their decision and rendered their verdict. It was the soothsayer's obligation to pronounce on their verdict. The hen was the messenger of God and the ancestors in that order.

Hindowaa sat as rigidly as a granite rock by the riverside. He was watching the soothsayer's mouth and every movement of his body.

"*Ndakei* Hindowaa, welcome again to Rogbohun," the soothsayer said. "I feel as if I was born here, just as I used to feel when I was in Kono."

Hindowaa was not interested in what the old man was saying. His heart felt as if it might jump out of his chest.

"I know you are anxious about the hen. The sacrifice of the hen is not very common. I can only remember a few as a practitioner in my profession. When it works, it is one hundred percent certain that all the problems addressed will be resolved. I know this from experience."

This time it's only Hindowaa and the medicine man were present in the room. The soothsayer's wife was not there; nor were any of Hindowaa's relatives. And there was no interpreter, only the concerned parties. The soothsayer had acquired a working knowledge of Mende and could therefore communicate reasonably well with Hindowa.

"The first time ever I asked a client to perform this type of sacrifice was in Kankan in Guinea," he went on. "I was a novice practitioner under the guidance of my Master, the grand Quaranic teacher, of all time in Guinea."

Hindowaa was already drenched in sweat and his stomach had started aching. The saliva in his mouth had increased and tasted unpleasant. Finally, the soothsayer told him,

"In your case, the hen came back. It came back indeed, but it was found at the periphery of the town. The previous hens came straight into town. Yours was spotted pecking with other chickens, but at the periphery of the town. What this means is that we should expect most of your dreams to come true, but a few will be unfulfilled. That is why the hen did not come straight to town. This is the good news I have for you."

Hindowaa had to excuse himself to go outside and spit out the saliva which filled his mouth.

"How do we know which of our desires will not be fulfilled even if they are only a few?" Hindowaa asked the medicine man on his return. It was the first time he actually said anything since the medicine man started talking.

"Hindowaa, if God and the ancestors wanted to reveal that to us, they would have done so. I ask you to wait. This is not the first time I have done this. So give the whole process time. Things will manifest themselves in good time."

As he left Rogbohun that day, Hindowaa thought about the soothsayer, and how fearsome he always looked. He thought about the wishes, which might not be fulfilled. Would Kunaafoh come back so that she could be married off to the Chief? Would Giita have more sons? Would his sons in Freetown be safe with Fanday now that Kortu had died? Would his next wife give him sons? These concerns weighed heavily on his mind as he returned to Talia that day. He went feeling uncertain about everything. Only time would tell.

CHAPTER THIRTEEN

Giita had lived long enough to appreciate that some divine law ruled her world. It was a law, which dictated that some people had to go though a painful process of survival. Since her husband said he would marry another wife, she had been paralysed with the fear of living with a co-wife, some very young girl. She had thought about her daughter, Kunaafoh, who had once said that if her father married another wife, Giita should abandon the relationship and go and live with her parents. Giita knew that Kunaafoh was too young to comprehend how society had held her hostage. She knew her parents would never support such a move. However, she appreciated her daughter's concern and innocent advice. How could she possibly dare to defy the small town mentality and rigid social norms that were so overwhelming in the community? She asked herself.

She was on her way to a small town north of Talia to see whether there were pregnant women there who were about to have babies so that she could secure the placenta for the sacrifice which she was to offer in fulfilment of the soothsayer's prescription. This item was the most difficult to find. She had already contacted all the pregnant women in Talia and there was not a single woman who would be having a baby soon enough to meet the terms of the sacrifice, nine days before the new moon.

When she was crossing a small river that morning, Giita saw her reflection in the water. She felt sorry for herself as she pulled her wrapper above her knees so that it would not get wet. Yes, everybody keeps asking me what has gone wrong, she said to herself. I have lost weight. I, Giita who was once so plump and attracted men's attention whenever I passed them. Now people tell me I am thin. I am not even pregnant. I wish I were pregnant and fat or pregnant and thin.

She stood for a while in the river as she washed her face and gargled some water before proceeding. The water was cold, but refreshing and clean. If only I can meet a pregnant woman, ready to give birth, she thought, but some of the soothsayers have failed to reassure me about that. Only one has assured me that I will eventually find a pregnant woman who will give birth and be willing to give me her placenta. She continued to talk to herself as she continued her journey.

She had not come across any other early morning traveller so far, but she was not afraid because she knew the path well. The sun had risen, but as she went through the thick forest, she was not aware of the sunshine ahead of her. It felt dark as she navigated her way through the forest that morning on the meandering path.

The thick forest and bush through which Giita was going provided her with temporary mental stimulation to focus her thoughts on the placenta she needed, an essential element in the fulfilment of her cherished dream of having more sons for her husband. As she approached the end of the long meandering bit of the path through the forest, she heard voices of people coming from the opposite end. She slowed down her pace to determine whether the voices were those of women or men. She saw the men in front with machetes in their hands and women trailing from behind with loads on their heads.

"Good morning, my people," Giita greeted the men since the women were trailing from behind.

"Good morning, woman," the men greeted her almost in a chorus and paused.

"You are undertaking an early journey, is there anything wrong or urgent?" one of them asked Giita.

"I am just going to Gondama to attend to an urgent matter," Giita responded in a subdued voice. "I shall be back before the end of the day".

"And where are you coming from, if I may ask?" another man enquired.

"I am from Talia," she replied.

"Oh, you people in that town, you have suffered a lot this season," another man sympathised. "The child that went missing and the death of Hindowaa's brother in Freetown are too many losses for one family."

The man who asked Giita where she was from, had heard the pain in her voice when she said that she was from Talia. He thought for a moment, then cleared his throat and spat by the roadside before taking out a piece of kola which he broke in his mouth.

"Who are you going to see?" he enquired. "We are just coming from Gondama this morning. We know everybody there."

"Do you know *Kinie* Hindowaa in Talia?" Giita asked. "He is my husband. We have been married for many years and have three children,

139

two boys and a girl. After that I have not had any more children. He has threatened to marry again because he wants more sons in the family. Because of this concern, I went and consulted with a soothsayer who advised me to make a sacrifice so that I would give birth to sons. I have secured all but one of the items. I need a placenta, and in Talia, the prospects are not good. All the pregnant women there are not likely to give birth between now and when the new moon comes out. This is my predicament. I am going to Gondama to see if there are pregnant women there who would be willing to help me."

The people were astonished because they had never heard of such a sacrifice. They thought it was very strange. A placenta should be buried and not sacrificed. Who would give up her placenta for such a project? they asked themselves.

"These are some of the things we do that annoy the spirits of our ancestors," one of the women remarked as she untied a knot at the end of her wrapper and took out a packet of snuff. She pinched a little and emptied it into her mouth as the others watched.

"Nine days before the new moon is not very far from now. This is my worry," Giita told them.

She got sympathy from the people, especially the women.

"Hmm. What a sorry state to be in. I understand your story my sister," another woman said. "I have personal experience. In my own case, my husband went ahead and married two women. I mean two. He did not want to take chances, so he married two. They were both younger than me. My sister, what I went through is not good to talk about. I had three girls for him; very beautiful girls who married and we received lots of bride price. Our marriage ended. However, I remarried later and had three sons for my present husband. I am happy. I now have three girls and three sons even though they are from two husbands. So I will advise you to have faith in God and the ancestors."

Giita appreciated the story and felt consoled as they went their separate ways. She was now almost half way to her destination, Gondama, and as she continued on her way, started wondering what the future had in store for her. She knew she would come across more travellers as she went. People travelling between Talia and Gondama frequently used that path. She and Hindowaa had travelled along it countless times. This time, she was alone and her mission was different. Her brother and uncle had not accompanied her because the distance was shorter compared with the one to Gbahama. Moreover, her mission to Gondama did not require the presence of her relatives.

"I wonder what I have done to our ancestors, she said to herself. Sometimes I feel strongly that I have done something clearly wrong and they are punishing me by depriving me of more sons. All my sisters have given birth to more sons. My husband keeps reminding me of this. I now believe that I have done something wrong. But what is it? I have not committed adultery and I was a virgin when Hindowaa married me. I have honoured the ancestors in appreciation of any good thing that has happened to me. Each time I gave birth safely, I poured libation and thanked all our ancestors. I respect my husband and my in-laws. I bear no malice against my neighbours and above all, I am not a witch."

The morning sun had now taken over the sky and the sunshine was brilliant. As she passed through a rice farm, she thought about the group of people she had met going to Talia. She had forgotten to ask them why they were going there. Perhaps they were going to board the only vehicle in the area and travel to some other town. They might have been going to the main junction to shop. This was a daily activity in the area.

From a distance, she saw a red dog coming towards her. The dog stopped abruptly when it saw her but she was not afraid. She knew from experience that there was someone behind the dog, even more than one person. As Giita approached, the dog moved a bit into the bush as if to give her space. After she had passed, the dog came out and continued its journey. Giita had still not seen anybody else. When she heard voices from a distance, she was relieved. This was the second group of people she was meeting that morning

"*Awuwaa bondeisaa*, (How are your relatives?)" she greeted the group. They stopped and exchanged greetings.

"*Nyahapui* (meaning, 'woman') where are you coming from so early in the morning and where are you going to?" one man asked Giita. Early travel always meant some degree of urgency or seriousness, so people were concerned whenever they met a person or persons travelling in the morning, though people also undertook early morning travel to get to their destination in good time or to avoid the heat of the sun.

"I am coming from Talia and going to Gondama," Giita replied.

Again, there was a moment of silence. Talia had come to symbolize tragedy in the area as Kunaafoh's disappearance and Kortu's death were still fresh in people's minds.

"Do you have a relative there?" One woman asked Giita.

"No," Giita answered.

"Then it must be something serious that made you to undertake such an early morning journey without an escort," another woman commented.

"Yes, you are right," said Giita. "I do not have anyone there. I am going there to find out about something, which I have to do. It is a woman's business. I want to get there early enough to transact my business and return today. That is why I am travelling so early this morning".

"Let us move away from the men and talk about it," another woman suggested. The men will wait for us. They can even go ahead. We will catch up with them. It is still early."

The other women agreed and they all came together, leaving the men to walk away. They were eager to know what had made Giita travel so early that morning.

"My sisters, my story is a long one and I do not intend to bore you with it. I need to make a sacrifice so that I can have more sons. I already have two sons out of three children, but my husband is not satisfied. He has threatened to marry another woman at the end of the current Sande session in Talia - a young girl - who will give him sons. I have consulted a soothsayer who advised me to make a sacrifice of several items. I have acquired all the items but one. I need a placenta to sacrifice and burry under a virgin kola nut tree. In Talia, I have made all the necessary enquiries among pregnant women, but there is no one about to have a child in time for the date I should make the sacrifice. That is why I am going to Gondama. If I do not find one, I shall continue to another town. This is my mission," Giita told the three women who had listened carefully.

"Ah my dear, I pity you. I know many women who have gone through this type of pain. My late mother was one of them," said one of the three women.

"My own experience was with my auntie," said another. "She was a beautiful woman in our town but only had two children, a boy and a girl, for the husband. Do you know what the husband did? He married two more women. The two women had five children between them. Only one of those children was a boy. Our ancestors knew what they were doing. People are not satisfied with what the ancestors decide. That is why sometimes we keep having problems that we don't understand. We continue to defy and even challenge our ancestors. When they get angry they sometimes punish us severely."

"My own case is different from yours," said the third woman. "Ah, me, I have four boys and no girl. You think my husband is sympathetic because I do not have a girl? I am longing for at least one. He told me not to worry. That was what he told me, but I do not feel complete as a woman without a daughter. I feel lonely. I know that when the boys marry, I will lose them. Girls are different."

Gitta was consoled by the concerns of the other women and felt that her story was universal. She asked the women whether they knew any pregnant women in Gondoma who would be having their babies soon.

"To be honest with you, my sister, your situation is not an easy one," one of the women replied. "I have never heard of such a sacrifice in my life. I had a friend who was also involved in making sacrifice to have sons. She consulted a soothsayer and was told to sacrifice forty-seven birds eggs, not hens, birds. She was not time bound. She succeeded in getting the eggs and conducted the sacrifice, but had to wait for almost two years. She was rewarded with sons, but that was a long time ago. I know of some pregnant women in Gondoma. On the other hand these days, it is not easy to determine who is pregnant. The young girls, unlike our parents and us, do not even want people to know they are pregnant. Look at the way they dress. They put on trousers and even restrain their bellies. Now, they have special dress for women who are pregnant. So these days it is not easy to be one hundred per cent certain who is pregnant or not."

The other women laughed, amused by the way the woman emphasised the restraining of bellies.

"I only know of five pregnant women so far and all of them are about six months pregnant. That means they will not be able to help. It is a pity," another of the women told Giita.

The third woman said, "I know that two of *Kinie* Dowie's wives are pregnant. The younger one must have been pregnant for over seven months, but I do not know when she is due to deliver."

143

"If I don't succeed in finding a woman who is about to have a baby, I shall go back to Talia and contemplate my next step," Giita told the three women as they said good-bye. They expressed sympathy and love for Giita as they went on their way, walking briskly to catch up with the men ahead of them.

It was about midday when Giita arrived at Gondama. The town was virtually empty when she arrived as most of the inhabitants had gone to their farms. Some of the others had simply gone to other places around Gondama or to the main junction where people went shopping.

Her hosts were waiting for her, however, because they knew she would arrive that day. She had not informed them about the motive for her mission, only sent a message that she would come to see them about a matter that was strictly confidential. They had therefore waited anxiously for her to arrive.

When they assembled in her hosts' bedroom, Giita told them about the urgency and gravity of her mission. After describing her predicament, tears flowed abundantly from her eyes. The hostess wept in sympathy with her and the host said, "I never knew Hindowaa could behave like that, my dear Giita. But you never told us. We are distant relatives and I could have taken time to try and persuade him not to take such a decision. I know that there is nothing wrong in taking a second or third wife, but not for the reason he has put forward. I have four wives, but I did not marry them because of sons."

"I had spoken to many elderly people when Hindowaa threatened to marry because he wanted more sons. Many people spoke to him in Talia, including his very good friend and confidant, Nyake, but he developed deaf ears about it," Giita told her hosts. "The marriage will take place soon and the wife-to-be is about the same age as my daughter. Imagine, a child to be my co-wife! Even if I have sons now, it will make no difference because he has made a commitment to marry her at the end of the current Sande session."

"Ada, do you know of any woman in this town who will be having a child soon?" the host asked his wife. "You are a woman. I have seen a few women whose bellies look big, but I cannot say how long they have been pregnant or how soon they will give birth."

"My dear, this is a delicate subject. You don't go about asking women how far along their pregnancies are and when they expect to have the baby. People will begin to wonder what type of person you are.

You can only do such a thing if you and the person are very close friends or you are relatives. You know our people consider pregnancy a fragile and sacred condition. They are concerned that if you show interest, you may be up to no good. Witchcraft is a menace in our town."

The husband concurred, and even Giita agreed with the hostess's observations. She came to the conclusion that her mission had failed, though she was grateful to her hosts.

It was just a little past midday when she decided to go back to Talia and continue the search for a placenta. The host accompanied her far beyond the outskirts of the town before letting her go. He knew then that Giita would be safe, and calculated that if she walked fast, she should be in Talia about the time people were having their evening meal.

Giita remained optimistic that she would get a placenta. Having acquired an inner strength, she was able to remind herself that she had never undertaken any enterprise and failed. This particular enterprise was too important for her to contemplate failure. She believed that the ancestors would come to her rescue no matter what the odds were. With that rock-like conviction, she arrived in Talia just about the time Hindowaa and the rest of the household were having their evening meal.

As she was undressing to go and take her bath, she heard an exchange of greetings on the veranda where Hindowaa and others were eating. The greetings went on for a while, so Giita went to find out what was happening.

The visitors were a man and two women who were travelling to Gondama but could not proceed because it was now dark. Under normal circumstances, the travellers would have continued their journey to Gondama since it was not a long distance away, and the man had a walking stick and a machete. They also had an Aladdin lamp, but decided to seek shelter for the night because one of the women was expecting a baby at any moment. The reason the travellers could not proceed beyond Talia was for fear that she would give birth that very night. They sought shelter from the Hindowaa family even though they did not know them. They could easily have stopped by any other house in Talia and asked the same favour. Sleeping arrangements were made for the family. The man joined Hindowaa and the men eating on the veranda and the women later ate with Giita and others.

When the travellers appeared that night, it was dark, so dark that no one had noticed the physical condition of the pregnant woman.

145

Fortunately, she was one of those women who did not have a history of prolonged labour. By the time people woke up in the morning, they found out that she had delivered a very healthy baby boy. The baby was named Kapinde meaning, 'a son born at night'. If it had been a baby girl, she would have been named, Magbinde, meaning, 'a baby girl born at night'.

The occasion was one of the happiest in Giita's life, for as a result of the birth of Kapinde in their house, she was able to secure the much sought after placenta and meet all the requirements for the sacrifice. It was the turning point in her burning desire to have more sons for her husband. She agreed that her ancestors had favourably responded to her prayers and had signed, sealed and delivered her destiny. It was now left to time to produce the desired results. She waited anxiously for the future.

CHAPTER FOURTEEN

Hindowaa saw his father in a dream so vivid that he felt it was real. His father was saying, "Son, son, do you hear me? Why are you now so different and distant from me? I relied on you as the elder son and the only son of your mother and look at what you are doing to me. I feel betrayed. Look how much debt you have piled up and in the process you have also forced Giita to become indebted. Soon, you will mortgage the family house. What has gone wrong with you? Are you mad? Do you know what you are doing to Giita? If you continue like this I shall curse you. Yes, I shall curse you and you know what that means. You can marry if you want to marry. You can marry ten wives, if you want to, but not for the reasons you have advanced. I have discussed your current plans with your grandfather here with me and he has asked me to intervene. That is why I have decided to confront you tonight. Do you know why your brother died, your brother Kortu? It was because he did not want to bring shame to the family. He was a good son. He defended your sons and in the end, the family name was vindicated. Look at your own current behaviour, Hindowaa. I ask you to behave yourself. I shall not come back to you on this matter."

"Father, allow me to explain myself, please don't go. Please don't go away from me. I beg you, please listen to me. I am doing this in the name of the family. I want the family's name to be preserved in perpetuity. I want your name and the land to remain forever. Please understand my own point of view. Please. I beg of you, don't go away. I beg you please, don't go away, please, please."

Giita woke up when she heard her husband talking to himself that night. It was about two in the morning and she was confused. Since their marriage so many years ago, that was the first time she had heard her husband talking in his sleep. It was loud and clear.

"*Kunaafoh ngi keh* (Kunaafoh's father), what happened to you?" Giita asked her husband anxiously. "What happened? You were talking in your sleep. You called your fathers' name. It was frightening. You spoke so loudly that I woke up. This is the first time this has happened. Are you all right?"

Hindowaa was sweating so profusely that his entire body was wet. He was also trembling noticeably and looked frightened. He held his head in both hands. He looked as if a wild animal was chasing him. He was confused and in a state of panic.

"It is my father, *Kunaafoh ngi nje* (Kunaafoh's mother), it is my father. He is the one. I dreamt of him," Hindowaa answered.

"It is just a dream, my dear. But what kind of a dream was it? Look at you!. What happened in the dream? Tell me." Giita said.

"Let me talk to mother in the morning. I shall tell you later. I don't think it was a good dream. I have never dreamed like this since my father died. He abandoned me abruptly in the dream even when I was pleading with him. Father has changed. He is now a different person. He has lost patience. I shall talk to my mother about this dream."

Listening to him, Giita felt disappointed that his mother had to be informed before her, even when they were in the same room, on the same night that the dream occurred. However, this time, she kept her feelings to herself and waited for her husband to come back to her after seeing his mother.

The next day, Hindowaa's mother noticed that something was wrong with her son, her only son. Hindowaa did not know how to approach his elderly mother about his dream of his father. He knew how she reacted over such matters and did not want to upset her. He feared that his mother would not take kindly to hearing about such an encounter between father and son.

"Hindo, (his mother always called him Hindo which means, 'man') are you well?"

It was late in the afternoon. Hindowaa was sitting on a low bench and his mother was enjoying the comfort of the only hammock on the veranda. She was smoking the old clay pipe, which she had inherited from her mother many years before.

"Yes mother, I am well. You know me very well. I am all right." Hindowaa replied, but *Yeea* Kigba looked worried and concerned over her son's appearance.

"Hindo, I am your mother," she insisted, sitting up and putting her pipe aside. "I gave birth to you. I carried you in my stomach for nine months. Tell me the truth. You are not all right. You don't look all right. I know it and I can feel it. What is wrong with you, son? You don't look like the Hindowaa I carried in my stomach for nine months."

Hindowaa reflected on the series of questions his mother had asked him, one after the other, before saying, "I came to tell you what

148

happened to me last night. I waited until I summoned enough courage because I thought the sensitivity of the event it might affect you in unexpected ways. That was my main concern."

Hindowaa told his mother. *Yeea* Kigba looked at her son. For a moment, there was absolute silence.

"Mother, it is about the dream I had last night, the dream...it was...." Hindowaa hesitated as he watched his mother's reaction when he mentioned the word 'dream'.

"Yes, the dream, what about the dream, my son, what about it? Tell me," she urged him.

"Last night I dreamt of my father. Mother, it was not a nice dream. He scolded me for wanting to marry another woman to bring more sons into the family. He threatened to curse me. He said he had discussed the matter with my grandfather in the after-world where they both now reside. I was shouting in my sleep and Giita woke up and, woke me up. I was sweating. I was shaking. Mother, it was very frightening. I have never had such a dream. It was terrible. It seemed very real. Now I don't know what to do about the pending marriage."

"Did you tell Giita and discuss it with her?" *Yeea* Kigba asked her son.
"No, mother, I told her I would discuss it with you first before telling her."

"And what did she say."

"She said nothing, mother."

"Good. Don't tell her or anybody else anything. If she does not ask you, don't tell her anything. Ah, my son," she added. "It sounds like a very serious dream. Anyway, don't mind your father. I know him very well. He will not do anything. I have told you repeatedly that you have my blessing; your mother's blessing is what matters more. It was I who carried you in my stomach for nine months; I suckled you for two years and a half. I carried you on my back until you almost grew a beard. Where was he? Tell me, where was he? I know him. I say your mother's blessing is what matters. You shall marry and God and the ancestors will give us more sons. That is all I have to say to you. So you shall go ahead and marry and leave the rest of the matter to me. I shall talk again to him when next I visit his grave."

Hindowaa's mother spoke in a very frank and convincing manner. By the end of the day, Hindowaa's mood had changed for the better. He felt good and his usual generous appetite was restored, because in the evening he ate very well and felt sound in both mind and body.

Not long after the dream about his father, news started spreading about the imminent wedding of Hindowaa to Boi-Kimbo, the queen of beauty during that year's Sande Society celebration. It was the talk of the town and beyond. Hindowaa, as was customary, had officially informed the Paramount Chief in the town and the other dignitaries of his intentions, so it was no longer a rumour. The parents of the bride were also aware of the arrangements being made by Hindowaa and the entire family for the occasion. However, many in Talia were concerned that Hindowaa was about to undertake an expensive marriage. Where would he get the bride price and the money for the other expensive arrangements for the ceremony? People were curious, because Hindowaa owed money to many people in Talia. He owed even the woman who baked pancakes in Talia. Hindowaa had not taken these concerns into consideration. He felt that people would wait until after the marriage before addressing the issue of debts he owed, all in the process of trying to have more sons. However, two days before the marriage was to take place, several people from whom he had taken loans to facilitate his consultations with the soothsayer, invaded his house, vowing they would not leave until he discharged his obligations. Some genuinely felt that Hindowaa had cheated them. They reasoned that, in order to marry, one had to have money and asked themselves why Hindowaa would want to marry if he was insolvent? Some threatened to take court action to get their money from Hindowaa.

"My good friends, I welcome all of you here today," Hindowaa told his creditors. "I know why you have come, but before you start, let me offer you some kola nuts. In a moment, we shall be drinking some palm and raffia wine which I had secured."

After he had spoken, one man cleared his throat and coughed lightly. The kola nuts were passed around and a woman came from the house with two gourds of palm and raffia wine.

"Hindowaa, why the rush to marry?" one of the creditors asked, sounding angry. "The girl will not run away. Pay back the money you owe me. You gave me the impression that you were hard up and could not afford travel expenses. I loaned you my well-earned money and now you are spending so much money to marry."

He took a gulp of the raffia wine and cleared his throat again. Another man said to Hindowaa, "*Ndakei*, that is not the way a big man should behave. You should honour your name, big man."

The others laughed at the joke, but his words were painful to Hindowa who had not said anything about the debts he owed his friends in Talia. He sensed that someone had hatched a conspiracy against him, and his first suspects were Giita and her sympathisers, including, Nyake. Nyake was one of the creditors even though he had not come with the others. Hindowaa had previously vowed that if he were in need he would not approach Nyake because his friend would tell the rest of the town that he had borrowed money from him. He pleaded eloquently with his debtors, saying, "All I can do at this moment, my friends, is to appeal to you to bear with me until tomorrow. I shall do some consultations and I hope this matter will be resolved to the satisfaction of everyone. I beg you and I apologise for the inconvenience I have caused all of you. I hope this will not spoil our good relationship in this our town. We should stand by each other when we are in need. We have always done so. This is what makes Talia better than other towns. Don't allow bad people to come between us and spoil the good name of our town."

The creditors were persuaded and because they liked Hindowaa, decided to give him the extra time he had asked for.

The compound of the Paramount Chief was the biggest in Talia. It was always crowded with people who went there to visit. Some went there to gossip and tell the Chief the things they thought he wanted to hear. They told him all sorts of things about all the suitors of the girls who were graduating from the Sande Society.

Many other visitors came there to eat; they would come in the morning for breakfast, they would come for lunch and the evening meal. Some would come to discuss private matters, such as their domestic problems. The Chief's many wives were used to the perennial visitors. They spent hours in the kitchen cooking for their husband's numerous visitors and gossiping about them. They knew the visitors who would not surrender a single penny to them as an expression of gratitude. They also knew the generous ones and always looked forward to entertaining them. For a long time, the Chief's many wives liked Hindowaa, and he had enjoyed their company. However, when they got to know that Hindowaa was prepared to give his daughter, Kunaafoh to be married to the Chief, they developed a careless and sometimes even hostile attitude towards him. Hindowaa sensed their change of attitude and now felt uncomfortable and unwelcome in the Chief's compound. That was why he had gone very late in the evening to see the Chief.

By the time he got there most of the wives had gone to bed or had disappeared into their huts. Many of the regular visitors had also disappeared. He had timed his visit this way because he wanted to confer with the Chief in private. The Chief offered such private audiences to only a few citizens of his chiefdom. Hindowaa was one of them. Moreover, Hindowaa had promised the Chief his daughter, Kunaafoh, as a wife. The Chief was waiting despite the fact that Kunaafoh had disappeared because Hindowaa had told him that consultations with the soothsayer had revealed that Kunaafoh would resurface one day. The Chief was convinced that Kunaafoh would return. Such disappearances had happened a long time ago in other areas under his jurisdiction and the missing people had showed up in the end. As far as he was concerned, Kunaafoh would not be the exception.

Hindowaa was seated on a long bench on the veranda of the Chief's circular hut. There were only three more visitors remaining and he was praying that the three would soon leave. He wanted the Chief's attention. He was cursing the other visitors under his breath. The Chief looked tired but would never ask his visitors to leave.

"*Mahee, maalo sinaa,* meaning 'Chief, goodbye, we shall see tomorrow'." Two of the visitors took leave of the Chief, which pleased Hindowaa. There was a moment of silence as the two visitors walked away towards the gate of the compound.

"They are always together," the Chief remarked.

"They have been like this for a long time. Nobody knows what unites them so tightly," said Hindowaa.

"Well, they are hunters, they hunt at night. They also married into the same family; their wives are from the same family," the other visitor informed the Chief and Hindowaa. He was called Ngawojah.

"Ha ha, but tell me, have you ever seen the animals they hunt? Have they ever sent you a pound of their catch?" Hindowaa asked. "No, no, but they eat at everybody's house."

"Occasionally, they send me some meat, very small. Even my wives have realized how small a portion they send for me. Others send me big portions and some even give me the entire catch," the Chief said. The night was still young. But it was dark and humid.

"Chief, I am sure they never miss a meal in this compound," Hindowaa suggested, to which Ngawojah replied, "I have known those two since we were children. The fact is that they took this greed from their parents. In fact their fathers were also hunters. That is how they inherited the hunting profession. So, you cannot blame them, it is in the family."

The Chief smiled and coughed. He was amused. He knew that what the visitor had said was true. Hindowaa also laughed.

"Well, I can tell you something from experience. There are many people like that here in Talia. They always know when food is ready at your house and they come just in time," Ngawojah remarked, as, much to Hindowaa's delight, he too rose to take his leave. Hindowaa remained the Chief's last visitor for that evening.

When Ngawojah took leave of the Chief, Hindowaa felt that his prayers had been answered at last. He had been longing for the moment when he and the Chief would be alone.

"Chief, can you believe that *Kinie* Ngawojah is accusing someone of greed. Can you imagine?" he said. "They say he taps the best bamboo wine in this town, yet I have never tasted a drop of it free of charge. Perhaps because you are the Chief, he will give you some, but if the rest of us don't buy his wine, we don't even smell it, let alone be given a gourd."

"Talk quietly, he may not have gone too far, and the night has ears," the Chief told Hindowaa jokingly. He confirmed Hindowaa's observations, though with some qualifications.

"To be honest with you, he always gives me his wine. And let me tell you the truth, he brews the best bamboo wine in town. He has been on it for a long time. But you are right, everybody says that he is not very generous with his wine."

"So why is he talking about other people being greedy? Does he think he is generous? I buy his wine sometimes and he looks me in the eye and takes the money. He has no shame. When he sees me, he greets me properly. He has no conscience."

The Chief was amused, but not impressed. Most of his visitors came to him and told him stories about each other. His mental file was full of such stories, but as leader of his people, he continued to listen to them.

"Chief, I know that it is now time to go to bed. I am sorry that I am still here." Hindowaa apologised, to which the Chief replied, "You know that I am used to this. Sometimes I stay here with people until midnight. It is my job. I enjoy being with my people. You know that, so don't feel guilty. When you kill me then another Chief will take my place. He may or, may not be like me, willing to stay up until late at night listening to complaints from members of the community. It is my job."

"But Chief, it is a good quality which your late father passed on to you. We are happy and we shall pray to have you for a long time. As long as your father lived," Hindowaa said.

That was not the first time Hindowaa had had an audience with the Chief. The Chief had met him and the rest of his family when, Kunaafoh was a child going to school. There was something about Kunaafoh that the Chief loved even then and in her absence he remained emotionally attached to her. He was so convinced that he would one day marry Kunaafoh that he continued to be kind to his future father-in-law and his wife, Giita.

"Chief, before I go on to tell you why I am here to see you this evening, I want to confide in you as I have always done, something that happened to me recently," Hindowaa continued. "I have already discussed it with my mother. I dreamed of my father very recently. It was a terrible dream. I have never had such a dream. I talked in my sleep until my wife woke up. When I woke up, I was sweating and trembling so much that Giita was frightened. My father was angry that I want to marry another wife and, according to him, for the wrong reason. He also threatened to curse me. I brought this to the attention of my mother but she told me not to worry and I should not abandon my current plan to marry."

The Chief listened carefully as Hindowaa spoke, nodding his head as if he too supported the plan to marry another woman. Afterwards he told Hindowaa, "I knew your father so well that I can imagine his feelings regarding all these developments in your life. I wish he were alive. He would have guided you in the right direction. For now, I advise that you listen to your mother. As she said she knew your father very well. I believe she did."

"I thank you very much for your comments. I have always appreciated your advice," Hindowaa replied. "After I told my mother about the dream, she advised me not to talk it over with anyone, but I am happy I have spoken to you about it. If I had consulted Nyake, he would have spent the entire day trying to lecture me about dreams. He thinks that he is the wisest man in this town. I don't want to imagine what he would be like if he were the chief in this chiefdom. Chief, I hope you will bear with me this evening. I am here to see you on another urgent matter."

The Chief listened patiently. He was used to the Hindowaas of Talia.

"Chief, as I said, I am here to plead with you on another serious and urgent matter.. I have a problem. You know that my marriage is pending. You also know how much I have had to spend in efforts to get Giita to have more sons. I informed you of my numerous travels in connection with this matter. During all this time, I have had to take loans from friends. I never bothered you, though at one time I thought about coming to ask you for assistance. Now that I am about to marry, I got a rude shock yesterday. All my friends to whom I owe money came to my house and demanded that I pay them back. I was surprised. Why all of them at the same time? I was even surprised that it was only Nyake who did not come with the others to ask for their money."

Hindowaa paused for a moment as if to give the Chief time to digest his long story of woe, then he continued. "I sensed some conspiracy in this matter. I believe it is Giita who is behind all this. She is jealous and yet she has stopped having children. Now she goes behind my back and conspires with people to humiliate me. Chief, I am in a tight spot, that is why I have come to plead with you to assist me by talking to these people, my so-called friends in Talia, to give me time. I will pay them after the wedding. I will not run away. Why are they all in a hurry to harass me? Why? Please, Chief, talk to them for me. I promised I would come back to them. I hope that you will summon them and plead on my behalf. They will never refuse your plea as Chief. I want you to intervene, please, I beg you. Do this for me in the name of your honourable father whom we all loved so much. And Chief, what I do not understand is the fact that some of these friends have, at one time or the other, enjoyed my hospitality, my generosity. They don't think about the past, the things I have done for them. Just because I am not now in a position to take care of all my debts, they decided to hang heads together to harass me and humiliate me. I shall not run away from Talia, this is my root and my umbilical cord was buried here. Don't they know that? Where do they think I shall run to?"

Hindowaa now sounded agitated and the Chief responded calmly.

"I have heard you Hindowaa. I am aware of your situation. I promise you I shall do my best to talk to your friends to whom you are indebted. You are my future father in-law. I owe this to you and I shall oblige accordingly."

Hindowaa was effusive in his gratitude. "Chief, I do not have adequate words to thank you," he said. "I shall tell my mother immediately I go to the house. She had assured me that she was confident you would be more than willing to oblige. No doubt, as a mother she knows you more than I. On behalf of my late father who was your good friend, my mother and I thank you most sincerely. May you live long."

It was charcoal dark when Hindowaa left the Chief's compounded and started walking to his house. On his way out of the compound, he met an old man at the gate who asked him if the Chief was in. Hindowaa said the Chief had gone to sleep and everybody in the compound had gone to sleep. He walked away and disappeared into the darkness of the town, feeling very grateful to the Chief, and confident that he was once more in control of his household which had been threatening to fall apart.

CHAPTER FIFTEEN

It was generally believed in Talia that Boi-Kimbo was very pretty, the prettiest of all the graduates from the Sande Society that year. She was not only the prettiest among those who graduated; it was also acknowledged that she was the best dancer and singer. Her beauty and other qualities had captured Hindowaa's attention even before she was initiated into the Sande Society. Boi-Kimbo's bright eyes, and clean, well-formed teeth set against her dark gums tantalized men as often as they saw her. Some referred to her as the beauty queen in Talia. Above all, she was a virgin and was perceived to be fertile. These characteristics made Hindowaa wallow in a sea of euphoria. He was looking forward to the day he would marry her and possess her as his second wife. He had made up his mind. It was just a matter of time.

Giita had come to the conclusion that no sacrifice would now stop her husband from marrying Boi-Kimbo. She had resigned herself to the painful reality of having a co-wife of Kunaafoh's age. She cursed Hindowaa, when she recalled how he had assured her that she would be his only wife. Now she could understand why Hindowaa had made such a promise. After all, she had been like Boi-Kimbo when Hindowaa saw her - pretty, voluptuous, a good dancer and singer and above all, a virgin. What else could Hindowaa had wished for? she wondered.

When both families assembled in the evening at Hindowaa's home, all the necessary arrangements had been put into place for the marriage transaction. Hindowaa's mother was at the centre of the occasion. The Paramount Chief and Nyake were also present as well as the local dignitaries, both men and women. Boi-Kimbo was seated on a mat on the floor, dressed in bright coloured clothes. Her mother and Hindowaa's mother sat beside her. The three of them were waiting for the Paramount Chief to speak.. Hindowaa's mother watched her son as he continued to focus his eyes on Boi-Kimbo.

"Do you people know why marriages are contracted during the ginger harvest?" The Chief asked the audience. The people were surprised at the question. At first nobody volunteered a reply and there was silence until a woman in the audience said, "Chief, the ginger harvest is the time when we sell our produce and have money. When we have money we can afford to marry and pay the bride price."

"You men, are you not ashamed that a woman can respond correctly to my question?" the Chief asked the men. There was no answer and he went on, "The ginger harvest has been very encouraging this season as well as the rice harvest. I am happy that the women's society has come to a successful conclusion. There were no reported incidents, like sickness among the girls in the grove. We thank God and our ancestors for protecting our children during the entire initiation period. We also thank our *Sowie* (the head of the Sande Society) who conducted the initiation successfully."

Everybody was attentive as the Chief continued to address the audience.

"You all know why we are assembled here this evening. I do not intend to prolong this ceremony. Both families are here and I have the pleasure of forwarding the bride price money to my *demia* (in-law), Kimbo. The accompanying items have been assembled here. We are all happy that Hindowaa is taking a wife from a very decent family. Is there anybody here who has a contrary view on this matter?"

There was no comment from the audience.

"I now call on *Kinie* Nyake to pour libation to our ancestors in appreciation of all they have done to make this marriage a reality and free from any hindrance."

All eyes turned to Nyake who cherished the honour.

"Before I pour the libation," he said, "I want to make one observation. From the beginning of this ceremony I have noticed the conspicuous absence of Giita. I do of course understand that sometimes, circumstances dictate the presence or absence of people from such occasions. I, however, hope that both wives will co-operate with each other and make Hindowaa a happy husband. My friend Hindowaa has suffered a lot, which is why he decided to take a second wife. We all wish him well. We also wish the best for those among us who will be doing what Hindowaa is doing this evening. I promise them that we have every intention of patronizing all the forthcoming marriages by our friends here."

After Nyake had spoken, he took a mug of palm wine and stepped outside the entrance of the house. He then thanked the ancestors, lavishing praise on them for the care they had taken of the community, the abundant harvest they had provided, and the fact that Talia had not had any natural disasters and continued to enjoy nature's bounty. He spoke eloquently about the Hindowaa and Kimbo families. People were happy as they acknowledged what Nyake said by nodding their heads. Some said, "*toonya, toonya*", meaning "true, true" and drank their palm wine. Hindowaa and his mother were happy, *Kinie* Kimbo and his wife and other relatives who had come to witness the ceremony were happy too. The Chief was happy because he had successfully presided over the ceremony.

The Chief and Nyake left for home about the same time. It was now dark but the other people stayed behind and continued to eat and drink. The Hindowaa household was in a jubilant mood that evening and all of the following day.

Nyake had an obligation to accompany the Chief home even though two local police escorts were with them. As they walked towards the Chief's compound, he said, "Chief, I had warned Hindowaa not to proceed with this wedding. Why is he rushing despite all the problems he has. He stopped talking to me for some time because of my advice. The man is in debt and he continues taking more debt to marry. I understand he made efforts to get money from his sons in Freetown, but they were unable to give him even a penny."

"Hindowaa is a stubborn man," the Chief replied. "We all know him. He came to me a couple of times over this issue of his wife not having any more children. I counselled him. I did. I told him that a number of my wives have never had sons. I said to him, 'look at Jebeh, a woman I adore with all my heart. She has given me four girls. Look at Katumu, she has had three girls for me. What can I do? It is God's will.' But remember, I have other wives who continue to give me sons. This is God's decision."

"Chief you are right. I also told Hindowaa the same thing one night when he came to visit me. We were drinking when he started to tell me what he considered his problem with Giita. Giita is such a nice woman, a good wife. I asked him one question - whether Giita had ever confessed adultery. He said no. Had she confessed that she was a witch or ever practised witchcraft? He said no. Had Giita ever tried to disrespect any member of his family? He said no, only that his mother did not get along very well with Giita because Giita had stopped having children. Otherwise, he had no serious problem with her. Chief, this is a friend I have known for many years. When he makes up his mind about something, he pursues it to the end, no matter what the consequences. But one day when the ancestors show that they are angry with him, he will understand what I have been telling him and come back to me for consultations. Then I shall tell him exactly how I feel about it."

Nyake accompanied the Chief into his compound, then took leave of him and returned to his house.

That night, Giita felt as if she was bereaved. It was her first experience of having a co-wife. Many women of her age had told her their experiences with co-wives, especially when they are younger. She had heard all sorts of stories and she had never looked forward to sharing her husband and living in the same house with another wife. She thought about her own daughter. Boi-Kimbo was about Kunaafoh's age. That thought troubled her as she sat alone on the darkened veranda at the back of the house. She had had enough time to reflect on her condition and her eyes were flooded with tears. Abruptly she got up from the bench she was sitting on and wiped the warm tears from her eyes. She looked into the darkness of the night, adjusted her wrapper, stood for a while then sat down again.

"Boi-Kimbo, a child of my daughter's age is going to be my co-wife, yes my mate, she said to herself in the darkness. Let me tell you Boi-Kimbo what my daughter Kunaafoh once said to me when I told her that her father had threatened to take another woman because he wanted more sons. Her reaction was spontaneous. She told me that if her father did that, I should pack up and go to my parents in the village. We were at the river washing clothes. I can still see the anger on her face as she stood and looked at me with pity and anger. Poor child. Kunaafoh is a child like you. She could not understand how I would be able to put up with the indignity and humiliation of sharing my husband with a child of her own age. She was right. I know and feel the indignity, the humiliation and anguish I will have to endure. But Kunaafoh could not understand what I told her my parents' reaction would be if I went home and told them my reason for leaving Hindowaa - that they would not accept me and would tell me to pack up and return to my husband; that they would send me back with a relative and would in fact, apologise to Hindowaa for what they would consider my misbehaviour - that my mother would summon me into her room and tell me to endure for the sake of my children. That would be the justification. She would tell me

160

that if she had not endured in her marriage, her children would not have been blessed. Yes, that is what she would tell me. My parents would also have another consideration, but would never mention it to me. No. They would not, because they would think I did not know the other reason, and a very important one for that matter. If they were to welcome me home, they would have to refund Hindowaa's fat bride price. This is a very important consideration. But would Kunaafoh understand this type of logic? No. She said I would get another husband, another man, because I was still beautiful and attractive. Poor child. I pity her. Well Boi, I do not wish you the same ordeal I am going through. You may be lucky and escape this female ordeal. I wish you well and welcome you into the House of Fear."

There was a long interval before she continued emptying her anguished mind that evening. She wanted to take a break because she believed the spirits of the night needed a break. After a while, she took up her troubled thoughts again, saying to herself, the night is still young, dark and beautiful.

"I do not believe evil spirits are around me tonight. My ancestors will protect me. I do not blame Hindowaa. No. I do not blame him. It is my father that I blame and shall continue to blame. I hope he knows what is happening to me now while he is in his grave. I know that he is monitoring developments here on earth and knows what is happening to the daughter he gave in marriage to Hindowaa without asking about her opinion. Do fathers care about the feelings of their daughters? I wonder. All he wanted was to give me away and take his fat bride price. My feelings did not matter. They did not matter. No wonder Hindowaa wants Kunaafoh to marry the Paramount Chief who could be her grandfather. Does he care about the tender feelings of a tender young girl? I wonder. Why deprive a child of love? How do you expect a child like Kunaafoh to love such an old man? No, you don't love, you fear, you fear the man like you fear your father. This is how I have survived in this House of Fear. Not House Of Love. You are ordered around. You have to go to bed as early as possible. You lie in bed waiting. You sleep, no; you lie and wait for him. If he goes ahead of you, you will be asked why you are late. What were you doing? You become a child again, an adult child. Ah. My co-wife, Boi-Kimbo the little girl, does not know what she is getting into. She is like Kunaafoh, young, virginal and innocent. What is her choice? I do not blame her or bear malice towards her. I went through it. It is a matter of time. Boi-Kimbo, your beautiful features will surrender to the elements, your body will sag, and your firm breasts will be different after you have children. It is a matter of time. Hindowaa will preside over the deterioration of your beautiful body. He did it to me. What will Boi-Kimbo's mother do? What will she do? She has no say in the matter. She is a woman. She has no voice. All she is doing now is praying for Boi-Kimbo to have children, sons for the husband. Boi-Kimbo's mother has no voice. One thing I know and I am happy about is that now when I go to bed, I shall sleep when it is not my turn to sleep with Hindowaa. The three nights I have in the week to be away, shall be my happy nights. Yes, because I will not be interrogated if I come to bed when I want to. I shall stay with my friends and talk and gossip. When the moon shines, I shall enjoy my freedom to gossip with friends or go and visit people. Yes, I shall enjoy those three nights. It will be like going to visit my parents in the village. So, I have three nights every week when I shall go to bed when I want to and won't have to appear in court for cross-examination. Poor Boi-Kimbo, she does not know what life she is coming into. I don't blame her. She does not know that she is like a contract worker - hired to do a specific task. If you do not fulfil the requirements of the contract, you are disposed of like a piece of cloth that is not needed anymore. That is the name of the game. Boi-Kimbo, you are beautiful and young. But you are a contract worker. Hindowaa wants you to produce sons. Sons are the requirement. If you don't produce them, well, you should be prepared for the consequences. Yes, the truth is that when I was hired I was not told this part of the contract. I was said to be pretty like you. I was the talk of the town, like you. I remember how men used to make flattering comments when I passed by. That was a long time ago. I did not have any sense of old age. I lived in youthful bliss. Hindowaa was monitoring every movement I made but I never saw him. Why? I saw boys of my age. I admired many of the boys with whom we used to play outside. We played hide and seek during the moonshine. When it rained heavily we went out under the rain and had fun. It was one of my happiest moments. I remember very vividly one boy who always told me that when he became a man he would like to marry me. He used to admire the beads I had around my waist, and I remember, I had beautiful beads around my waist. The boy had seen me naked when we went to the river to wash clothes. I adored him. He was tall and slim and could swim like a crocodile in the river.

162

His friends admired him. He did not marry me because my father had his own plans. I hope he is aware of my present condition. I hope he is aware that Hindowaa never told me the nature of the contract I was signing. I never signed it. No. I had no choice. The contract was signed, sealed and delivered to me by my father in consultation with Hindowaa. Is this justice? My father was the one who did all this. However, I bear him no malice just as I bear no malice towards Boi-Kimbo. I shall cooperate with her. She is innocent. She is my child. Yes, she is my child. I remember now what it means to be a child. Kunaafoh once made the entire household laugh for days and days. That was the first time she saw herself in a big mirror. She had never seen one before. She ran and came to me saying, 'Mother, mother, I saw my twin sister in the room. I greeted her but she refused to speak to me. Please come with me and let her come out so that we play together.' Her twin sister. It was her reflection in the mirror. Well, that is what sweet innocence means. It is sweet and harmless. It was the talk of the household for a long time. Boi-Kimbo, you are an innocent child. One day you shall see the true reflection of this house in the mirror. I shall do everything to protect you, because one day Kunaafoh might find herself in a similar situation. But Boi-Kimbo, you came late into this marriage. Hindowaa is an old man now. I met him when he was younger, much younger. His energy has now been diluted. The best of his youthful energy is gone. It is the residue that you will be dealing with. There is a big difference between your energy and his energy level. Let me tell you this, whenever he drinks bamboo wine, not palm wine, I mean raffia wine, that night, you forfeit everything. All he does is snore. He snores very well. It is musical and changes vibrations as the night progresses. After some time you will get used to it. As I said, he is not a young man. Both of us should contemplate the grim possibility of widowhood. Ah, it would be painful, especially for a young person like you. You will lose the dominant position you enjoy as the favourite wife and the young wife. All those privileges will disappear in an instant. Think about how painful it will be for you. I say these things because I can see my daughter in the same situation. I know that Kunaafoh will come back and her father will not hesitate to marry her to the Chief. When she marries, she will not be told about the contractual nature of the relationship, in the end, she will become the victim of an unfulfilled contract to which she was not a signatory. In law, that is not a good contract. But what will she do? It is a bad contract in a bad situation but that does not make it null and void. If you complain, they will tell you that is tradition, it is custom and above all it is culture, it has been like this since our forefathers and who are you, Giita, who are you, Kunaafoh, who are you and Boi- Kimbo to challenge it? You do so at your own peril. This is where we are and this is where I now find myself, a victim of a bad contract."

All of a sudden, Giita realised she had been outside for a long time. The town was silent. People were sleeping. The animals too were sleeping. Nature was in a state of blissful slumber. Only Giita and the spirits of the night were awake, but she was not afraid.

"This is the first time I have spoken to myself for such a long time. If someone in Talia spotted me talking to myself he or she would say I have gone mad because my husband is taking another wife. The news would spread like harmattan wind in this town." Giita said aloud as she walked into the house. The night was advanced and she went to bed, feeling relieved after she had released her thoughts on her condition in The House of Fear.

CHAPTER SIXTEEN

Talia was used to all sorts of gossips. It was almost the trademark of the town. Gossip took many forms. There were the little pieces of gossip that came and disappeared almost immediately because people took no notice of them. Then there was the gossip that lingered for some time, but had little weight. That also vanished and people continued to go about their business as usual. However, gossip that became persistent arrested the attention of the majority of the people of Talia.

Maamusu had dropped her seven-year-old daughter at Giita's house late in the afternoon one day. She was Giita's good friend and they gossiped a lot. Most people referred to them as the best of female friends in Talia. Maamusu had a valuable asset, which had further served to cement her relationship with Giita. She had finished elementary school. She had wanted to continue her education, but her father married her off as soon as she finished elementary school and graduated from the Sande Society. She read letters and answered correspondence for people in Talia. She knew many of Giita' secrets because she helped her correspond with her children in Freetown. Maamusu's school-going daughter had lice on her head and she had dropped off the child at Giita's house so that Giita would help to rid her head of lice. The child was being harassed by her colleagues in school because of the lice.

"*Mba*, sit down over there, I shall be with you soon," Giita told Maamusu when she came to collect her daughter. She had finished undoing the girl's hair and was putting the medicine on her scalp.

"Welcome, *Mba*, welcome. I think that everything will be all right after this treatment. What we should concentrate on is to avoid her getting lice again. It is not nice. The child is always scratching her head."

"*Mba*, let us go into the room," Giita said when she had finished with the child. "I want you to see something."

Maamusu felt a little anxious till she realised what her friend wanted her to do. Giita had done it many times before and always requested it be done in secret.

When they entered the room, Giita went straight to one of her boxes and brought out an envelope. It was a long letter from her son, Kafo. He had written to his mother through somebody who was travelling from Ginger Hall to Talia. The boy had given strict instructions that the letter should be given only to his mother and to no one else. The person had complied and had delivered the letter to Giita.

"*Mba*, here, it was delivered to me yesterday. *Kinie* Foday sent his son to come and call me saying he had something for me from Freetown. I rushed out immediately and collected it. Please open it and let me know what my son is saying. I want to know what is happening at Ginger Hall. You see, unlike his senior brother, Kafo always finds time to brief me about developments at the house in Ginger Hall."

Giita was speaking as Maamusu hurriedly read the letter from Kafo before telling her friend of its contents.

"He said he sends his greetings and wishes you well," she told Giita. "He says that he and his brother are fine. He says that since his last letter to you, his uncle's wife continues to behave strangely to both of them. He believes that it may be due to the effect of Uncle Kortu's death. He says that one day, he eavesdropped at Auntie Fanday's room and thought he heard her singing and then talking to herself. The room was locked but he could hear her singing and talking. She was threatening that one day she would come to Talia and confront you in connection with what he told you in one of his previous letters to you. However, he says that despite her strange behaviour, she has not done anything bad to them so far."

"Thank you very much, *Mba*, you see what I have been telling you about Fanday. She believes we are enemies. So what do you expect me to do? She has her own problems. I have mine. One thing I can tell you *Mba*, one day, she will regret everything she has said about me. That is all I can say. Please *Mba*, when you have time, please come and help me reply to my son. Please, I beg."

"Giita, do you have to thank me for this?" Maamusu said, teasing her friend. "How many times are you going to be thanking me? What are friends for? Imagine, what you have done for me over so many years. I had stopped thanking you. Now, I am going to take my daughter and thank you very much for doing her hair. I appreciate your help and time, so we are going to continue thanking each other forever. I have read your son's letter for you. You have thanked me. You have treated my daughter's hair and I have also thanked you. However, I wanted to discuss something very serious with you. It has been on my mind for some time and keeps giving me sleepless nights."

166

Maamusu's serious tone made Giita sit upright and stare at her friend in surprise.

"What are you talking about, *Mba*?" she asked. Maamusu did not respond immediately, as if she was organising her thoughts. Giita looked impatient. "*Mba*, I am waiting," she said.

When Maamusu answered, she was visibly angry and upset.

"I heard something which surprised me. In this town, everybody knows we are the best of friends. Therefore, I would expect that if anything happened to you, good or bad, I would be the first one you would tell or consult, especially if it was a good thing. To hear it from people outside, people I don't trust, puts a question mark on the quality of our friendship. This thing has really upset me."

"*Mba*, I don't know what you are talking about," Giita said in an equally serious tone. "I swear by my Sande Society. I swear, I do not know what you are talking about."

A moment's silence ensued and the atmosphere between the two friends was tense. Giita summoned someone in the house to take her friend's daughter home as it was getting dark.

"Ndeve, come and accompany the girl home. Her mother is not likely to be going home for soon... *Mba*, your observations worry me a lot," she said afterwards. "I agree with you that if something bad or good happens to me, you will be the first person I will tell before anyone else. You know that, and that is the honest truth. I am saying this from the bottom of my heart. When did you start doubting my sincerity?"

"*Mba*, I have never questioned your sincerity, never." Maamusu told Giita, realising that her suspicions had made her friend angry, "but what I heard in town made me believe that you had no intention of telling me until I found out by myself. This is the reason I am angry with you."

"Ha, Ha. This town is full of rumours, nothing but rumours. My mother who gave birth to me, listen to my own trouble today," Giita remarked. Maamusu laughed and the tension eased. Giita enquired in a light-hearted tone, "So what is amiss? What have you heard about me that is so nice and I have refused to tell you. Tell me."

Maamusu thought for a moment, then looked around her, came close to Giita and whispered in her right ear.

"*Teeh bia quihun*, they say you are pregnant."

167

Giita was speechless even as Maamusu began to examine her contours for any sign of pregnancy.

"Ah, my friend, this is a very dangerous place," she said at last. "*Mba*, you are a woman, you know as well as I do that there are times when you miss your period. That does not mean you are pregnant. Yes, I missed my period and I mentioned it in a casual way to someone. I think after that, the person sent a message to the Talia Broadcasting Service to be transmitted in town. I know the person, because there is only one person I told while we were having a casual conversation at the river. I am going to undress for you before you leave this room so you can see for yourself if I am pregnant or not. Yes, I shall undress completely, from head to toe for you before you leave. I have nothing to hide from you."

Maamusu was convinced after Giita told her what had transpired.

"*Mba*, no wonder when you came in I saw you obviously examining my body," Giita said and the two women laughed. "But," she went on, "*Mba*, I wanted to tell you how I am feeling these days. Yes, I have only missed my period for one month. However, lately when I wake up in the morning, I feel like vomiting. On a few occasions, I have actually vomited. I also feel like eating sour limes, and my appetite is not what it used to be."

Maamusu smiled.

"You know, *Mba*, you are right," she said. "I have four children. I am the first wife of my husband. Let me tell you what used to happen to me each time my husband married another woman. I am telling you, I know how this female body works. The first time he married, I actually felt I was pregnant. I had all the symptoms of pregnancy. To tell you the truth, it was because of jealousy. I was very jealous, I became thin and people thought I would die if I continued like that. My mother was worried as well as my sisters. I was not pregnant. My husband was not even bothered because all his attention was on the new bride. *Mba*, I suffered a lot and it never stopped happening. Each time he married a new wife, I would have the same symptoms of false pregnancy. I understand your situation."

When Maamusu was leaving Giita's house, she met two other women, Adama and Ngadie, who had come to see Giita that same evening, and they exchanged greetings. As they entered the house, Adama and Ngadie greeted Giita in a chorus. They sounded happy.

168

"Come in and sit down," said Giita ushering them in. "How have you both been doing?"

"We are doing fine, and you?"

"Well, I can't complain," Giita replied. "I now have a co-wife and this has reduced my chores in this house, especially cooking when guests are around."

Giita observed the two women exchange glances and wondered why they had come. They visited her from time to time, but never at night, just as she had only visited them during the day. They were not close friends. She guessed that the women whom she regarded as some of the most vicious gossips in Talia had come because of the rumours about her pregnancy. Otherwise, why would they have come all the way from down town just to visit at night? She was not pleased about it but waited for them to broach the subject.

"*Aaa bii hini?*" Adama asked, enquiring about Giita's husband.

"He has gone to bed," Gitta replied in a cold manner. She was trying to send a message to them that she was not impressed by their visit, but they ignored it.

"The night has not even started, it is still early and he has already gone to bed?" Ngadie remarked.

"How can you ask such a question?" Adama protested. " The man has just married a young girl. All these men are the same. I am saying it out of experience. My husband did the same thing each time he married a new wife."

Giita had already started feeling agitated over her visitors' questions and comments. Their next remarks annoyed her even more.

"Your co-wife deserved the praise she got at the graduation ceremony. She is really beautiful and looked well mannered. I like her a lot," said Adama. Giita did not respond.

"Giita, we are here to sympathise with you," Ngadie said. "We know how much you have suffered over the years. How Hindowaa had to marry because he wants more sons. We know. Some of our relatives and loved ones have had similar experiences. That is why we women sympathise with you."

Giita still did not respond.

"My dear Giita, we are here because we heard something that is nice. We are here to express our joy about what we have heard. In fact we are hear to congratulate you. Is it not so, my friend?" Adama asked her companion.

"Yes, it is true what my friend has said," Ngadie said. "That was why we decided to come in person. We wanted to come tomorrow, but we felt that many people would be coming to congratulate you, so we decided to come before the crowd."

"Yes Giita, we are happy to hear that you are pregnant," Adama chimed in. "We pray that you get a son, or even twins this time around."

"Who told you that I am pregnant? Who told you?" Giita asked, not hiding her irritation.

"No Giita, don't be annoyed," Ngadie said, hoping to appease her. "We have been hearing this rumour for some time now and we thought that where there is smoke, there must be fire. We are happy about this development, that is why we came."

"Do I look like a pregnant woman? Tell me, do I look like one?" Giita asked them in such a caustic tone that Adama began to apologise.

"Giita, we are sorry, we did not mean anything bad. We came here out of concern. If our interest has caused you any distress we apologise. We are really sorry and we hope you will forgive us if we have offended you," However, unappeased, Giita lashed out at them and the entire town.

"I know Talia," she said bitterly. "Ever since I married in this town, I have realised that people spend most of their time gossiping. They are idle and they are hypocrites. That is why I have few friends, very few friends. Yes, Hindowaa has married a new woman, so you came to see how I feel about it. That is why you have come here pretending that you heard I am pregnant. Let me make it clear. I have pregnancy symptoms, but this does not mean that I am pregnant. It happens sometimes to women. Some women have this tendency when they are under stress. However, I did not tell the whole of Talia. I only told one person during a casual conversation and that person was Naataa. I intend to confront her about it soon and if she does not apologise, I shall wring her neck like a chicken."

After that, Giita's visitors left in a hurry feeling embarrassed and unappreciated. Giita felt relieved that they had gone. She was certain that many more such delegations would arrive at her house and made up her mind that she would not tolerate anybody else who came to find out about her pregnancy. Shocked that Naataa had broadcast what had been just a casual mention of her condition, she was also preparing to confront her.

"My sister, I never thought that Giita would react the way she did," Adama remarked as they walked home in complete darkness. "After all we only came to congratulate her on her pregnancy because we knew what she had been going through. Now look at the way she treated us. Is that nice?"

"I don't blame Giita, I blame you Adama," Ngadie told her friend angrily. "When this rumour was circulating, you were the one who insisted we pay a visit to Giita to find out whether it was true. I told you that it was not our business. I said we should wait and see whether her stomach would start showing. But no, you could not wait. You were in too much of a hurry."

"So you are blaming me for the insults we received from Giita?"

"All I am saying is that you show too much interest in other people's business," Ngadie replied in an aggressive tone. "Even *I* am sometimes afraid of you, Adama. I am telling you the truth. Have less to do with other people's business."

"Ngadie, between you and me, who likes interfering in people's business? Tell me."

"You want to pick a quarrel with me tonight because I told you the truth," Ngadie remarked. "Don't you think what I told you makes sense? Who is responsible for our coming here tonight? When you suggested it what was my initial response? You tell me. If we had stayed at home and taken care of our children we would not have suffered the humiliation Giita put us through."

"I don't want to pick a quarrel with you tonight," Adama said. "I think that you have had me in mind for sometime now and you were just waiting for an occasion to vent your frustrations on me. Otherwise I don't see the need for all this talking."

"One thing I know about you is that you don't like the truth," Ngadie lectured her friend. "The fact is that we had no good reason for going to see Giita. We are all aware of her problems in this town. They are not unique. One thing is certain; we would have received adequate information about her condition anyway. This is Talia, nothing is a secret here and we would have been informed. Instead, look how much time we wasted going to see Giita just to be humiliated, thanks to you. I think we deserved what we got this evening. The next time we hear any rumours, we will think twice before we take action."

Adama did not reply and, knowing she was on the defensive, Ngadie continued to lecture her.

"Adama, you never accept your fault and that is not good. We are not perfect. It is virtue to own up when you make a mistake. What happened to us tonight is your fault because of your curiosity about other people's business."

"Talk quietly, people are now sleeping," Adama told her crossly.

"Don't talk to me as if you are talking to your children," Ngadie responded, adding, "Tell me something. When you went to visit your sister-in-law this afternoon, did you drink any alcohol?"

"Are you suggesting that I am drunk? Do I look drunk or have I behaved like a drunken person? Ngadie, are you trying to provoke a fight?"

"Adama, we are not children. Don't talk about fighting. You see, that is what is wrong with you. You like to evade reality. Admit to what I have said. *You* brought this whole mess on us."

"No. I will not admit it, Ngadie." It was now Adama's turn to lecture her friend. "If you had seriously advised against it when I suggested that we visit Giita, I would not have insisted, but when I made the proposal, you agreed willingly and came along. If you felt that I was wrong to suggest the visit, you should have told me so and I would have complied. You did not. So why make such a big fuss about it now that things have gone sour. *Bo do ya, lef me saaful* (Don't bother me)."

The atmosphere between the two friends was quite acrimonious by the time they reached home. They did not talk to each other as they negotiated the entrance into the house and disappeared into their respective rooms where they found their children fast asleep, unaware that their mothers had been involved in verbal combat. There was no victor or vanquished.

Giita's other visitors were some of the elderly and respected women of Talia. They came with the same concerns, to determine whether she was indeed pregnant and also to advise her and sympathise further over the consequences of her inability to have more sons. These visits, unlike the previous ones, did not generate any animosity, however. Giita waited for a couple more days before confronting, Naataa, the author of the rumours that she was pregnant. She had thought about it and decided on the best course of action to take. Being one of the respected women in Talia, she was not prepared to tarnish her well-earned reputation by confronting the rumour-monger in Talia town itself, so she spent some time monitoring Naataa's movements. On the next Sunday afternoon, she saw Naataa with a fishing net, heading towards the river. Concluding that Naataa was going fishing, she took up her own fishing net, took leave of her mother-in-law and followed her.

It was a pleasant day and those women who had gone fishing the previous day had reported that because the level of the river had risen, there was an abundance of fish to be caught. By the time Giita arrived at the river, Naataa had already cast her net a couple of times and caught some fish, which she had deposited in her calabash. Giita saw that the fish were fresh and still alive. Naataa had spotted Giita but pretended to be busy with her fishing and ignored Giita's attempts to catch her attention. So Giita grabbed the calabash and threw the entire catch into the river, saying, "I am here to teach you a lesson, you child of a harlot."

Naataa, who was a younger woman and respectful of Giita, was thoroughly shaken by the verbal attack. She had never heard Giita utter an obscene word. She had never seen Giita angry.

"*Ngo*, Giita, what I have done to you?" she asked in a frightened tone, "Please tell me. If I have wronged you I shall apologise. I don't want to pick a quarrel with you; you are my elder sister."

She was still standing in the river with half of her body buried in water.

"You come out of the river and let me teach you the lesson of a lifetime," Giita told the frightened woman who had broken out in a sweat even though she was standing in water. "I am going to undress for you to see me naked so that you can go and tell the whole of Talia that I am pregnant."

"*Ngo*, Giita, oh, I now understand why you are angry. Please, I never meant it in a bad way. Someone might have quoted me out of context. I know how Talia is. I beg you to forgive me. I will never do it again. I am on my knees begging you. Forgive me for the sake of your children. Please."

Giita calmed down after Naataa's plea for forgiveness, especially when she heard other women coming to fish. Believing Naataa was sincerely contrite, she felt her heart melt, so to speak. She went into the

173

river and began to fish with Naataa and when they were ready to leave, gave Naataa some of her own abundant catch to make up for the fish she had thrown into the river. The two women walked home talking about Talla and its receptivity to all sorts of gossip. Giita and Naataa never fought again and after that incident held each other in high esteem. The rest of the day passed by peacefully.

Giita's pregnancy symptoms assumed a regular pattern. Only one month had gone by since she missed her monthly period. However, she believed her feet were becoming swollen and her appetite went into hibernation. She also developed a taste for sour foods. Hindowaa was growing concerned about her condition and decided to summon the best female soothsayer who specialized in determining whether a pregnant woman would give birth to a boy or girl, whether she would have twins and how the child would look. She had made Talia famous because of her profession and many pregnant women found their way there to consult her.

"We have now reached a situation that warrants consulting Mamie Yegbeh," Hindowaa told Giita one evening. It was her turn to share the matrimonial bed, Boi-Kimbo having completed her three days and three nights' rotation.

Since Yegbeh was now an elderly woman, she often went to bed early if she did not have clients. Giita had a very trying day following her husband's suggestion that they see Yegbeh, first, to determine whether she was pregnant and second to find out whether she would have a boy or girl. The day seemed to go by faster than any other that she could remember.

"*Yeea* Giita, I have been praying so that you get a positive result when you go this evening to see the female soothsayer," Boi-Kimbo, her young co-wife, said sweetly.

"Oh, I thank you very much for the kind thoughts. Thank you my child," Giita replied. Boi always referred to her as 'mother Giita' and Giita appreciated the girl's politeness and humility.

When Hindowaa and Giita arrived at the soothsayer's hut, they found her lying on the ground on a brand new mat bought for her by one of her grandsons.

Without much ado, Hindowaa and Giita sat down.

"What can I do for you, my children?" the soothsayer asked. She knew the couple very well.

"We are here to determine Giita's condition. A whole month has passed and she has missed her monthly period. We want to know if she is pregnant and if she will have a son," Hindowaa replied.

"Do you know, another couple has just left here with the same problem," the soothsayer told Giita and Hindowaa. She was now seated up right on the mat and had begun to position the four peanut shells. "I will not tell you the name of the couple because I don't want people to quote me. You know Talia is full of lies and gossip. The most recent gossip is that two women almost fought at the river yesterday. No names were mentioned, but they say it is true. I can assure you that by tomorrow, we shall have all the facts."

Giita felt sweating break out between her legs as they continued to watch the soothsayer study the positions of the peanut shells she had cast on the mat. Both she and Hindowaa were familiar with the ritual.

As the soothsayer watched the shells, she gave an indication that all was not well.

Hindowaa and Giita waited in anxious silence.

"My children," she said at last, "The time is not yet ripe. It will come. Even the ancestors have agreed that Giita will be pregnant. But the time is not yet ripe. I have seen so many cases like this. I too went through such moments when I was married. Sometimes my late husband would tease me. I used to have all the symptoms of pregnancy. One of my known symptoms was aggression and being quarrelsome. In fact because of that, two of my children, a boy and a girl were called Manja and Kanja (meaning 'a girl and boy born of a woman who was quarrelsome when she was pregnant'). Now, the way I see the peanut shells for the second time is very revealing. When Giita gets pregnant, she will have twins, a boy and a girl. The wife you have married will also have twins. They will be girls. If this does not happen, cut off both my ears."

Hindowaa paid the consultation fee and they took leave of the old woman. That pleasant evening, he and his wife walked home, absolutely certain that Giita would eventually become pregnant again and give birth to twins, a boy and a girl. They walked away from the soothsayer's hut, looking forward to Giita's pregnancy and continued to await the ancestors' decision as time progressed into infinity.

CHAPTER SEVENTEEN

It was well known in Talia that Hindowaa had a very good appetite. Those he invited to share meals would acknowledge that he had a generous appetite, especially when Giita cooked his favourite sauce which was potato leaves and goat meat. This was one of the reasons Giita loved her husband. He appreciated her cooking. People said her culinary expertise was among the factors that sustained their marriage. However, as time went by, it was said that with his marriage to Boi-Kimbo Hindowaa had developed a wolf's appetite that was beyond imagination.

Boi-Kimbo, the new bride, was grateful to Giita who had helped prepare her for her new status as Hindowaa's wife. Giita told her what Hindowaa liked and disliked, his favourite foods, and also his favourite sauce, which was potato leaves cooked with goat meat. She said it was Hindowaa's mother who was responsible for Hindowaa's love for food because their mother-in-law was good at cooking and could prepare almost any sauce very well. Boi-Kimbo too was known to be a good cook. Her culinary talent, compared well with her artistic talent for singing and dancing.. Hindowaa was a lucky man in this regard, having two exceptionally talented cooks as his wives. Many of the perennial visitors at his house acknowledged the fact that Giita was a very good cook and admitted that Boi-Kimbo was equally good.

In Talia, many things made news headlines and people spent their time talking about them. Those who frequented Hindowaa's house argued which of the two wives was a better cook. The debates took on a sinister dimension when it became the talk of the town that Hindowaa's newly improved appetite was due to the fact that Boi-Kimbo's mother had taught her daughter to cook using special condiments. They had been provided by a medicine man, so the story went, in order to make Hindowaa love her more than he loved Giita. All Boi-Kimbo had to do was to add the potion to the sauce she was cooking. People said that Hindowaa's appetite became as voracious as a vulture's whenever it was Boi-Kimbo's turn to cook.

Maamusu continued to visit her friend Giita regularly. Sometimes, when she visited, Giita would ask her to accompany her to the river to fetch water. She might also ask her to accompany her to visit an older woman who was not well. This strategy was devised by Giita to ensure that she and her friend had some privacy, since this could not be guaranteed at home. On one particularly beautiful day, Giita asked Maamusu to go with her to the river. Maamusu asked for a bucket so that she too would bring back some water for her household. Giita obliged and Maamusu balanced the big bucket on her head. As they walked towards the river, she said to Giita,

"Remember when I told you the last time that mothers-in-law can be vicious when it comes to promoting the interests of their children, whether they are sons or daughters? Well, the rumour you mentioned is correct; I have also heard it in town. That is why I decided to come and see you today."

"Maamusu, to be honest with you, I have more important things on my mind these days," Giita replied. "These are the things you have to put up with when you have co-wives. I knew that such issues would crop up where there are two or more wives. Yes, I have noticed how much appetite Hindowaa has acquired these days. I monitor the amount of food he eats when I cook and when Boi-Kimbo cooks. I have known him for a long time, so I know there is a big difference between when I cook and when Boi-Kimbo cooks. The difference is even greater when there are no guests and he eats alone."

"What is unfortunate is that we cannot prove our suspicions. Do you think we can consult a reliable soothsayer on this issue? But again, what difference would it make? What would be the purpose of doing so - to reduce Hindowaa's appetite when Boi-Kimbo cooks and increase it when you cook?" Maamusu asked, and the two friends burst out laughing. The idea was so amusing that they looked at each other and clapped their hands, saying, *"ahyee jooh."*

"Look at the child," Giita remarked without bitterness. "She looks so innocent. They say it is her mother who is behind it, and the poor girl cannot refuse. She is a good girl and I have never suspected her of any mischievous behaviour. You see what we mothers can do to our children?"

"But Giita, how can you be so innocent yourself? When it comes to men, you cannot talk about the girls of today as children or innocent. They learn faster than if they were in school. My dear, I am saying this from experience. I too have mates. They looked young and innocent when they got married but learned faster than I ever imagined. So stop talking about Boi-Kimbo's innocence. As you say, the mother is also helping her to learn fast so that she can guarantee her survival in the House of Fear, as you call it."

After this lecture Giita was silent for a moment as if she needed to collect her thoughts.

"There is a lot of sense in what you have said, my sister," she replied. "The children these days are not as innocent as our own generation. Some of them even know about sex before they are initiated into Sande. They know many things of which we were innocent at their age. If you notice, they look at men straight in their eyes. In our day, you dared not; you bowed your head and refused to make contact with men's eyes. My sister, you are right, those days are gone, 'the good old days'."

Maamusu concurred with her observations.

"But tell me, Giita," she asked, "is she pregnant yet? Have you suspected any symptoms of pregnancy? It is some time now since the marriage took place. When I was married, I got pregnant within three months. Her mother should be helping her in that respect rather than to increase Hindowaa's already huge appetite."

"Leave our husband alone, about his appetite," Giita pretending to chide Maamusu as they chuckled. "I give him credit for that; at least I know that after I have laboured in the kitchen and cooked for him, he will eat well. I feel good and secure in the knowledge that he has not gone and eaten somewhere else, or been fed by another woman. These days, you never know. You know as well as I do that many women complain that their husbands don't eat much at home. Who knows? In the case of our own husband, we cannot complain about his appetite."

Both of them chuckled again.

"One thing you never told me, though, and I have waited long enough," Maamusu said putting on a solemn expression that made Giita confused.

"Maamusu, what is it again? What is there in my life that I have not told you? Tell me. I don't have a boy friend. I don't involve myself in that kind of thing; it is not my nature, and I never caught my mother doing it. You know that. We both have that in common," she replied, eager to know what her friend was insinuating.

"Well, not long ago, I learned that your husband is a very good sportsman," Maamusu said and Giita felt even more confused.

"I don't understand what you are saying, Maamusu, please don't confuse me this afternoon. I beg you in the name of God. My hands are full of problems."

"Are you not aware that Hindowaa won a prize a long time ago, maybe before you and I were born? The white man had a competition on Empire Day and there were lots of sporting activities. They said Hindowaa won first prize in the eating competition. I am sure if you ask *Kinie* Nyake and others they will tell you. But don't tell them that I told you. I was told by some people long time ago."

Both relieved and amused, Giita said,

"To be honest with you, and I swear by my Sande Society, Hindowaa never told me that story. Maamusu, you know our men, don't sit and talk with us. They would rather go to their peers, like to Nyake, or go and spend the time with the Chief. Let me tell you, I shall never ask him if he does not tell me himself. Anyway, to come back to your previous question about whether Boi-Kimbo is pregnant. I have been careful not to give her the impression that I am watching her body to find out if she is pregnant, but, I can confirm that she is. I have been expecting her to tell me herself, and I am still waiting. Who knows, she might do it one of these days. I hope so."

By this time, they had filled their buckets with water and had started walking home.

"How far do you think the pregnancy is?" Maamusu asked.

"My best guess is about two to three months, because when I remember my first pregnancy, when I was two months pregnant, my stomach was exactly like Boi-Kimba's," Giita answered.

"But, you cannot go by that," Maamusu pointed out. "Even when one of my co-wives is three months pregnant, you will think that she has only just finished eating a bowl of rice. Her stomach is so small. Even when she is nine months pregnant, her stomach is just like an average calabash."

Giita was impressed with her friend's observations, but still insisted that in her visual estimation, her mate was about two to three months pregnant.

"You know, Maamusu," she said, "despite our reservations about the innocence of today's children, I am still thinking that my mate is one of the few exceptions. She is truly innocent, and were it not for the fact that her mother is too busy trying to make her mature quickly, she would keep her innocence. She reminds of my only daughter, Kunaafoh."

"Before I forget, did you hear that your friends almost fought?" Maamusu asked Giita as they continued on their way."

"What friends are you talking about?"

"Adama and Ngadie."

"What would they be fighting about?"

"You remember the night they came to visit you after I left, that was the night. I hear that on their way home they had an argument which had almost degenerated into a fight by the time they got home."

"To be honest with you, this is the first time I am hearing such news," Giita commented. "I would like to know why they were quarrelling."

"The story goes like this," Maamusu said. "They were not comfortable about the way you treated them when they came to visit and congratulate you about news that you were pregnant. They did not like the way you treated them, so on their way home Ngadie blamed Adama for suggesting that they should come and visit you and for the humiliation they suffered when they came. She scolded Adama for having too much interest in other people's business."

"But why should they fight? I only gave them a piece of my mind. I shall do so again if they come my way. Maamusu, I am just fed up with the hypocrisy in this town. Both Ngadie and Adama are always involved in people's business. Why don't they spend their time talking about their broken homes? Both of them have been without husbands for a long time. Have I visited them? Have I asked them about their problems? Why are they after me? Their former husbands have since remarried; why can't they stay home and find a solution to their miserable existence instead of passing from house to house in Talia trying to find out what is happening. So what stopped them from fighting?"

"It was too dark, I suppose. As for that Ngadie, when you see her, she looks as if she cannot lick palm oil," Maamusu said in disgust. "They say she is very deep and capable of spoiling other women's homes, including those of her so-called best friends. I even heard that she had something to do with Adama's problems with her husband. Look at her properly. You can see that her eyes are hard. She looks dangerous."

180

It was late in the afternoon by the time they reached Giita's house. Maamusu could not stay and continued on to her own house.

When Giita arrived home with the water on her head, she saw Boi-Kimbo sitting on the veranda. She looked downhearted as she rose and came forward to help put down the bucket.

"Good evening, *Yeea* Giita," she greeted her senior mate, calling her 'mother' as usual.

"What is happening? Boi-Kimbo you don't look yourself," Giita remarked.

"*Yeea* Giita, I have something to tell you. I have nobody else to confide in. You are the only person I can talk to and feel confident it will stay confidential. For the short time I have been here, I know that this town is full of gossips and malicious people. But what have I done to people? They are already saying bad things about me," she answered and began to cry.

Giita tried to comfort Boi-Kimbo, putting her left arm around her shoulders.

"What is the problem tell me," she asked kindly. "If there is anything I can do to help, I promise I shall do it. Stop crying."

Boi-Kimbo wiped the tears from her eyes.

"*Yeea* Giita can you believe that people are saying that I put medicine in our husband's food so that he can eat more of my food? I feel very miserable. I have been in this marriage for less than six months and they are already making my life miserable. What have I done to people?"

"Boi-Kimbo, this is Talia; it is part of the nature of this town," Giita told her. "You have to make up your mind not to listen to what people say or gossip about you. If you don't adopt that attitude, you will be miserable. I have gone through what you are just beginning to experience. It is unfortunate, but that is the reality. They will say many more things about you. You know my own story. I have only two sons and one daughter. They have put me under stress and even suggested that my daughter, Kunaafoh, is responsible for my misfortune, that she has an evil eye and that is why I cannot have more than two sons. It is very disheartening. I thank God I am still alive."

"*Yeea* Giita, I cannot even enjoy my food these days. I keep asking myself why people are so nasty to me? I understand your friends; Ngadie and Adama are among those spreading lies about me. I don't know them and they are not of my age group. If they were of my age group, believe me *Yeea* Giita I would confront them. I am not afraid to fight with my peers, but these ones are even older than my elder sisters."

"You don't have to fight with anybody over such things," Giita said to her young mate. "I know the people you are talking about in this town, gossip and lies are their trademark. I have a suggestion which will help us both if you accept it. It will also disprove what the gossips are saying - that you put medicine into Hindowaa's food to make him eat more and love you more. Since most of the time he is away when we are cooking, when your turn comes, let me prepare the sauce and give it to him. He will not know who cooked the food since he never comes to the kitchen. When my own turn comes, you will do the cooking and give it to him and we shall see what happens."

The proposal excited Boi-Kimbo, so they both agreed to go ahead with the experiment Giita had suggested.

"I am glad about what you have suggested, *Yeea* Giita," Boi-Kimbo said, "but I still feel like confronting your friends. That Ngadie looks like a witch, but I can beat her - put her back flat on the floor. I am not so confident that I can do the same to Adama. She is too big for me to challenge for a fight."

"You will not fight with anybody, as long as I am around," Giita said firmly. She was speaking with the experienced voice of a married woman who had lived in Talia for many years. "Try to avoid their company," she went on. "They are hypocrites. Avoid them. They will try to come near you as if they want your friendship, but all they want is to find out what is going on in your home; they want to find out about your marriage. Women like that are even ready to have an affair with your husband."

Boi-Kimbo listened attentively to Giita and took her advice.

One day, Hindowaa travelled to a nearby village and said he would come back late that evening. That was when Giita and Boi-Kimbo decided to carry out their plan. It was Boi-Kimbo's turn to cook as she was spending her three days and three nights with Hindowaa. The two wives agreed that Giita should prepare Hindowaa's favourite dish made with potato leaves and goat meat. It was not all that late when Hindowaa arrived, looking happy. He had brought back two live chickens which he had acquired in the town he visited, and told his wives how he wanted them prepared for the next meal. As usual, he took a warm bath, which Boi-Kimbo had prepared for him, then came to sit in a corner of the sitting-room. Because his normal visitors expected him to be away, no one had turned up that evening, though the more notorious of his food-loving visitors had been known to come and wait for him for as long as necessary.

Boi-Kimbo brought his food and he sat alone in front of a little mountain of rice, accompanied by potato leaf sauce cooked with goat meat. Both Giita and Boi-Kimbo went outside and sat on the back veranda, enjoying roasted corn which was sending out an appetising aroma. It was the harvest season for corn and rice, and at the fireplace near where they were sitting, lots of corn was being roasted. This was a familiar scene in many other households during the season of plenty.

"Shall I go and see if our husband has finished eating?" Boi-Kimbo asked her mate.

"If he has finished, he will already have gone to bed and be there waiting for you," Giita remarked. Boi-Kimbo was smiling as she entered the house. Giita was right. Hindowaa had finished eating and had disappeared into his bedroom. As both wives had anticipated, their husband had levelled the entire small mountain of rice, and it was evident that he had thoroughly enjoyed the food cooked by Giita. The co-wives' experiment had worked and they went to bed happily.

CHAPTER EIGHTEEN

The news started circulating in a piecemeal manner, but after some time, generated its own momentum. At its peak, people started calling it '*viivii*', meaning 'a thunderstorm'. However, *viivii* happens toward the end of the rains and this was the dry season; so it was not *viivii* as people knew it. It was a social thunderstorm that had hit Talia - a heavy social thunderstorm. Households were busy trying to see how they could cope with the storm that had taken them by surprise. That was the only way people in Talia could describe this particular news that was circulating in town. Most of the old people agreed that they had never known of any event that had such a magnetic appeal for people. It was also the coincidence of the two events that had made such an impact. It was too amazing to ignore. So the town was buzzing as people gathered in small groups to discuss the news that Giita was pregnant and the missing Kunaafoh was alive and well.

At first, the only people who had reliable information that Giita was finally pregnant were herself and Hindowaa. It was three months since she became pregnant and this time she knew for certain that it was not a false pregnancy because for three months, she had not completed her menstrual cycle. She knew it; her husband knew it and the soothsayer had confirmed it. She had also confirmed that Giita, like Boi-Kimbo, would have twins. She could not determine the sex of the twins, but she was positive that Giita would have twins. They could be two boys or two girls, or a girl and a boy.

The news that the Catholic nun, 'Sister Kono', had delivered a letter for Hindowaa, came to light in the course of the next day. When the nun arrived at Hindowaa's house, she met only his mother and had given her the letter for the urgent attention of her son. Letters and telegrams were treated very seriously in the community, so *Yeea* Kigba had gone to the farm herself to deliver the letter and after that she and Hindowaa immediately returned to town to await the arrival of Maamusu and Giita from the riverside. In the presence of Hindowaa, *Yeea* Kigba, Giita and Boi-Kimbo, Maamusu had read out the letter. It was from Kunaafoh, telling them that she was in place called Ireland. People later said that Giita fainted with joy. Apparently Kunaafoh had also said that she was aware that her mother was pregnant with twins, a boy and a girl and she would come home to witness their birth.

Hindowaa and Giita were not sure how the news that Kunaafoh was safe and well became known because apart from the immediate family, only the trusted Maamusu was privy to that information. Giita, who had been a victim of malicious gossip and believed that there were too many hypocrites in Talia, had told Hindowaa that they should keep the news a secret until Kunaafoh herself arrived, for fear that the same malicious people might do some mischief out of jealousy.

However, the people of Talia were jubilant when they heard the news. They remembered having gone through a mourning period when Kunaafoh disappeared and how the town had been thrown into confusion in their efforts to find the girl. They had sent out all their professional hunters and fishermen to search the forests and rivers to determine if Kunaafoh had drowned, or had been taken by the spirit of the forest, or by the mermaid. The exercise had yielded not a single clue, so Talia had gone into mourning. The Hindowaa household had experienced a flood of sympathisers which lasted for forty days and forty nights. Those had been trying days for the Hindowaa family and the whole town of Talia.

Kunaafoh, the story was told, was already in the process of qualifying to become a nun as well as a medical doctor. That would make her the first female medical doctor in the region. Hindowaa and his family were delighted and joyfully awaited her return with the rest of Talia. Some people were troubled though when they heard that Kunaafoh was not dead but had appeared in another country. Those were the ones who had been so sure that Giita had sacrificed her daughter to the spirit so that she could have sons, and had gossiped about her. The hardened sceptics among them said they would wait until the day Kunaafoh returned before approaching Giita to confess and ask for forgiveness. Those who had heard the rumour wondered whether the malicious gossips would approach Giita, confess their suspicions and ask her to forgive them for defaming her.

Hindowaa was aware that some people, especially Nyake and the Chief, would be offended by the secrecy he and his wife had maintained over Giita's pregnancy. After all, some people had been genuinely concerned over Giita's condition and had wished her well in her search for sons. He had thought about this and started to prepare himself, should such a situation arise, especially with Nyake and the Chief, his future in-law.

Maamusu had been the first to visit Giita after the news broke that her friend was definitely pregnant. When she arrived, she found that Boi-Kimbo, Giita's mate, had gone to the garden to collect vegetables and that Giita was getting ready to go to fetch water, and invited Maamusu to accompany her.

"Have you been down town yet since this morning?" Maamusu asked as they walked towards the river.

"No, I have not been out of my house this morning," Giita replied. "This is my first trip outside."

"My dear, Talia never changes. You are the talk of the town. If you just walk a couple of houses down from your house, you will see people gathered in little groups. People have been congratulating me, saying that at last you made it. Some have even gone to the extent of asking me if I know whether you are expecting a boy or girl as a result of your real pregnancy. People can be *so* inquisitive."

Giita made no comment and Maamusu went on in a somewhat injured tone, "Well, even though you did not choose to tell me, I must say that I am happy it has happened at last. I knew it would happen. We thank God and our ancestors. They have answered our prayers."

"You see Maamusu, sometimes it is good to surprise people," Giita finally responded. "Yes, three months ago, I knew I was really pregnant, but my husband and I decided to keep it a secret and not tell anybody, not even his mother; and I am glad we kept to our decision. I did not intend to offend you, my dear. You are my best friend, but we made a decision not to tell anyone until I had confirmation of my pregnancy. It has been a very difficult time in my life, and you know it. Now, I know for sure that I am really pregnant and I thank God and our ancestors."

"I understand, and don't blame you for taking such a decision. I know that this town is full of malicious gossip. I have had my own share of it. You know what I went through; how I almost lost my husband when rumours spread like wild fire that I was having an affair with the Chief. Let all those who made my life miserable with that outrageous accusation perish in hell fire," Maamusu said. Her tone had turned bitter as she recalled the incident.

186

On their way back to Giita's house after collecting their water, Maamusu said, "Now, you are going to have many visitors, people who will come to congratulate you, the good, the bad, the not so good and not so bad.. They will all come. I am sure Adama and Ngadie would want to come but since the good treatment you gave them the last time almost led to a fight, they will be more circumspect this time, I hope."

"Those two will not come, unless they are spineless and insensitive to insults. How can they possibly come to my house? No, I don't believe they will come," Giita replied.

"Perhaps," Maamusu said," but if you asked me for my view on this matter, I would say that if they did come you should, welcome them and show them hospitality. There are times when we have to try to be above pettiness. Let them get the message that you are above their cheap gossip and that you are more mature than them. If you treat them that way, they will feel the pain of their cheapness. I am telling you Giita, I know these Talia people. *You* are from another town. *I* was born and bred here. I know them like I know the palm of my hand. They are small-minded people."

"Maamusu, you are a true friend. What you have said makes lots of sense and I promise that if they come to see me again I shall be nice to them."

The two women smiled at each other, and for a while neither of them spoke. Then, as they were approaching her house, Giita said, "My sister, I have been very impressed and touched by my mate. She has been very sweet. Do you know, she came and congratulated me, hugged me and kissed me when she knew about my real pregnancy? The child is really innocent. Both of us even plotted against Hindowaa and it worked. She cooperated so fully that; in the end, both of us were happy. People wanted to sow discord between us saying Hindowaa preferred the food Boi-Kimbo prepares for him to mine. We proved that Hindowaa could not distinguish between food prepared by me and that prepared by Boi-kimbo."

"What are you telling me?" Maamusu exclaimed, stopping in her tracks. "People say what? No, my friend, you are joking. You mean Talia has now reached the stage that people are poking their noses into domestic matters. I don't believe you."

"Maamusu, I am telling you the truth, nothing but the truth," Giita insisted. "My mate herself was shocked at how low people can go. I wanted to ask her whether she was familiar with such things in her home town. My dear, sometimes when I reflect on all that is happening in Talia, I just say to myself, the people are idle, malicious or both. How else can you explain it?"

"Giita, I am shocked by this information," Maamusu said. "God help us in this town. But then, I should not be surprised; in Talia anything is possible. And I can vouch for one thing. This type of gossip can only come from women. We women!"

By the time Giita and Maamusu arrived at the house, they found visitors waiting to see Hindowaa who was still in his room. Among the assembled visitors was Nyake, Hindowaa's friend and confidant. They had all come to congratulate Hindowaa and Giita on the news of the pregnancy. Some of the people in the town sent to say that they would come in the evening - especially at mealtime when there will be food and palm wine, Hindowaa said to himself.

When Hindowaa finally left his room, on his way to the veranda, Giita told him that there were many visitors waiting for him, so he went back to bring some kola nuts along with him. He hoped that some of the well-wishers would have been thoughtful enough to bring some palm wine to grace the occasion, though he had made ample provision himself.

"Biwah, ndakei Hindowaa, biwah, biseh." people greeted him in a chorus as he entered the veranda.

They had already seated themselves while awaiting their host. Hindowaa was dressed in a beautiful cotton gown and trousers with a hat of the same fabric. He looked so relaxed that morning that his visitors smiled as they saw him. He greeted each of them and began to offer them kola nuts. While he was doing so, one of the visitors began to scold him, saying, "Hindowaa, now that you are making everything a secret, let me not hide it from you, I only came because my neighbour here forced me to. Even from your very good friends here you hide the good things that happen to you. What has happened to you? Are you not a *Ngumbuwaa*? What are you afraid of in this town?"

"Kinie Largo I thank you," said Hindowaa's friend, Nyake, nodding to show how much he agreed with what had been said. He felt that Hindowaa no longer trusted him and that was why he had not given him even a hint about Giita's pregnancy and Kunaafoh's existence. Yet he was one of those who had been seriously involved in the search for

the girl when it was revealed that she had gone missing. He was angry and looking for a confrontation with Hindowaa, so he went on, "If I had introduced the subject along those lines, some of you here would have said that I have a big mouth. You would also have said that Nyake has a free mouth. You would also have said that I am not afraid to tell people the truth. I am sure you would have said many more things. My friend and colleague, Largo, has eloquently expressed the facts. He is right on this matter. All of you here know how we were all concerned about the sad happenings in this household, yet now we have had to hear this good news from rumours. Hindowaa owes us an apology which should come in the form of palm wine so that we can pour libation and ask our ancestors to forgive him."

"Before we close this matter, I would like to go on record as having spoken in support of all that my two friends have said," It was *Kinie* Kposowa's turn to address the group on the veranda. "I still recall how we were involved in praying for our brother to be rewarded with sons as he and his wife travelled around the area seeking the intervention of the best medicine man. They spent a lot of money on transportation. They accumulated debts. They got our sympathy. Now, when our prayers were answered, it took three months for us to know, and we only knew through rumours. Let me add that, in support of what Largo and Nyake have said, we need more than palm wine. Hindowaa should also add raffia wine to complete the libation."

Every body agreed with *Kinie* Kposowa, so Hindowaa had no choice but to say with humility,

"I am not going to argue with all that you have said. I am apologising to all of you and I want to assure you that such a thing will never be repeated. Yes, I owe you an apology on behalf of myself and my wife. To demonstrate my sincerity, while I shall provide both the palm wine and the raffia wine, I also intend to live up to tradition and provide a big meal where I shall slaughter several he-goats in accordance with our Wunde Society custom. Thank you very much my good and dear friends."

Satisfied with the apology, the visitors applauded Hindowaa's speech.

"Well done, Hindowaa, you are forgiven. Well done, *Ngumbuwaa.*" Even Nyake observed light-heartedly, "Let us praise our brother and friend. He has done a remarkable job at his age. Giita is pregnant and the

189

new, young wife will soon be pregnant, if she is not pregnant already. The man has decided to be more potent in his old age than when he was a youth. I hear that the senior wife is expecting *twins*."

At this, the visitors laughed so much that one man almost choked. Hindowaa joined in the laughter while trying to find himself a comfortable seat. Someone had taken his place of honour - his hammock.

"Boi-Kimbo," he called out to his younger wife.

When Boi-Kimbo answered the summons, Hindowaa told her to go and bring the two gourds of palm wine and two gourds of raffia wine that the tapper had brought for him. The gourds were big and heavy, so Boi-Kimbo brought them one after the other. As she served the drinks, another man studied her form and joked, *"Ndakei* Hindowaa, I shall see you privately so you can tell me your secret. We are of the same age, but I must admit that I cannot do as good a job as you have done. You should definitely tell some of us the secret."

"I agree with you," another man piped up. "I am much younger than Hindowaa and yet I am unable to perform such a miracle. Hindowaa must show us the recipe for such a performance."

"Yes, give us the recipe. Give us the recipe. Give us the recipe," the men chorused merrily. They sounded as if they were already drunk.

"Where is our pregnant wife? Where is she? I want her to come and pour some wine for me," another of the visitors teased Hindowaa.

By the time they left Hindowaa's house that morning, it was now reliably established that Giita was three months pregnant.

In down town Talia, Ngadie and Adama were by now in a state of painful indecision. Adama was itching to go and see Giita, but Ngadie was reluctant, remembering that previous visit when it had been rumoured that Giita was pregnant and it turned out not to be true. One morning while they were sitting on their veranda, Adama had once again tried to persuade her friend to visit Giita with her, evoking a stern response from Ngadie who had had enough of the subject.

"Adama, let me remind you again," she said, "we went to visit Giita to express our happiness on hearing that she was pregnant. We were sincere about it. Remember the way she treated us? You and I almost fought over the incident and now you want us to repeat the same mistake. If Giita is the one feeding me, let me die or let me eat grass. *I am not going there even if she is pregnant with ten babies."*

"You see Ngadie, I have always cautioned you to be tolerant with people," Adama replied. "We are not all the same. As for *me*, the way I see it is that tolerance is a virtue."

"I have heard all that before. But remember that we went to see Giita in all sincerity. Ok, she had problems, but so do we all. Just because we don't put our own problems on our heads does not mean we don't have them. Remember that Krio saying that goes, *'all kondo lay beleh na gron; yu nor no us wan im beleh dae at am* (All lizards crawl, so it is difficult to tell which one has a stomach-ache)? How can you justify insulting someone who tries to sympathise with you. How can you?"

"I like the proverb you have just repeated," said Adama. "I also know one which says you should not pinch someone's buttocks if he or she is carrying you on his or her back."

For the first time since their tense conversation began, both of them laughed, but Ngadie still went on to say, "As for me, Adama, despite what you have just said, I am a woman with pride. I do not intend to compromise my dignity. I shall not go to see Giita. We now know that she is three months pregnant. I wish her well and a safe delivery and hope that she has sons. I mean that; sincerely, but to drag myself along to visit her again, I swear by my Sande Society, I will not."

"Ah, Ngadie, you see what I always tell you? You have a very hard heart. You behave like a man with a hard heart. It is not good for a woman to be like that. I am warning you as a friend. Stop being so hard-hearted. It is not good. A woman should have a soft heart that is why we are mothers; we should be soft hearted."

"Adama, I don't accept your views," Ngadie said firmly. "If you are soft-hearted people take advantage of you. And it is not a matter of being soft or hard-hearted. It is a matter of principle. If having principles means I am hard-hearted, then I intend to stay that way. Why after Giita humiliated us, do you still insist that we visit her? I am beginning to suspect your motive."

"If we have reached the point where you are suspecting my motive for visiting Giita, then let us abandon the subject," Adama told her friend and began to gossip.

"You know Ngadie," she said, "what baffles me is the fact that Hindowaa promised his young, lovely and educated daughter to the

Chief. You know that our Chief is one hundred per cent illiterate. How do you explain that?"

"Adama, that was an arrangement made before the child disappeared. I do not believe that any reasonable parents would put their daughter through such an ordeal. The Chief cannot even speak Krio. Of all his numerous wives only about four can speak or understand Krio. When the child comes back she will be an adult and I do not believe she will accept such a proposition from her father."

"You see how you reason?" Adama said, "Ngadie, when did a daughter ever refuse to marry to a man proposed by her father? What is her choice in the matter? Tell me, if you were educated and had the white man's knowledge until you could write it with your teeth, would you refuse a marriage arranged by your parents? That child has no choice? It is our culture, my dear."

"Tell me. Do you know of any other case of a woman doctor who came from the white man's land and married a Chief who cannot read or write. I told you that the man cannot even talk Krio. If I were faced with a situation like that, I tell you, I would run away and become a runaway wife. They would never see me again." Ngadie told her friend.

She had become rather agitated at the thought of being in Kunaafoh's position, so to calm her down, Adama said, "Ngadie, I am sorry, you don't understand our culture. Let me tell you what would happen to you if you did that. Your father would curse you, and you know what a father's curse means for you and your future and the future of your children? And let me tell you, your mother would never again enjoy peace in that household because she would forever be the one blamed for your action. I know what I am talking about. My dear take it easy and let us wait and see what happens when Kunaafoh comes."

Adama went back to trying to persuade Ngadie to visit Giita with her, but they had still not agreed on whether or not to go as the morning advanced into midday.

"Are you coming from up-town, Ndiamoh?" Adama asked a man who was passing in the street. She was referring to that part of town where Giita lived, for she was still longing to visit Giita, under her principle of tolerance.

"No I went into the forest to check on the animal traps I left there last night," the man answered barely pausing. "I was not lucky this time. Your neighbour made a big catch; he is right behind me."

As the day grew warmer, Adama and Ngadie agreed to a ceasefire and amicably dropped the idea of visiting Giita before she had delivered her twins.

Hindowaa's mother was one of the happiest people on the day the news of Giita's pregnancy broke. She had, however, expressed her displeasure that both Hindowaa and Giita had kept her in the dark about it for three months. Giita had scrupulously avoided her during that time so that she never suspected that her daughter-in-law was pregnant. Now she felt she was again being kept in the dark about something and, one evening when they were in the sitting-room, she raised the matter with her son in Giita's presence. Boi-Kimbo was in the bedroom as it was her turn to sleep with her husband for three nights.

"I suspect that you have not been forthcoming about certain things, Hindo," she said. "I don't know what is happening to you," *Yeea* Kigba always called her son Hindo, instead of Hindowaa.

"Yes mother, you are right," he replied. "I have a serious issue on my mind. Something that is causing me sleepless nights. It is not an easy subject to contemplate."

"What are you talking about?" *Yeea* Kigba asked, her eyes showing deep anxiety. "What is it again in this household? Child, we have had so many problems. I hope this time it has nothing to do with my in-laws."

"*Yeea*, it does not concern this household as such," Giita said, answering for her husband. "What is worrying Hindowaa is the question of Kunaafoh marrying the Chief when she eventually comes back. She will be a doctor and a nun so it is not possible for her to marry the Chief or anybody else, for that matter. This is the problem we now have. *Yeea* Kigba, you recall that your son promised to give Kunaafoh to the Chief. That was a long time ago. We had promised that the year Kunaafoh graduated from the Sande Society, she would be given to the Chief because the Hindowaa family had never given him a wife."

"You people make my heart ache," her mother-in-law said, throwing up her hands with impatience. "What is the problem? Kunaafoh is a woman now. She should get married and we have decided that the best thing for her is to be married to our Chief. I do not see the problem. What has Kunaafoh being a doctor and nun got to do with her marrying the Chief? Is the Chief not a man? I will stand firm so that my granddaughter marries our Chief. Hindo, if you don't do that I shall be

193

angry with you. I am warning you not to change your mind on this issue and bring shame to this house."

"Mother, things are not as simple as you see think," Hindowaa told his mother. "The situation has changed and I am in a dilemma. That is why I want to go and see the Chief this evening and explain to him the new circumstances. I hope he will understand. Mother, nuns do not marry, this is the truth about the Catholic religion. Fortunately, the Chief has not given me any money or items for an engagement.. We may have to look for another woman for him, but not Kunaafoh."

"Hindo, I don't understand what you are saying," *Yeea* Kigba said, thoroughly annoyed by Hindowaa's words. "I am serious, I do not understand. You want to tell me that women who go to the white mans' land, should not marry? What is this nun business, which I am hearing for the first time? Are nuns not women? Let me not hear about your nun anymore. Is she not a woman? What are you suggesting? Tell me. Tell me, I am your mother; I carried you in my belly for nine months and suckled you for a long time. Do you know that of all my children, it was only you that I had a problem delivering? I almost died in the labour. Now look at you telling me nonsense about my own grandchild. You children of today, you challenge your parents. I wish your father were alive. *Chai, Chai*, your mother who brought you into this world!"

"If you were to ask me, I would suggest that we suspend this matter until Kunaafoh arrives and gives her own opinion about it," Giita told her husband and mother-in-law. *Yeea* Kigba turned her back on them for a moment, then stood up, shook her head and clapped her hands as if in disbelief, before turning back to them, and pointing her finger directly at Giita.

"Ah. Ah. What did I hear you say, Giita?" You said what? Ask whose opinion? My granddaughter's opinion? Did your parents ask for your opinion when they decided to give you to Hindo? When did that idea germinate in our society? Tell me. Do you also know that we face the embarrassing situation that Kunaafoh had not even been circumcised when she disappeared from this town? Now you are sitting here suggesting that we refer this subject to her? For what? For discussion? Are you out of your mind this morning or did you not sleep well last night? You people make me sick in the stomach. *Ngewo gbomumaa*, (God help us!)"

Hindowaa was sweating, but Giita remained quite unmoved by her mother-in-law's performance. Boi-Kimbo had not fallen asleep since she went to bed awaiting Hindowaa's arrival, so she heard almost everything that they were saying in the sitting-room. She also was not impressed by what Hindowaa's mother said. She had decided that she would like her children to be educated and marry educated people. She herself would have loved to go to school and become an educated woman.

It was late in the evening that Hindowaa visited the Chief's compound. He had hoped that by the time he got there, the perennial crowd of visitors would be reduced to manageable proportions. The Chief had been kept well informed about all the latest news in Talia before Hindowaa's arrival. He greeted Hindowaa warmly.

"Ah, my *ndemia*, (meaning 'in-law') welcome, welcome. I knew you would be coming to see me. I have already heard the good news. Congratulations. Most of the people who visited you came to see me today to convey the good news. God and the ancestors have answered our prayers at last. We people in Talia always pray to God when any person is in need of prayers, and fortunately God has been kind to us. Your wife is pregnant and your daughter has been found," he added with a chuckle, "You have even worked hard and Giita is pregnant with twins."

Other visitors agreed with the Chief. Some laughed while others just nodded their heads.

"But when is my wife coming?" He asked, and went on, "This is the most important thing for me. I know now that she is alive and well and she is coming as a doctor. God loves Talia. The first woman doctor in the region will be from Talia and the Chief's wife. I am looking forward to it with infinite delight."

The crowd applauded, but Hindowaa said nothing. He looked confused and disorientated. He stayed on for a long time at the Chief's compound but this time others had their own agenda to discuss with the Chief and were in no hurry. In the end, Hindowaa had to leave the Chief's compound without being able to discuss his concern, the fact that Kunaafoh could not marry the Chief after all. It was a very worrisome development in his household. Fortunately, this time, he and his wife saw eye to eye on the matter.

Hindowaa decided to wait for an appropriate time to bring this sensitive subject to the Chief's attention. He had a very powerful argument for what should happen when Kunaafoh eventually returned as a medical doctor and a nun, but it was a closely guarded family secret which was not disclosed to the public.

When Hindowaa, arrived at his house, Boi-Kimbo was still awake, waiting for him in bed. *Yeea* Kigba and Giita had planned to give him a big surprise and they thought the time was right.

"How is the Chief?" *Yeea* Kigba asked.

"He is all right. As usual there were many people there. They don't give the Chief time to rest or sleep. The place is always crowded. They should give him time to think and reflect," Hindowaa replied. And his mother said, "Hindo, you don't sound like your usual self. Is there anything wrong with the Chief, any palaver?"

"I did not have the opportunity to discuss Kunaafoh's coming with the Chief or the fact that she will not be marrying him. It is a delicate matter and he is the Chief. We have to treat it very carefully. That is my main concern."

Yeea Kigba made no comment. Instead, she asked in a playful manner, "Have you noticed anything different about Boi-Kimbo lately?"

Hindowaa thought for a while.

"No, mother."

"Well, Giita and myself have good news for you. She is pregnant."

Giita and his mother watched his expression change from anxiety to pleasure as he exclaimed, "That is good news!"

"But how come you did not notice that she is pregnant?" his mother teased him. 'The pregnancy is almost two months old. I mean, don't you ever look at your young wife when both of you are together?"

"Well, you know that I see her mostly when it is dark," Hindowaa answered.

"And you never even touch her when it is dark?" The question embarrassed Hindowaa and he felt himself blushing. Giita almost burst out laughing. The family stayed together late before retiring to bed.

News of Boi-Kimbo's pregnancy made no great impact on Talia. It was not even an event worth the gossip that Talia was known for. After all, a girl of Boi-Kimbo's age was expected to be pregnant a few months after marriage. The only person who was very excited was

196

Hindowaa's mother. Like her son, her preoccupation was the sex of the children that Boi-Kimbo would have. She was busy praying that both Giita and Boi-Kimbo would have sons. She prayed when she went to bed at night and prayed when she woke up in the morning.

"Didn't I tell you the last time that you were pregnant?" Giita informed her mate, as they sat on the veranda. "I knew it when you told me that you felt like vomiting after eating. I also noticed how succulent your breasts were looking and your general attitude to food. Let me tell you, pregnancy can be a difficult period in the life of some women, but others manage it, some with very few problems, though they are in the minority. Sometimes, you will even dislike your social environment and small things will irritate you. Some people become less talkative when they are pregnant while others become aggressive. It is a life experience by itself."

"How are you doing, my wives?" *Yeea* Kigba enquired gaily as she joined Giita and Boi-Kimbo on the veranda. Before they could answer, she went on, "I am always happy when I see you both together in this house, because it is not always easy to find co-wives who get along. I was not lucky in my own case. My mate and myself never got on well. We fought, did not speak to each other and wished bad things on each other. Can you imagine that?"

Boi-Kimbo rose from her seat and asked her mother-in-law to sit down.

"No, you sit down, my child, you are a pregnant woman now. *I* should give you the seat. If you stand up, you will strain the babies. It is good to be pregnant when you are young. You shall see the difference later in life. For now, enjoy it because when you reach a certain age and you are pregnant, it is a big burden. Ask your mate, Giita. She knows what I am talking about."

"That is just what we were discussing," said Giita.

Giita often thought about the old female soothsayer who had told her that if her pronouncement that she would have twins, a son and daughter did not materialize, Hindowaa should cut off her two ears. Convinced that she had heard the truth on that occasion, Giita felt reassured as she waited for her dreams to be fulfilled and her tribulations to come to an end. It was just a matter of time now.

Even in childhood, babies had fascinated Boi-Kimbo, and as she grew into adulthood, her delight in these angelic creatures made her long to have her own. If only there was a way to make the months go faster so that she could hold her baby, in her arms. That thought was still engaging her mind as she fell asleep that night. She hoped that the baby would arrive sooner rather than later. That was a thrilling time for the two wives of Hindowaa.

CHAPTER NINETEEN

For three consecutive nights, people in Talia heard the continuous barking of dogs in the early hours of the morning. It was unusual. The dry season weather conditions also changed suddenly with clouds forming the way they did in October and November and thunderstorms threatening. Indeed, the atmosphere felt as if a huge thunderstorm was on its way. Some people found it strange that nature could change its complexion in such a short time and they waited apprehensively, particularly concerned about the strange barking of dogs for three consecutive nights.

The continuously barking dogs were heard all over Talia and elderly people were particularly worried because, so some of them said, they could not recall any remotely similar occurrence in the history of Talia. As for the sudden change in the weather, people recalled that they had witnessed something like it in the past when the current Chief's father was about to die after a long illness. They said it rained for two days even though it was the height of the dry season, but that was a long time ago.

Though the unexpected change in the weather and the barking of the dogs were significant, they were relegated to the background of Talia's social history on account of Giita's now obvious pregnancy. It was the talk of the town and the soothsayer who had predicted it became immensely popular overnight with his credibility reinforced in Talia and beyond. As her pregnancy advanced, Giita continued to dream about the twins, the boy and the girl. She would dream about washing them in liquid herbs to improve their health and protect them from evil spirits. She would dream about going to the soothsayer to get amulets which she would tie around their arms or feet as precautionary measures so the children would grow up healthy. She dreamed about the names she would give to the twins, the boy and the girl. The Mende people have names for twins boys and for twin girls. They also have names for twins that are boy and girl. Giita planned to give Hindowaa's name to the boy and her mother's name to the girl as their second names. She kept dreaming about them for as long as the pregnancy lasted and even started composing the songs she would sing to them when they cried. The songs would reflect her struggle to have more sons for Hindowaa.

When the children smiled, she would welcome them and thank them for fulfilling her wish. She would observe all the taboos regarding twins and tell people who came to visit not to touch the twins on their heads since that is one of the taboos about twins in Mende culture. She would watch them grow and enjoy Kunaafoh's delight in her twin siblings. Kunaafoh would also be around to treat the twins whenever the need arose. Oh, how lucky and happy they would all be, especially, Hindowaa and his mother. They would be looking forward to more sons now that the soothsayer had opened the way. Giita was a happy woman who felt that her tribulations had ended. She often touched her big stomach and whispered to the twins, telling them how much she was looking forward to receiving and welcoming them; then she would smile and touch her big stomach again.

Since Hindowaa was expecting his two wives to give birth, he took time to prepare for the occasion. He also thought about Giita's twins. He knew he had devoted much of his time and energy to ensuring that Giita had more sons and he was happy that his efforts had not been in vain. He was now sure of having three sons and that more would come after Giita had given birth to the third one. He also looked forward to welcoming his daughter who had brought honour to the Hindowaa family, by becoming the first female doctor in the entire chiefdom. He was prepared to communicate with his late father and grandfather to thank them for having answered his prayers. He knew that his mother would be happy and there would once again be peace in the house. However, he would not agree with her that Kunaafoh should marry the Chief. It was impossible. That matter would be addressed when the occasion was right. He looked forward anxiously to the birth of the twins, knowing that his friends in Talia would expect him to celebrate the occasion in grand style. As he waited, he made up his mind to do exactly what his friends expected of him when Giita delivered the twins.

Yeea Kigba, Hindowaa's mother was longing for the birth of her grandchildren and as she waited for their birth, reflected on all the efforts she and her son had made for Giita to have more sons, and for Kunaafoh to resurface. Oh, how she looked forward to the day Giita would deliver her grandchildren, especially the grandson. She had been in the forefront of the struggle for her son to have more sons. She had had to push her son on the issue of having more sons, because Hindowaa had been as slow as snail about taking action on the matter.

She had had to confront him aggressively because she realized that Hindowaa was a bit of a weakling, unlike his late father. She had even become suspicious that Giita possessed an evil spirit which affected her ability to have more children. She was now remorseful, and promised herself to confess her suspicions and ask for Giita's forgiveness. She would do that later, after Giita gave birth. She was looking forward to the twins, her grandchildren. She would sing to them, cuddle them and hug them. She would take them over the way she had done with Hinga, Kunaafoh and Kafo. However, the twins were going to be even more special because, as Mendes believed, they would have some psychic qualities and would need to be treated with maximum care. As was the custom, the family would build a small shrine in the house and tend to it appropriately. It was going to be one of the happiest periods in her life and she waited impatiently for it to begin.

Kunaafoh had monitored events and developments at home, and she too was refreshing her mind about all her mother had to endure as she tried to have more sons. She had witnessed her mother's woes and shared moments of her mother's challenges as she navigated her way through a turbulent society that demanded so much of her. Her mother's daily concern over her inability to have more sons had stressed Kunaafoh's own innocent mind. She too had prayed to God to grant her mothers' wishes, and as she went through her studies to become a nun, she had prayed even harder. She was delighted that she would be coming home to see her mother give birth to her twin siblings, and even began thinking about how much pleasure she would derive from taking care of them. Twins had always had a fascination for her so she was captivated with the idea of having twin siblings.

Kunaafoh also thought often about coming back home to her motherland. She remembered how she had once seen the beauty and tranquillity of Freetown by the ocean, where transport ferry-boats crossed each other on the waters of the Atlantic Ocean as seagulls flew overhead, apparently, navigating fishermen to their destinations. She was intrigued by the flight of the seagulls as they dived into the sea and emerged with tiny fishes sandwiched between their beaks. As the day ended, she would watch the calm, beautiful day, merge peacefully into the night. That was not such a long time ago, she thought, and looked forward to her triumphant return to Talia and the welcome she would receive.

Hinga and Kafo were relieved that their mother's desires were about to be fulfilled. They too were in high spirits as they looked forward to receiving their twin siblings. The idea of having twin siblings had never occurred to them, but now that it was a reality, they cherished it. Kafo had asked his elder brother, Hinga, what would happen if he hit his twin brother or sister on the head. He was curious about many other things he had been told about twins and he looked forward to having a boy and girl as twin siblings. The brothers thought the occasion of the birth of the twins would also provide an opportunity for the family reunion they had missed. Kafo, the spoiled son, was eagerly looking forward to that. It was now just a matter of time and a short time at that, before they would all be together to witness the birth of their siblings.

Fanday also looked forward to witnessing Giita give birth to the twins. She convinced herself that the moment would be the best time for a reconciliation with Giita. She would admit that there had been an undeclared state of war between them, but would also let Giita know that the sayings to which she had always subscribed, should be invoked, namely, 'a family tree can bend but will never break', and that 'blood is thicker than water'. Consequently, she thought the birth of the twins and the appearance of Kunaafoh would provide an opportunity to mend fences with Giita and the rest of the family.

Ngadie and her friend, Adama, were engrossed in their thoughts about Giita's pending delivery of the twins. Each of them had two children from two different men. As they watched their children playing that afternoon, they had been jolted by the realisation that Giita's pregnancy was confirmed beyond any doubt and that she would be having her twins soon.

"Ah, to be honest with you, I envy Giita, Ngadie. I do, and I am sure you will also agree with me," Adama remarked. "I would have loved to have twins. I don't know why, but I always wanted to and I admire parents, especially mothers, with twins. There is just something about twins that has always fascinated me."

Ngadie looked at her friend and smiled. "I agree with you," she said. "This is one time I can support what you have said. Believe me, I also wish I had had twins. I have always loved twins. Having them makes you feel different in the community. You stand out, and people look at you differently - the mother of twins, or - the father of twins. It is just wonderful."

The Chief and Hindowaa's friend and confidant, Nyake, admired Hindowaa's iron will and determination in his efforts to have sons. The Chief admitted to Nyake that he owed Giita an apology and would do so after she had had her children. He confessed that he had had the suspicion that Giita had an evil spirit and had sacrificed her daughter in order to have sons. He said he had looked into Giita's eyes during the period of mourning and her tears did not seem genuine. During his rule as Chief, he said, he had known of women who had bewitched their own children and had participated in the mourning ceremony with wet eyes, even though they were the culprits. He was now convinced that the tears of his future mother-in-law had been genuine. He looked forward to seeing Kunaafoh again, imagining how she had grown and matured. No one had told him as yet, not even Hindowaa, that Kunaafoh had become a nun, and as such, no longer a potential future wife.

"We all owe her an apology and there are many more in this town who will have to swallow their pride and offer their apologies to Giita – such a pleasant woman in this town," Nyake agreed. "I know many of them who used to pass by my place and gossip about her. I am happy that in the end, God has rewarded her." Nyake also admitted that he too had not come clean about his suspicions on the matter and looked forward to confessing and ask for Giita's forgiveness.

Maamusu, who was among Giita's most honest and devoted friends in Talia, had come to the conclusion that Giita was more like her sister rather than a friend. They had come a long way and relied on each other when it came to addressing their mutual domestic problems. She pictured in vivid imagination Giita's twins as her own children. It was a good feeling for her, a mother of four children. She would help Giita take care the twins. She would wash them, feed them, sing to them and play with them. Oh, she thought of the songs she would sing as she used to do with her own children. When the children cried in the absence of their father, she would sing a song to tell them not to cry, that daddy would be coming back soon. If they cried when their mother was away, there was a song she would sing to them. When the parents returned, she would say, 'You see, I told you not to cry, that mother would be coming back. Here she is. You believe me now?' Then the child would smile and she would kiss it and say, 'I love you because you listen to me and therefore things happen.' She was the solid pillar who had given Giita strength during her trials and tribulations. Because she was the friend closest to Giita's body and mind, she knew Giita would be delivering her twins shortly. As these thoughts about her friend were fresh, Maamusu decided to visit Giita since she knew Giita appreciated her presence at any time. Her husband and children were not at home when she left for Giita's house. Since it was not a long distance away, she made her way there in a couple of minutes. She found Giita sitting on a bench made from palm fronds with her belly half exposed and remarked, as they chatted, "When I am pregnant, my belly is not usually big like yours. You used to tease me about it, but as for you, ever since I have known you, you have always had a big belly when you are pregnant. This one is the biggest I have seen."

"Yes, you are right. I always have big belly when I am pregnant." Giita replied. "Maamusu, that is what pregnancy means, a big belly. But you should also realise that this time I am pregnant with twins," "I have some friends whose bellies are so small when they are pregnant that when they pass you, you will never notice that they are pregnant. They only look as if they have just had a big meal. In fact they say that such women have an enormous appetite."

Both of them laughed as Maamusu went on. "Talking about people whose pregnancy does not show, look at your mate, Boi-Kimbo, she could pass for someone who has only become slightly plump. She is among those lucky women whom pregnancy makes more attractive - just round and succulent. There are men who have an unlimited appetite for them."

As her friend chuckled at this naughty remark, Maamusu said, "Giita, since you became pregnant, you have not been ill at all. Have you acquired immunity against illness? As for me, when I am pregnant, I get ill often. The mornings are my worst time."

"I do get ill when I am pregnant. But this pregnancy has been good for me. The twins are cooperating," Giita smiled. "I don't like taking medicine even when I am not pregnant. I have to be seriously ill before I take medicine. Most times, I do not talk about my illness. Hindowaa knows this part of me and my mother-in-law also knows it. I usually suffer and keep it a secret to my self."

With the stoicism she had described to Maamusu, despite her advanced pregnancy, Giita continued to do all her domestic chores and never missed her turn to sleep with her husband. She stayed strong and as fit as a fiddle.

Late one afternoon, the wind started blowing and again the clouds darkened, giving a warning of rain, though this was the dry season. Both Maamusu and Giita were baffled by the erratic nature of the weather but nevertheless decided they would go and fetch water from the river. As they walked away from the house, it became windier. The gusts lifted their wrappers. They had to hold on to them with one hand and the empty buckets with the other, but undeterred, they continued their trip to the river. As they walked along, Giita thought about Kunaafoh. They had visited the river many times just like she and Maamusu had been doing. It was at the river that she and Kunaafoh used to come and engage in mutual problem-solving conversations, and in the end, they would cry and console each other. It seemed so long ago. They were now half way to the river and Giita said to her friend,

"I hope that by the time we come back my mate would have finished cutting the potato leaves so that I can finish cooking before our husband arrives from the farm. Today, we have decided to give him his favourite meal."

"It is not your turn to sleep in the room, is it?" Maamusu asked.

"Maamusu, my stomach is too big now. What difference would it make anyway? He has to eat whether it is my turn or not."

All of a sudden Giita, who was walking in front, stood still and fell silent. She let her bucket drop and clutched her belly. The wind was relentless. Maamusu rushed forward and held her friend who now showed signs of pain. As the worried Maamusu held her, Giita began to sweat.

"Maamusu, I am not feeling well," she said. "It is my belly. I can't make it to the river."

Two other women who were on their way to the river stopped and helped Maamusu walk Giita to the house, going slowly. The discomfort in Giita's belly had increased by the time they arrived at the house and was now recognised as the onset of labour pains. As the pains continued, the traditional midwives were summoned to attend to Giita. They belonged to the sorority of elderly Sande women, and were the best that Talia had to offer. They decided to move Giita from the house to the Sande grove in the forest. Giita's labour pains grew more intense, but still the babies were not delivered.

The news about Giita's prolonged labour became known to the entire town of Talia. Darkness had still not enveloped the town, but the weather had become even more menacing, though it had still not rained. There was a vigil-like gathering at the Hindowaa house. The only vehicle in Talia arrived, bringing Kunaafoh, her brothers, Fanday and 'Sister Kono'. There was instant jubilation, and a festive atmosphere replaced the tension, even amid Giita's suffering. The birth attendants in the grove were informed about the arrival of Kunaafoh and her siblings and the atmosphere there also became euphoric though Giita remained in extremely painful labour. Hindowaa's mother was among those present in the grove. She was watching for the arrival of her grandchildren and her eyes almost popped each time Giita was forced by the birth attendants to take a deep breath in order to force the babies out.

Giita was in such pain by now that she was barely conscious, and totally unaware of the arrival of her children and Fanday. As time went on, the birth attendants became worried. Some of them speculated that Giita's prolonged labour might be associated with evil spirits and that perhaps she had a secret that needed to be revealed before she could deliver her twins safely. Giita, however, was in no position to speak. Other people felt that her prolonged labour was due to three factors, her advanced age, she was having twins for the first time, and she had not given birth for a long time. There was nothing to be done to remedy that situation either.

Kunaafoh asked to attend to her mother, but her request was refused in spite of her vehement protests. They said she was a child because she had not been initiated in the Sande Society. It was absolutely impossible for a woman who was not a member to attend to such matters. It had never happened and would never happen. Kunaafoh protested in vain. 'Sister Kono' also asked if she could be of assistance, but her request was turned down and even considered an affront to the midwives. How dare she, a non-initiate, ask to enter the grove and in the process render it profane, they said. It would be sacrilegious. Other, more optimistic, people were of the view that Giita would eventually give birth, saying that traditionally, twins were not easily delivered, hence the spiritual powers associated with them. This case would not be an exception.

Meanwhile, Giita was in intense pain, suffering even as the midwives continued to attend to her. Maamusu kept crying and pleading with the midwives to assist Giita to deliver her children quickly, because she was becoming more tired and weak as the seconds sped.

The crowd outside Hindowaa's house had increased. All of Giita's children and many other people such as Fanday, 'Sister Kono', Ngadie and Adama, the Chief and Nyake were present. They were all waiting. As Giita's labour continued, some of the women began to cry out of sympathy for they had had similar experiences and knew how much she was suffering.

Some of the midwives continued pleading with Giita to confess anything she might have done to offend the spirits or ancestors so that she could deliver her children safely, but she was almost unconscious and could not respond. However, with great efforts and in the presence of Kigba, Maamusu, and Boi-Kimboy, the twins were eventually delivered. The girl came out first and then the boy, so the girl was the senior sibling. There was wild and spontaneous jubilation among the birth attendants and all those present. Their joy resounded outside Hindowaa's house and was immediately received with vibrant enthusiasm by the expectant crowd, gathered to witness one of the more memorable events in the history of Talia. Then the rain that had threatened for hours, came down and drenched the town, dispersing the crowd assembled outside Hindowaa's house. The twins cried lustily, announcing their arrival in Talia. According to custom, the girl was named Jinaa and the boy, Sao. But Giita never saw her twin children or heard their cries. Death cheated her of the pleasure for she died soon after their birth, *in search of sons*.

Printed in the United States
By Bookmasters